UNFORGETTABLE

Eric James Stone

UNFORGETTABLE

This is a work of fiction. All the characters and events portrayed in this book are fictional, and any resemblance to real people or incidents is purely coincidental.

A Baen Books Original

Baen Publishing Enterprises
P.O. Box 1403
Riverdale, NY 10471
www.baen.com

ISBN: 978-1-4814-8244-8

Cover art by Kurt Miller

First mass market paperback printing, May 2017

Library of Congress Catalog Number: 2015030725

Distributed by Simon & Schuster
1230 Avenue of the Americas
New York, NY 10020

Pages by Joy Freeman (www.pagesbyjoy.com)
Printed in the United States of America

It took me only a few seconds to unlock the chain. Pushing the handlebars, I sprinted alongside the bike before hopping on and beginning to pedal.

I chanced a look over my shoulder. The man was still running after me, but he was falling behind. I wove through pedestrians on the sidewalk until I got into the street, then pedaled away.

Once I was sure I had left him more than a minute behind, I pulled over to catch my breath. I got out my iPhone and checked the time. It would be a little after eight a.m. on the East Coast of the United States. Perfect. I don't have any contacts listed in the phone—not because storing phone numbers would be a security problem but because it would forget them after I entered them. So I dialed a number I had memorized.

A computer-generated female voice on the other end answered, "How may I direct your call?"

"Edward Strong," I said.

The phone rang a few times, then someone picked up. "Strong here."

"Mr. Strong," I said, "in the lower drawer on the right side of your desk, there is a manila file folder labeled 'CODE NAME LETHE.' I need you to pull it out and read the cover letter. There should also be an authentication protocol sheet in there."

Having to go through this sort of rigmarole every time I reported in was an inconvenience. But what else could I do?

My name is Nat Morgan. And even though they don't remember me, I work for the CIA.

To my dad, David Rodger Stone,
who has gone to seek a newer world.

ACKNOWLEDGEMENTS

I want to thank my agent, Joshua Bilmes, for believing in this novel, and Baen publisher Toni Weisskopf for taking a chance on it.

Caleb Warnock is the man most directly responsible for my getting on the path to publication, and taking his Writing in Depth class was one of the best decisions I ever made.

I owe a great deal to all the teachers I've had over the years, but there are a few who stick out in my mind as having encouraged my creativity during my schooling: Diane Pepetone, Lenelle Davis, Pat Gledhill, Breck England, Melinda Welch, Donna Parker, Elouise M. Bell, and Marion K. "Doc" Smith.

Then there are the writing workshop instructors and classmates from whom I learned many of the skills I used in writing *Unforgettable*: Orson Scott Card and my fellow 2003 Literary Boot Campers; Tim Powers, K.D. Wentworth, the Writers of the Future judges, and my fellow winners from 2004 and 2005;

Dave Wolverton and my classmates from his 2004 Novel Writing Workshop; and Jeanne Cavelos, the guest instructors, and the Odyssey Class of 2007.

I'd also like to thank those who participated in the 2008 Codex Novel Contest, which really helped to motivate me in writing this novel. My in-person writing groups were also invaluable in giving me feedback, particularly the Rats with Swords, who read the whole novel.

Some of the following people are included in groups I mentioned above, but I want to thank them specifically for their feedback: Alethea Kontis, Alex Haig, Amber Sistla, Amy Lau, Ben Olsen, Brandon and Emily Sanderson, Cavan Helps, Charmayne Gubler Warnock, Dan Wells, Darja Malcolm-Clarke, Drew Olds, Ellen Van Hensbergen, Heidi Summers Creer, Isaac Stewart, James Goldberg, Janci Patterson, Jean Huets, Juliette Crane, Karla Bennion, Kirsten Lincoln, Laura Anderson, Laurel Amberdine, Lee Ann Setzer, Lesley Hart Gunn, Matt and Brooklyn Evans, Matt Rotundo, Maya Lassiter, Meg Stout, Nikki Trionfo, Pat Esden, Rachel Whitaker, Spencer Ellsworth, and Vylar Kaftan.

Finally, I want to thank my wife, THE Darci; my parents; and the rest of my family for their encouragement and enthusiasm for my writing.

UNFORGETTABLE

Chapter One

Sometimes the most important part of stealing something is not letting the victim know someone stole it—particularly when it comes to stealing information from a computer. It's a task that requires a thief of immense subtlety.

Or someone like me.

I chained my bicycle to a lamppost in front of the London headquarters of Jamshidi Oil, Ltd. The glass doors parted before me and I strode to the reception desk. I held up a courier envelope and said, "Package for a Mr. Kazem Jamshidi."

The blonde receptionist looked me over. I'd like to think that she was appreciating my physique in my skin-tight cycling outfit, but realistically, I'm a little on the scrawny side. I do a lot of running in my job, and I can't afford any extra pounds.

She reached out for the package but I pulled it back.

"Sorry," I said. "Mr. Jamshidi has to sign for this personally."

"I'll see if he's in." She picked up a phone.

I knew he was in: his bald head and fat face had been visible through the window of the chauffeured Mercedes-Benz sedan that had pulled into the underground parking garage ten minutes ago.

After a brief conversation, the receptionist said, "Someone will be here shortly to escort you up."

A door at the far end of the lobby opened and a stocky black man in a gray security guard's uniform emerged. Based on the personnel files I'd reviewed while prepping for this job, I recognized him as George Vance, a former amateur middleweight boxer. Hopefully I could pull this off without resorting to fisticuffs, or else things might get a bit painful.

"Thanks," I said to the receptionist before walking over to meet the guard. "Package that has to be signed for by Mr. Jamshidi himself."

"Hold out your arms," George said in a bored voice, holding up a metal-detector wand. I complied, and he ran the wand cursorily around my body. It squealed a bit next to the specially modified iPhone clipped to my belt and the metal on the clipboard I held in my left hand, but didn't make a sound as he checked the package in my right. That made sense, since I hadn't put any metal in it.

He made me take off my knapsack and show him that it was empty, except for a PowerBar and a water bottle in the side pockets.

Satisfied, he said, "Follow me." We entered one of the elevators at the back of the lobby, and he inserted a keycard into a slot before pushing the button for the fourteenth-floor penthouse.

As we ascended, I surreptitiously slid a penny-sized

transmitter off the metal of my clipboard and into my left hand.

An olive-skinned, black-haired young man sitting at a desk looked up when we stepped off the elevator. Behrouz Salehi, according to the personnel records, was Mr. Jamshidi's personal assistant. The reception area was furnished in opulent fashion, with thick shag carpeting, overstuffed leather couches, and incomprehensible—and probably expensive— abstract sculptures on white pillars. A floor-to-ceiling glass wall looked out over smaller buildings toward the Thames.

I walked over to Behrouz's desk, fumbling with my clipboard while reciting my line about Mr. Jamshidi. When I was close enough to the desk, I dropped the clipboard. I bent over to pick it up, using the desk as support—and pressing the sticky side of the transmitter to the underside of the desk's surface.

"I have authority to sign for him," Behrouz said, with an English accent that, to my ear at least, betrayed no evidence of his Iranian birth. Jamshidi hired lots of people of many nationalities, but his inner circle was exclusively Iranian.

Having already planted the bug, I could technically accomplish what I needed to by delivering the package to anyone on this floor. But I'd never met a multibillionaire before, so I said, "Sorry. My instructions are that he must sign for it personally."

"Who is it from?" Behrouz asked.

"HM Revenue and Customs." I figured this was the most important possible sender, because no business can afford to get on the bad side of the Tax Man.

He picked up a phone and spoke briefly in Farsi.

After listening to a reply, he nodded to me and said, "Mr. Jamshidi will be right out."

I counted off seconds in my head. If I reached sixty, I would just let Behrouz sign for it. But at forty-three, the wooden door behind him opened and a man in a blue pinstripe suit came through. If he was wearing the pinstripes to make himself look thinner, they weren't working. Or maybe they made him look only three hundred and fifty pounds instead of his actual four hundred.

I hurried over to him, holding out my clipboard. He took it from me, signed, and handed it back. I gave him the package and, without having said a word to me, he returned to his office and closed the door.

Now I just needed to get out of there. I headed for the elevator as quickly as I could without seeming suspicious. I couldn't be sure if Jamshidi would open the package immediately or—

An incoherent yell from the office made me suspect he had. I would probably yell in much the same way if I opened a package full of live cockroaches. So a calm trip down the elevator with George was out of the question. I sprinted for the door with the green exit sign over it, next to the elevator, and banged the bar to open it.

Descending the stairs three steps at a time, I could hear George's footsteps following me. And I couldn't be sure, but it sounded like he was gaining on me. Why'd I have to get stuck with a security guard who was in better shape than I was?

As I passed a door with the number 10 painted on it, I pulled my water bottle from my knapsack, opened the top, and emptied it behind me as I ran. "Don't slip on the water at the tenth floor," I shouted. Just because he was chasing me didn't mean I wanted him to break his neck. I just wanted him to slow down a bit.

It worked. The footsteps behind me stopped, and I heard him talking to someone, presumably on his radio, telling them to block the exits. A few moments later, his footsteps resumed, but a bit more cautiously.

I exited the stairwell at the seventh floor. If the building schematics were right, a large janitorial closet was located to my right. It was there, but locked. I slipped my carbon-composite lockpicks out of my waistband and had the door open in less than ten seconds—but that was long enough for George to come in from the stairwell and spot me.

Giving him a friendly wave, I stepped into the closet and closed the door behind me. It locked with a click.

It was pitch dark inside, but the schematics had shown a light switch by the door. I fumbled around until I found it.

The doorknob rattled, then George yelled, "Come on out of there. You can't escape."

I used my knapsack straps to lash the doorknob to a shelf of cleaning supplies, just in case someone with a key arrived within the next minute. Then I sat on a stepladder, caught my breath, and started counting off the seconds.

George stopped pounding and started talking on his radio. "I've trapped him in the cleaners' closet on seven." A pause. "No, there's no way out from there." Pause again. "He's a quick little guy, but now that he's cornered, I should be able to handle him. You check on the boss. He did something to him."

I made a silent objection to being described as a "little guy." Granted, George outweighed me, but we were both about six feet tall.

My count reached forty.

"Cockroaches?" George's voice was astonished. After a pause, it grew even more astonished as he said, "What do you mean he doesn't know who brought them? It was the guy I've got locked up here. I saw him give the boss the package with my own two—"

And then, just as if someone had switched to another channel showing a completely different episode of the George Vance Show, he continued, "—secure here on seven. I'll come up and help you look."

That was it—he'd forgotten me. No one ever remembered me after not seeing or hearing me for a minute. Call it a talent, call it a curse, call it whatever—I didn't know why I couldn't be remembered, but that's what let me do my job.

Even after living for twenty-five years with my talent, I didn't understand why it worked, but I had figured out most of its effects and limitations.

Solid, physical evidence of what I did always remained, like the cockroaches, or the electronic bug I'd planted on the desk. But it seemed that any evidence of my presence that directly relied on electrons or photons always vanished within a minute after I was gone. That meant I disappeared from videotapes and undeveloped photographs. No computer could hold onto any information about me. And, since the neurons in the brain used electrical signals, it meant no brain could remember me.

The only way to store any information about me was to put it in permanent physical form while I was still around—printing a digital picture, for example. Even then, if I wasn't around, people's memories of that information would disappear a minute after seeing it. Not only that, but anyone they told about me would forget me, too.

I allowed some time for George to walk away, then I left the closet, took an elevator down to the lobby, and walked out of the building.

Phase One of my plan was complete. Now for Phase Two.

I walked around the corner to the white van I'd rented yesterday. This morning I'd painted a logo on the side, consisting of a black silhouette of a cockroach in the center of a red circle with a slash through it. I hopped into the back of the van and pulled on a workman's jumpsuit with the name Larry embroidered on the lapel.

Then I had to pull it partway off to get to my modified iPhone. I activated a special app that allowed me to play the recording from the bug I'd planted in the penthouse. I was pretty sure they would call an exterminator to deal with the dozens of cockroaches that would now be scurrying around Jamshidi's office, but it would be kind of awkward if I showed up before they called one.

Hearing Jamshidi's yell of surprise again was satisfying. Angry shouting in Farsi was interspersed with Behrouz speaking in an apologetic tone. The elevator dinged, and a few moments later Jamshidi switched to English, saying, "You are supposed to check all packages. How did all these insects get through?"

"I'm sorry, sir, but we just check for weapons," said a new voice, presumably a guard. "Company policy is we're not supposed to look at confidential documents."

Jamshidi let out an exasperated sigh. "As of now, company policy has changed. It seems we are being targeted by environmentalists."

Good—that meant he had seen the manifesto I had included in the package, calling Jamshidi Oil, Ltd., "an infestation of vermin that must be exterminated from the face of Mother Earth."

After some more instructions to the guard about tightening up security, Jamshidi said, "Call someone to kill these things. I don't want them laying eggs in my office."

I smiled.

A few minutes later in the recording, Behrouz was on the phone with an extermination company, and from his side of the conversation it sounded like it would be at least an hour before they could get anyone out. So I hung out in the van for forty minutes, then drove it around the corner and parked right in front of Jamshidi Oil, Ltd, so my artwork on the van would be clearly visible.

For the second time today, the glass doors parted before me and I strode to the reception desk. The same blonde receptionist looked me over, but of course she didn't recognize me as the courier from before. She wouldn't even remember that courier—I was completely gone from her memory.

"Somebody called for an exterminator?" I said.

"I'll have someone take you up," she said, then called someone.

George emerged from the same door as before,

and we went through a similar security routine. The metal detector whined about my keyring, which George demanded I remove from my pocket. He inspected it carefully and found a bunch of keys. He inspected my iPhone. Then he examined the contents of my backpack: a gas mask, various spray bottles, and a canister labeled "Roach Bomb."

"Gas mask?" he asked.

"I work with some pretty toxic chemicals. Trust me, you do not want to breathe them in."

He nodded. "Will we need to evacuate the whole floor?"

That would make my job easier. But it was no good telling him to evacuate the floor. The moment he forgot me, he would forget telling people to evacuate. People's memories would change to give them a reason why they were no longer on the fourteenth floor, but nothing would prevent them from returning. So there was no point.

"Let me evaluate the situation first," I said.

George took me up in the elevator, and we emerged into the waiting area outside Jamshidi's office. Jamshidi was there, talking on a cell phone, and he waved me toward his office door.

As I brushed past Behrouz's desk, I retrieved the bug I'd planted—no sense in leaving any traces, and I could re-use it on a future job.

Inside Jamshidi's office, a couple of smushed cockroaches showed up against the deep-pile beige carpet. The corner office had magnificent views of the London skyline out the two walls made entirely of glass. Jamshidi's desk, made of intricately carved wood, faced at an angle toward the glass corner so he could sit in his massive brown leather chair and look over the city. Behind the chair was a series of shelves filled with assorted books.

On the desk were two computers. One of them was my target, but I did my best to not look at it.

"Hmm," I said, making a show of peering around the room. "Looks like the bugs have already scurried into whatever nooks and crannies they could find."

Out in the waiting area, the elevator dinged.

"Only way to be sure of getting them all," I said, pulling the canister out of my backpack, "is to use this. So you'll need to clear the room."

George headed for the door while I brought out my gas mask. I was about to put it on when I noticed George had stopped in the doorway. I looked past him to see a second security guard and a man in coveralls with BugBanishers written across the front.

Against all odds, the real exterminator had showed up early.

I lunged forward and shoved George in the back. He went sprawling onto the carpet of the waiting area. I slammed the door shut, locked it, and started counting seconds.

My plan was still the same, just on a slightly faster timeframe. With a few twists, the cap came off the canister.

I had to take a moment to psych myself up for the next step: setting off the smoke bomb. When I was a kid, I was caught in a fire. Even without flames, smoke tended to make me anxious.

Someone pounded on the door.

Taking a deep breath, I activated the smoke bomb, then tossed it into the middle of the room.

As thick smoke billowed out of the canister, I put on my gas mask. Then I made my way to the desk and hid under it. If they managed to break through the door before the sixty seconds was up, that might give me the few extra seconds I needed for them to forget why they were breaking down the door.

The pounding continued, but fortunately the door still held.

The smoke in the room quickly became thick enough that I could barely see the chair three feet away. Even though I had the gas mask on, my breathing became labored. I knew it was psychological, so I tried to breathe evenly and concentrate on my counting.

Just as I reached twenty-seven seconds, the building's fire alarm blared to life. Good. That would give them reason to evacuate the floor as soon as they forgot about me.

At forty-three seconds, there was a splintering crash, followed by the thud of a body hitting the floor. Someone groaned, then coughed.

"Find him," said Jamshidi, shouting to be heard over the fire alarm.

Through coughs, George said, "He has a gas mask."

A male voice I didn't recognize said, "There's no way out of—"

Sixty seconds.

"—too thick, sir," continued the voice. "It's too risky. Let's get you safely out of the building."

I waited another thirty seconds to give them time to be on their way downstairs, then came out from under the desk. Jamshidi's brown leather chair was comfortable, although the armrests were set too wide apart for me to use. But I wasn't there to relax.

After pulling the keychain out of my pocket, I flipped through the keys until I found the one I wanted. With a strong tug, the blade of the key separated from the rest. The part that had been concealed served as a USB drive. I plugged it into the computer on the left, then leaned forward so I could see the screen through the smoke.

An antivirus program popped up a warning screen, which I clicked to cancel. The specially designed worm on the USB drive activated, automatically bypassing the login.

When I saw that his browser was open to a web page, I knew this was the wrong computer. My target was the computer that was inaccessible to remote hackers because it was not connected to the Internet.

I removed the USB drive and plugged it into the other computer. The worm again bypassed the login, and I had access to Jamshidi's secret files. Of course, they were mostly written in Farsi, but the drive had an automatic translation system on it.

Jamshidi was liquidating billions of dollars in assets— even the financial papers had noticed that—but no one seemed to know what he was doing with the money. My job was to find out.

My big advantage on a job like this was that I didn't need to erase the tracks of what I did on the computer—because computers forgot me, sixty seconds after my last interaction with it, all trace of what I had done would be gone. Jamshidi would never know his computer had been accessed.

My big disadvantage was that I couldn't just copy the files onto the USB drive, because after a minute it would forget I had copied them. Printing files would work—because getting them into physical form put them beyond the reach of my talent—but Jamshidi did not have a printer connected to this computer. And lugging up a printer full of paper might have raised a few questions from George.

So that left one other way of getting the information out: my memory. I would need to locate the key data and remember it. The problem was, I didn't really know exactly what I was looking for.

I brought up a list of translated document names and sorted them by most recent. A document with "Shipping Manifest" in the name caught my eye, and I opened it. It listed tons of computer equipment—three hundred and seventy-four tons, to be exact. Departure from the Port of London. Destination: Bushehr, Iran.

There were other shipping manifests with similar information. Whatever Jamshidi was doing required a lot of computing power.

I almost skipped over a document titled "Prophet," because I thought it would just turn out to be something to do with Islam, but then I wondered why Jamshidi would keep religious stuff on his protected computer.

The document popped open. I had just enough time to see the words "quantum supercomputer" before I heard someone cough behind me.

I whirled in the chair. Partially obscured by smoke, the vague shape of a man stood inside a lit rectangle. This was something completely unexpected: the building plans had not shown a secret door at the back of Jamshidi's office.

"Who are you?" the man demanded.

I whirled back to face the computer, then kicked

the leather chair backward toward the intruder, hoping it would block him temporarily. The USB drive was still plugged in, so I yanked it out. There couldn't be any physical evidence of my hacking or it wouldn't matter that no one remembered me.

As I rounded the corner of the desk and headed for the door, someone grabbed my right arm. I twisted out of his grip and lunged for the door. By the time I got to the stairwell, despite the fire alarm's shriek I could hear his footsteps close behind, punctuated by coughs as he tried to clear his lungs of smoke. For the second time that day, I ran down the steps.

As the stairs turned at the thirteenth floor, I looked up and saw my pursuer. He looked around fifty, with a fit, muscular build and a full head of black hair graying at the temples. He wore a white shirt, no tie. There hadn't been anyone like him in the personnel files.

I lost sight of him as I looped down the stairs. But his footsteps didn't slow. Just before reaching the tenth floor landing, I remembered that it was probably still wet from my water bottle. I slowed to a walk, stepping carefully, and took advantage of the moment to pull off my backpack. Since the smoke hadn't spread down here, I took off my gas mask, shoved it into the pack, and pulled out two spray bottles.

Breathing easier as I continued down toward the ninth floor, I shouted, "Watch out for the—"

A yell and a thud told me my warning had been too late.

"—water!" I finished.

I had to slow him down even more if I wanted to put a minute's distance between us. I unscrewed the top of one spray bottle and poured oil over the ninth floor landing. "It's slippery down here," I shouted. "Slow down!"

His footsteps didn't resume immediately, so my pace was more leisurely. As I reached the seventh floor, I decided there was no need to detour to the janitorial closet.

When I reached the fifth floor, I could faintly hear his footsteps again, but I estimated he was still about three floors behind me.

As I turned toward the third floor landing, the footsteps were louder, but I thought they were still far off.

Then I saw him less than a half-flight of stairs behind me. He had taken off his shoes, and in his socks he made so much less noise I had misjudged the distance.

With a burst of speed, I raced toward the ground floor. The man was in fantastic shape, especially for someone about thirty years older than me, and he continued to gain.

My second spray bottle—filled with concentrated capsaicin—was still in my hand. Pepper spray was always my last resort, because I hated to leave people temporarily blinded without any idea of what had happened to cause it once they forgot about me. But this guy wasn't giving me much choice.

I turned suddenly, aimed the nozzle at his face, then squirted.

He dodged to the left and mostly avoided the spray, but he stumbled and had to catch himself on the railing to keep from sprawling onto the landing.

I ran. If I could make it to my van parked right

outside, I was sure I could get a minute head start before he could get a vehicle to follow me.

Bursting into the lobby, I headed straight for the glass doors.

As he exited the stairwell only about ten seconds behind, he yelled, "Guards! Get him!"

There weren't any guards between me and the doors. There was no one in the lobby. The fire alarm was still sounding, so people must have evacuated.

But my van was gone—they must have towed it.

A moment of panic subsided when I spotted my messenger bicycle still chained to the lamppost. I dug into my left pocket for my keys while using my right hand to spray capsaicin randomly behind me, hoping that would slow him long enough to get my bike lock open.

Fortunately, the automatic doors were stuck open, maybe because of the evacuation. As I passed through, I dropped the spray bottle, switched my key to my right hand, and ran to my bike.

It took me only a couple of seconds to unlock the chain. Pushing the handlebars, I sprinted alongside the bike before hopping on and beginning to pedal.

I chanced a look over my shoulder. The man was still running after me, but he was falling behind. I wove through pedestrians on the sidewalk until I got into the street, then pedaled away.

Once I was sure I had left him more than a minute behind, I pulled over to catch my breath. I got out my iPhone and checked the time. It would be a little after eight a.m. on the East Coast of the United States. Perfect. I don't have any contacts listed in the phone—not because storing phone numbers would be a security problem but because it would forget them after I entered them. So I dialed a number I had memorized.

A computer-generated female voice on the other end answered, "How may I direct your call?"

"Edward Strong," I said.

The phone rang a few times, then someone picked up. "Strong here."

"Mr. Strong," I said, "in the lower drawer on the right side of your desk, there is a manila file folder labeled 'CODE NAME LETHE.' I need you to pull it out and read the cover letter. There should also be an authentication protocol sheet in there."

Having to go through this sort of rigmarole every time I reported in was an inconvenience. But what else could I do?

My name is Nat Morgan. And even though they don't remember me, I work for the CIA.

Chapter Two

I've been forgotten all my life. The day I was born, my parents left me at the hospital and drove home. They didn't realize it until a couple of hours later, when my grandmother arrived from out of town and asked where the baby was.

My mother cried all the way back to the hospital, feeling guilty because she couldn't even remember giving birth to me. It probably didn't help that my grandmother was in the back seat, telling her what a bad mother she was obviously going to be. When my parents returned to the maternity ward, the nurses were very confused, because no one had filled out the paperwork on my birth. They finally located me because I was the only baby left after they'd accounted for the rest.

After they got home, guilt over forgetting me made my mother cling to me. She sat in the rocking chair in the living room and held me for hours. To her shock, both my father and my grandmother forgot my existence after leaving the room.

Once I was old enough to understand, my mother read me the journal entry she wrote that night, still cradling me in one arm. She was exhausted, but terrified that she would forget me again if she fell asleep.

Which is exactly what happened.

For obvious reasons, I wasn't the easiest child to raise. My mother never complained to me, so it wasn't until I read her diaries that I understood how difficult it was for her, particularly at first.

She would be puzzled to hear a baby crying in the apartment and go to investigate. I would be in a crib in the room she and my father had decorated as a nursery back when she was pregnant. She would pick me up to try to calm me down while she figured out whose baby I was. Then she would remember that she wasn't pregnant anymore and wonder if I was hers and if she had amnesia. Then she would go and check her journal to try to figure things out.

I don't know how many times she went through that cycle of rediscovering me before she started pinning a note on my jumper that read "Tina, you don't remember him, but this is your baby, Nat. Read your journal."

Over the next few years, my mother set old-fashioned wind-up alarm clocks with notes on them to remind herself to feed me and check up on me. Even after I was old enough to find her when I needed something, she kept detailed journals of her interactions with me. Fortunately, she liked the feel of writing in a paper journal, because anything she typed into a computer about me would soon end up changed to read as if I had never been there. Eventually she discovered that if she printed something out immediately, the printed copy wouldn't change, so she would sometimes take pictures of me with a webcam and print them out to put in a photo album.

Because all the hospital records were on computer, there was no record of my birth, and since she and my father hadn't decided on a name before I was born, she wasn't sure what name they told the hospital for the birth certificate.

So she called me Nat, after Nat King Cole, because she hoped that someday I would become unforgettable.

Of course, that had never happened.

It was just my mother and me as I was growing up—my father couldn't handle it and left when I was just a few weeks old. After he left, he didn't remember having a son, just that he and my mother kept arguing.

The amazing thing about my mother is that she could have given up on me at any time, just like he did. All she had to do was abandon me somewhere, and a minute later she would have forgotten I even existed, and she could have moved on with her life because no one else remembered me either. Instead, she quit her job and lived off welfare in order to take care of me.

I was homeschooled, of course. It would have been too awkward having to reintroduce myself to classmates and teachers multiple times every day, constantly being the new kid.

I never had a friend for more than a day. If I spent all day with someone, they'd remember me while we were together. But eventually they had to sleep, and when they woke, the memory of me would be gone.

So I grew up unconnected to anyone but my mother, and even she needed to be reminded to read her journals so she would know who I was. I know it sounds like a strange life, but it was the only life I knew, and I was happy enough.

When I was eleven years old, my appendix ruptured. Because we had no car, my mother called 911. The pain I felt while waiting for the ambulance was the worst of my life.

In an attempt to distract me from the pain, my mother asked me to recite the Vice Presidents of the United States. "John Adams," she said, to get me started.

I didn't have a photographic memory, but my mother discovered early in my childhood that I was very good at memorizing things. She told me many times that my excellent memory was "ironic," which at first I thought meant it was magnetic like iron, until I finally looked it up in a dictionary.

When homeschooling me, she helped me develop my skills by giving me lists, like vocabulary words or state birds or elements of the periodic table, to memorize. When I was ten, I even memorized the first thousand digits of pi.

So, lying in my bed while the ambulance was on its way, I recited the Vice Presidents of the United States, followed by the capital cities of Europe and the plays of Shakespeare in chronological order. And by concentrating my mind on something other than my physical pain, I was able to bear it.

That memory training came in handy in other ways once I started working for the CIA. My Russian accent

might be terrible, and the grammar didn't come naturally, but I memorized large amounts of phonetically
spelled vocabulary without too much trouble. And, of
course, I had memorized the authentication protocol
sheet I used with Edward.

I still found it quite ironic that people could forget
me within a minute, yet if I concentrated I could still
remember lists of useless information I had learned
as a child.

One night when I was thirteen years old, my mother
shook me awake to the sound of sirens. From the
fourth floor of our high-rise apartment building, I
looked out my bedroom window to see fire engines
pulling up in the street.

By the time we got to the hallway, the fire was
in the stairwells. We went back into our apartment
to try the fire escape, but the fire had started below
us on our side of the building—the steps descended
into flames.

My mother screamed out the window for someone
to help us, then we huddled together low to the floor,
trying as much as possible to avoid the smoke filling
my room.

Suddenly, she rose to her feet. "My journals!" she
cried. When I started getting up to go with her, she
said, "Stay here." She rushed out the door, headed
toward her bedroom.

She came back a few moments later with some
of her journals cradled in her arms, but flames had
caught onto her nightgown.

I remembered what she had taught me about fire
safety. I grabbed the blanket off my bed and tackled

her to the floor, wrapping the blanket around the flaming part of her nightgown. "Roll," I said.

She rolled, and the flames went out.

But the smoke was thicker now, and we were both coughing. My lungs felt like they were burning, and I lacked the strength to even reach out to hold my mother's hand.

Through my squinted eyes, I saw two shapes enter the room. Firemen. One of them hoisted me over his shoulder and started out. I saw the other pick up my mother—and the journals fell from her grip as he lifted her.

"No! I need those," she said, but he ignored her.

The firemen carried us out and put us on stretchers.

I can still remember the way my mother's voice wheezed as she called my name, trying to make sure I was all right.

The paramedics rushed us both to the hospital.

In separate ambulances.

Later that night, I crept down the corridor in my loose-fitting hospital gown, hoping none of the nurses would notice me. At each door, I checked the digital sign outside each room, until I found the one with Tina Morgan on it. I opened the door and slipped inside, then closed it behind me.

After my eyes adjusted to the dark, the light coming through the open blinds was good enough that I could see my mother lying asleep in the hospital bed. I wanted to turn on the light, then wake her up and see if she remembered me, but I was scared she wouldn't. My only hope was to go back to our apartment and find some of her journals and photo albums so I would have proof when I told her that I was her son.

So I quietly said goodbye and slipped back out the door.

"Hey, kid!" a man said. "What are you doing?"

I turned to see a dark-haired man wearing a white lab coat over pale green scrubs, and I vaguely remembered that he was one of the doctors who had been checking out some of the other people rescued from the fire.

"It's my mother's room," I said. "We're fire victims."

"You need to get back to your room."

"I don't remember where it is," I lied.

"Come with me," he said. He led me to a nurses' station. Of course, with room assignments and even the door signs being computerized, there was no record of my being in the hospital at all, so I had to wait while they sorted things out.

After they put me in my room, I waited a few minutes, then snuck out. Obviously, I couldn't go home in the hospital gown, so I took some scrubs that were way too big for me from a locker, promising I would return them after I got the evidence I needed to prove to my mother who I was.

After all, I wasn't a thief.

Our apartment didn't even have a floor anymore. I spent hours looking through the still-smoldering debris that remained in the apartment below ours, despite being found and taken out several times by police who were trying to keep people away from the building.

It was evening and my borrowed scrubs were blackened with soot by the time I had to face the truth:

All my mother's journals, everything that connected her to me, had burned to ashes in the fire.

"But a DNA test would prove you're my mother," I said. It was a month after the fire that had destroyed all the evidence I was her son, and we were standing in the living room of my mother's new apartment.

She shook her head. "I don't know what scam you're trying to pull, but it won't work."

It was my third try, and the first two had ended this same way—she would rather believe her false memories of the past thirteen years than believe she had forgotten her own son.

I realized that in our old apartment, with my obviously lived-in room and the sheer accumulation of journal entries and photos, she had been able to convince herself she was my mother, but in this new home, it would take something more than a simple picture.

"Mom, please list—"

"Don't call me that," she snapped. She strode to the door and yanked it open. "Just leave or I'll call the cops."

Across the hall, a woman carrying two bags of groceries paused in her struggle to open the door and peered at us.

"Wait, I can prove the forgetting thing is real," I said to my mother. Raising my voice, I said, "Excuse me, ma'am, do you need a hand with those groceries?"

The woman answered, "No, thank you." She quickly opened her door and entered her apartment. The lock clicked behind her.

My mother scoffed. "What does that prove, other than your real mom taught you to be polite?"

"Just wait a minute, then go ask the lady across the hall if she's ever seen me before."

She stared at me. "You seriously believe this. You need help."

"Please, just try." I held up my hands in surrender. "If she remembers me, I'll leave with no more fuss."

After a moment, she stepped into the hall.

"Wait," I said. "It takes a minute."

When time was up, she knocked on the door. Footsteps approached on the other side, the lock turned, and the door opened a few inches. A chain prevented it from opening further.

"Excuse me," said my mother, "I know this sounds crazy, but you remember this young man offering to help with your groceries as you were coming in just now, don't you?" She pointed to where I stood in the doorway.

"No. And if he did, I wouldn't't'a let him. Can't trust kids these days. Probably run off with them."

"But you're sure he didn't—"

"Never seen him before. Go away." The door slammed shut, and the lock clicked.

"See," I said. "I told you, Mom. People forget me."

Her shoulders slumped as she turned to face me. "It can't be true. How could I forget my own child?" Tears brimmed in her eyes.

"It's not your fault," I said as she walked past me and sat on the couch.

"You look like your father," she said. "I should have seen it before."

I shrugged. "I don't remember him. You raised me."

"I thought the fire was a wakeup call," she said. "I was finally getting my life back together, finding a job, making friends. But it was you, wasn't it? My life for the past thirteen years is a blur because I can't remember you, not because I was depressed."

"It was me."

She let out a half-choked sob, which reminded me of how often I had found her crying in the mornings, and how if I asked her what was wrong, she always said it was nothing. It had been me, all along—every day as she woke up and discovered the truth, she had cried.

"I must have been a terrible mother," she said.

"No, Mom, you were the best." For the first time in my life, I saw the real sacrifices my mother had made to raise me. "I love you and always will, no matter how many times you forget me."

That only made her sob more.

"I'm sorry, Mom."

"For what?"

"For coming." I turned and walked out the door.

When I heard her call for me to come back, I began to run.

And so I was thirteen years old and living on the Dallas streets the first time I got caught stealing. Three weeks after I ran away from my mother, a store detective grabbed me as I stuffed a three-hundred-dollar digital camera inside my Dallas Cowboys sweatshirt. He took me back to his office to keep an eye on me while he called the police.

Until then, I had always gotten away just by running fast and turning corners. When I was out of sight for long enough, my pursuers would forget who they were chasing and why. But even after calling the cops this store detective watched me like I was his favorite TV show, and I was scared the cops would take me and lock me in a cell and then forget about me and I would starve to death.

Fear did not make me piss my pants, but it gave me a powerful urge, and I begged the detective to let me go to the bathroom. He finally relented and escorted me to the restroom, going so far as to follow me in.

I headed toward the urinal to relieve myself, but inspiration struck and I went into a stall instead.

The detective walked over and stood just outside the stall door. "No funny business," he said.

"No, sir," I said as I sat on the toilet seat. Then I held my breath. And despite the pressure in my bladder, I held that in, too. I sat as still as I could, not making any sound as I counted the seconds. Eventually the detective walked to a urinal, relieved himself, flushed, and walked out. Without washing his hands, I might add.

That's how I figured out that bathrooms were my friends.

After that first time I was caught, I realized that relying on my talent alone to get me out of tough situations was stupid. So I decided to learn how to pick locks.

I couldn't just go to lock-picking school. I couldn't even order a locksmith training course over the Internet like any civilized person, because when it came to computers, I might as well have had someone follow me around, hitting Ctrl-Z to undo whatever I had done.

So I traded some stolen jewelry for a used lockpick set at a pawn shop. And then, with the help of some library books, I taught myself to pick locks—first with the standard picks, and then with improvised tools.

The skill served me well in many ways. First, I no longer had to sleep on the street or at a homeless shelter, because I could get into nicer places while their owners were away. Second, I could steal the kind of stuff people tended to keep under lock and key. But most importantly, I had a way out in case someone locked me in a room and forgot about me.

Becoming a thief was only partly out of necessity. At the time, I was a friendless teenager who had just lost the only person who cared about me, and I was angry at the world. Stealing was my revenge.

But my mother had not raised me to be a thief. She taught me right from wrong, of course. But more than that, she believed I had a destiny.

"You have your talent for a reason," she would say. "God must have something special he wants you to do." I guess that was her way of justifying the sacrifices she made for me—that it was all part of some grand plan. She was so sure about it that I believed her.

Until the night of the fire.

I didn't date much as a teenager—or as an adult, for that matter. My talent did provide me with an initial advantage in meeting women, as I could try approaching a girl several times in order to find out what she liked. As for the end of a relationship, I never had to worry about breaking a girl's heart or being pursued by a jealous ex-girlfriend. A minute after I left, she would be over me.

While all that would have been great if all I wanted were one-night stands with women I'd just met, I

longed for something more than that. I would have
been thrilled just to have a real date. I lost track of
the times I'd take a woman out to dinner, only to
have her go to the restroom and forget she was out
with me. And begging a woman not to go to the restroom doesn't make a good impression. Neither does
following her to the bathroom and trying to carry on
a conversation through the door.

In that situation, bathrooms were not my friends.

When I was seventeen years old, I worked up
the courage to flirt with a cute cheerleader from the
local high school in the food court at a mall. After
a few forgotten attempts, she thought I was funny
enough that she invited me to a party at her house
that night, writing down the address with pink ink on
a paper napkin. I knew she wouldn't remember me,
but I fantasized I would just flirt again and maybe
we'd end up making out.

When I got to her house, the party was in full swing,
with some kids already drunk enough that they were
throwing up on the lawn. Her parents must have been
rich, because the house was huge—three stories tall,
with so many rooms filled with so many people that
after half an hour of searching, I still hadn't found
the cheerleader.

One guy heard me asking about her, and he said
she was his sister and he knew where she was. He
called it the "secret party within the party." I showed
him the napkin, and he said since she'd invited me
personally, he'd take me to her. Like an idiot, I followed him. He unlocked a door and shoved me inside,
then closed it.

It was not a secret party within a party. After I

managed to find a light switch, I discovered it was a windowless storage room.

I could hear him and his friends laughing outside, but soon they forgot me and wandered off. I reached for my lockpicks, and to my horror I discovered that in changing into nicer clothes for the party, I had left them in my other pants. I cursed myself for my stupidity.

Looking around the storage room for something I could use to unlock the door, I noticed lots of ceramic figurines, silver candlesticks, crystal vases, and other assorted fragile or valuable items. I realized that in finding a secure place to lock me up, the brother had put me in the same place that he and his sister had locked up the things they didn't want people breaking or stealing during the party.

I laughed when I found their mother's jewelry box. The party had turned out to be worthwhile after all.

Twenty-seven days before my eighteenth birthday, I was wandering through a mall looking for a good chance to steal something. As I passed a jewelry store, an employee took out a ring for a man and woman standing in front of the display case that held the really expensive diamonds. There was a pawn shop downtown that would only give me about five percent of what it was worth, but the rings in that case started at ten thousand dollars, so I figured it was worth trying a little snatch and run.

Like many mall jewelry stores, this one didn't have a door, so I just walked in, approaching the couple from behind, keeping them between me and the young man who worked for the store so he wouldn't

see me until I was close. I stepped up to the counter
right next to the woman, who was holding the ring,
and with a quick motion I grabbed it from her hand.

Just as I was about to turn and run she said, "Hey!"—
and I knew that voice. I looked at her face.

My mother. And she was looking at me with surprise
and disgust.

I froze, my heart pounding within me.

The dark-haired man she was with said, "Give
that back!" He looked familiar, and after a moment
I recognized him as the doctor from the hospital we
were taken to after the fire.

I looked back at my mother, and there was no love
or even pity in her eyes.

Then the employee reached for my hand holding
the ring, and I dropped it and ran, thoughts whirling
in my head.

My mother had not raised me to be a thief. She
had taught me right from wrong, taught me to be a
good person, and I had thrown that all away after I
lost her.

When I got back to the house I was currently
staying in—the owners were away on vacation—I
tried to put my mother out of my mind, but I kept
seeing her face. If she knew that I was living as a
thief, stealing from ordinary people, she would have
been very disappointed in me. She had believed God
gave me my talent for a reason, but I was just using
it for myself.

Even though she didn't know it, I had failed the
only person who had ever cared about me.

To distract myself from my shame and guilt, I
turned on the big-screen TV and flipped through the

channels. I stopped when I came to a car chase: two sports cars racing across the ice, one shooting at the other with a Gatling gun.

It was a James Bond movie. I let it distract me until I realized maybe I could put my talent to good use after all.

Chapter Three

I straightened the maroon tie I'd stolen from Macy's that morning and stepped into the interviewer's office. Becoming a CIA agent was my only choice if I wanted to go legit. I had to find a way to make this work.

The balding man behind the desk looked up. A placard gave his name as Tom Pendergast. From the look of his office—government-standard desk and chairs, tan file cabinet, no window, not even a family picture to add some color—Pendergast was a no-nonsense kind of guy. My stomach clenched even more. I had hoped for someone with imagination.

"You don't look twenty-seven," Pendergast said.

"I'm not. I don't have a Ph.D. in math, either." My words rushed out, and I sat in a chair to force myself to slow down. "I copied someone's resumé, just hoping to get the interview." It was a lot more complicated than that, but I needed to keep explanations simple for now.

Pendergast leaned back in his chair and pinched

the tip of his nose a couple of times as he looked me over. "You're what, eighteen?"

"Yes, sir." I rubbed the sweat from my palms onto the threadbare tan cloth that padded the chair arms.

"Fresh out of high school and watching too many James Bond movies? Tell you what—I admire your creativity." He grinned at me with enthusiasm, and for a moment I felt he might give me a chance. Then he continued, "Go to college, get a degree in something useful, and I'll guarantee you an interview when you graduate."

"I can't go to college. Anyway, I need a job that will pay me now, and I think you can use someone of my unique talents."

"I hate to disappoint you, but you're not much of a liar." He held up the resumé I'd sent. "A good candidate would have been able to walk through that door and convince me he was the man on this sheet of paper."

"I'm not a good liar," I agreed. "My talent is different. I have to show it to you."

"What is it?"

"You wouldn't believe me if I told you. You have to see it first. Write this down on a piece of paper: Nat Morgan promised to show me his talent. Then sign it and put the date and time."

He shot me a skeptical look. "I don't have time—"

"Please. I promise you'll be impressed."

"Nat Morgan's your real name?"

I nodded.

After a moment, Pendergast picked up a yellow legal pad off his desk and wrote. "Done. Now what?"

"Now I step outside for a minute and come back in." I stood up and walked out the door, closing it behind me.

After counting to sixty, I walked back into the office.

Pendergast looked up from his desk. "You don't look twenty-seven," he said.

"My name is Nat Morgan," I said, "and I promised to show you my talent."

"Sorry, I don't remember that. You'll have to make an appointment, because I'm supposed to see—"

"Look at your pad of paper."

"What?"

I pointed to the pad. "Read it."

Pendergast pulled the pad across the desk and looked at it, then looked at his watch.

"You must have snuck in here and written that while I was at lunch. How'd you get past security?"

"Is it your handwriting and signature?"

He leaned back in his chair and pinched the tip of his nose a couple of times. "You're a forger? It's pretty good work."

"I'm not a forger. The fact is you wrote that when I was in here a minute ago, but you forgot I'd been here after I stepped outside."

"I wouldn't forget something like that so quickly." But he stared at the writing on the pad.

"That's my talent: I'm forgettable," I said. "You know the old saying, 'out of sight, out of mind'? With me, it's true. A minute after I'm gone, no one can remember me."

He shoved the pad away. "I don't have time for this nonsense. You'd better leave before I call security."

This wasn't going as well as I'd hoped. "Don't bother," I said. I walked out of the office and closed the door behind me.

And sixty seconds after leaving, I walked into the

office for the third time. I hoped it would be the charm. There was no telling if I would ever again run into somebody bragging about having a job interview with the CIA the next day. I'd delivered a fake letter this morning telling him the interview had been postponed by an hour.

Pendergast looked up from his desk. His mouth opened.

"I don't look twenty-seven," I said, before he could say anything.

He closed his mouth abruptly, then opened it again. "I guess you get that a lot. I'd've pegged you at about eighteen. Have a seat."

I sat.

"Pretty impressive resumé," Pendergast said. "Nothing in it that says why you want to work for the CIA, though."

Telling him that I was tired of stealing things for a living probably wasn't the best idea, although I might have to give it a try later if nothing else worked. "I want to serve my country, and I think the CIA could best use my talents."

"Actually, someone with your math background might be better suited to the NSA," he said. "Their cryptography—"

"I'm not interested in cryptography. I'm interested in fieldwork."

"Been watching too many James Bond movies, huh?"

I was losing him again, before I even got far enough to tell him about my talent. He was going to write me off as just another spy wannabe.

"Call security," I said.

His brow wrinkled. "What?"

"Call security and ask them to send someone here."

"Why?"

"I want someone to check me to make sure I'm not carrying any weapons."

Pendergast's hand moved his phone. "If you've managed to sneak a weapon past security, that doesn't get you a job. That gets you a world of trouble."

"I'm not carrying. Just have them send someone."

He made the call, and in less than two minutes, a pair of security officers in navy blue uniforms came through the door. One of them methodically checked my body from head to toe with a metal detector wand, and then patted me down for good measure. All he found was the keys to my latest "house-sitting" location.

"He's clean," said the officer.

"Thank you," I said.

"As long as you're here, officers," said Pendergast, "why don't you just escort this young gentleman out of the building?"

"Wait!" I said, as one of the officers took me by the arm. "Aren't you even the least bit curious as to why I did this?"

Pendergast pursed his lips. After a moment, he said, "A little. So tell me."

"Not while they're in the room." Seeing he was about to object, I said, "I don't have any weapons. And they can wait right outside the room."

He nodded, and they left, closing the door behind them.

"What's your big secret?" Pendergast said.

Without saying a word, I stepped over to his desk, and picked up the pad of paper on which he had written earlier. I handed it to him.

He read it, then looked at his watch. "Who's Nat Morgan?"

I tapped my chest. I had to avoid speaking in case the officers were listening at the door. If they heard my voice before they forgot about me, it would keep reminding them of my existence.

"You came here under a false name?"

I picked up a pen from his desk, took back the pad, and wrote, "Is this office bugged?" I didn't care whether it was or not. It just gave me one more excuse not to speak. Each second that passed make it more likely the officers had forgotten me.

I gave him the pad back, and he read it. His face reddened, and when he spoke, his tone was angry. "Maybe it's all very funny to you, but the security of our nation is not a joke."

Knowing that I wasn't going to get the full sixty seconds, I hoped for the best and spoke quietly. "My talent is that I'm forgettable. I had to find a way to prove it to you, because you wouldn't believe me when I told you the first time."

"You've never told me."

I pointed to what he had written on the pad. "Do you remember me asking you to write this?"

"Obviously not. You must've faked it somehow."

"Call in the security guards. Ask them if they remember me."

He stared at me. "You're serious?"

"Go ahead. If they remember me, then have them escort me out of the building. But if they don't, please listen to what I have to say."

He went to the door and opened it. "Officers, could you step in here, please?"

The two of them came in.

Pendergast pointed at me. "Do you remember him?"

The officers looked at me, and I was relieved to see the puzzlement in their eyes. The one who had searched me said, "Doesn't look familiar, sir."

"Same here," said the other.

"I don't mean, do you remember him from some other time," said Pendergast. "I mean, you remember searching him in this office a couple of minutes ago, right?"

After a small hesitation, the one who searched me said, "Is this a joke, sir?"

"Officer," I said, "will you tell Mr. Pendergast what you do remember about the last time you were in this office?"

The officer looked at Pendergast, who nodded. "We came in and spoke to you, and then you told us to wait outside."

"Was there anyone else in the room?" I asked.

"Not that I saw," said the officer. "Of course, you must have been hiding somewhere."

After a few more questions, Pendergast dismissed the officers, then walked over to his desk and sat. He leaned back in his chair and pinched the tip of his nose a couple of times. "So, tell me about this talent of yours."

It took the CIA a while to find the right person to be my handler. Pendergast wanted the job and felt kind of possessive about me since he'd seen me first, so the higher-ups let him try. But I realized quickly that my handler had to be someone who wouldn't immediately dismiss me as a hoax every time I tried to contact him.

I went through four handlers before someone had the idea of assigning me to Edward Strong. He was career CIA, in his mid-sixties. No one ever flat-out told me why they thought Edward would be a good match, but my guess was it had something to do with the fact that he suffered from early-onset Alzheimer's disease. Medication had slowed the progress of his memory loss, but he was capable of forgetting people who lacked my talent. He knew his memory was bad, and so the fact he couldn't remember me didn't shock him. Plus, he could take notes in his own special shorthand, which meant he could take down my mission reports in a format that wouldn't disappear—and that would be proof to him that he really had dealt with me before.

The CIA didn't spend much time training me for combat—partly because my instructors couldn't remember what they had already taught me, which led to some wasted time. However, the most important reason was explained to me by my unarmed combat instructor, a petite blonde named Lydia.

"You're my instructor?" I asked, as she walked over to me in the training room.

"I am," she said. "Edward's just explained to me about your unique skills. Try to take me down."

"Take you down?" At five feet eleven inches, I was almost a foot taller than her, and I outweighed her by seventy pounds or more. I didn't want to hurt her.

"Yes, please," she said.

I reached out to grab her arm. She had me face down on the blue mat in less than five seconds. Her knee pinned my right arm behind my back.

She leaned in close to my ear and said, "You don't want to fight."

Even if she only weighed a hundred pounds, it all seemed to be concentrated on my lungs. "I don't?" I finally managed to say.

"No." She eased up, and I drew in a deeper breath. "You don't have the killer instinct."

"Can you teach me that?"

She laughed. "You can't teach instinct. Sometimes you can awaken it. But that's often a nasty process. Sometimes you can learn to fake it. But that's the wrong choice for you."

"Why?" I asked.

"Your talent is meant for someone who runs away and hides. That has to be your instinct. Training you to overcome that would be wrong. I'll teach you stuff to help you get away. But that's your focus: get away. Hide. Run, not fight. Don't try to be a hero."

The first time the CIA tried to book me on a flight, a few months after I joined, they ran headlong into the weirdness of my talent. The airlines all used computers to track reservations, so any details about my ticket would vanish.

So they tried booking me under an alias, figuring that the computers wouldn't know it was me. Those reservations disappeared as quickly as the first.

"It's no use," I told Edward as he hung up the phone after talking to the travel office. "There's no way I can fly anywhere, which means I won't be able to carry out any missions."

"Nonsense, my boy," he said. "Someone with your talents was born for a job like this. We just need to figure out the limitations on what is affected and work around those."

After some trial and error experimentation, we found a way: use an existing reservation made for someone else and informing that person his trip had been postponed. It meant creating new identity documents for me for every trip, but that was no obstacle for the CIA.

My assignments started off small, making dead drop deliveries. Then I was assigned to tail people they were interested in and report on their movements. Eventually the operations grew bigger and bolder. After only three years, I was back to stealing things for a living.

But now I was stealing them for the government.

Chapter Four

After seven years as a CIA officer, I had found my own ways of doing things. That's why, two weeks after delivering cockroaches in London, I was delivering pizzas in Barcelona just before one in the morning—that, plus the fact that if there was one thing the CIA hated more than not being able to break other people's codes, it was other people being able to break ours.

The headquarters of InterQuan loomed ahead of me, silhouetted against the clouds reflecting the nighttime lights of the city. InterQuan was Spain's leading competitor in the race to develop practical quantum computers, and according to a CIA source the company's engineers had just finished a prototype chip capable of—among other nifty things—breaking the encryption used for the secure lines to U.S. embassies worldwide.

My orders were to steal that prototype. I'd decided on a nighttime approach because cracking a safe during the building's working hours was more conspicuous.

Beyond the building's glass doors, the security guard sat at his desk in the lobby. Since I was carrying four pizza boxes, I hit the intercom button with my elbow and said, "Pizza." My Spanish might be lousy, but pizza was pizza.

I was working on the assumption that InterQuan, like many tech companies, fueled its operations with junk food and caffeine. If for some reason InterQuan was staffed entirely with health-food nuts, I would have to try a different approach.

The door lock buzzed, so I pushed my way into the lobby. I marched over to the guard's desk, where I deposited the pizzas. The warm scent of melted cheese escaped from the top box. *"Sesenta y dos euros,"* I said.

The guard said something to me in rapid-fire Spanish.

With a shrug, I said, *"No hablo bien. Americano."*

"Who order pizzas?" asked the guard. His English was slightly better than my Spanish.

"I don't know. They just give me an address, I deliver the pizzas, and I collect the money." I held out my palm and tapped it for emphasis.

The guard—Carlos, according to his name tag—scratched the back of his neck. "I not order, I not pay."

"Call upstairs," I said, holding my thumb and pinkie out next to my head in the internationally recognized hand sign for making a phone call. Then, pretending to remember something, I added, "Seventh floor. *Piso siete.*"

According to the CIA's source, that's where the prototype was. From outside the building, I hadn't seen any lights on that floor, and the parking lot was mostly deserted, but someone might still be working late up there.

Carlos got on his walkie-talkie and spoke with another guard. After some back-and-forth, he said, "Nobody there."

That made things easier. Just because witnesses won't remember me when I'm gone doesn't mean I want witnesses who could interfere while I'm stealing something.

Now I just had to shake Carlos. Muttering angrily to myself, I picked up the pizzas and turned as if to leave, then stopped, turned back and put the pizzas down. *"¿Dónde está el baño?"* I asked.

That was the most useful phrase in the world, for me at least. I could ask where the bathroom was in fifteen different languages.

Carlos pointed to a door off to one side. I went in, let the door close behind me, and started to count.

While I waited for Carlos the guard to forget me and find himself puzzled by the sudden appearance of four pizzas on his desk, I stripped off the pizza delivery uniform shirt I wore over my black long-sleeved tee and threw it in the trash. I pulled a black ski mask and gloves out of my pants pockets and put them on, checking in the mirror to make sure most of my skin was covered.

I didn't need the stereotypical cat burglar costume to hide my identity—my talent took care of that. But just because a guard wouldn't remember seeing me after I'd lost him didn't mean I wanted him to see me in the first place—they could be quite a nuisance in my line of work.

Underneath my shirt I wore one of the latest CIA-issue bulletproof vests, made from a flexible nanofiber that stiffened instantly to distribute a high-speed impact. My ski mask was made of the same stuff.

Bullets don't forget.

I cracked the door open and peeked out. The dilemma of the magically appearing pizzas had not stumped Carlos for long—he was helping himself to a slice. I hoped he would enjoy it, as partial payment for all the trouble he would be in after I stole the prototype. Guards like him made my job easier.

After a spate of well-publicized industrial espionage cases in which companies' own security cameras were hacked in order to steal the information, most high-tech firms had moved back to the lower tech of human security guards. But Carlos was evidence that such a strategy had its drawbacks—for the company, not for me.

Opening the door wider, I slipped out of the bathroom. Intent on his pizza, Carlos did not look my way as I walked briskly but quietly toward the elevators. I pushed the up button and then flattened myself against a wall, putting a potted plant in the line of sight from Carlos to me.

One of the elevators dinged and opened its doors. Carlos, with cheese stringing from his mouth to the slice he held, turned to stare at the empty elevator.

I waited for him to look away, but he didn't. Instead, still staring in my general direction, he put down the slice of pizza.

I couldn't afford to let him get close, or else I might have to start over from scratch. So I lunged through the elevator doors and hit the button for the seventh floor.

For a moment, Carlos looked at me wide-eyed, open mouth still full of mozzarella. Then he leapt from his chair and ran toward me. Even though I knew better,

I punched the 7 button several times in rapid succession as if that would make the doors close faster.

With a *ding*, the doors slid shut, leaving Carlos too far away to do anything but yell at me to stop.

Like bathrooms, elevators were my friends.

Between the third and fourth floors, I pulled out the emergency stop knob. Waiting here for a minute would allow Carlos to forget me. Even if he had alerted the other guards about an intruder, their memories of the conversation would change to something like an invitation to share the pizza.

After I restarted the elevator, I continued to the seventh floor. No guards greeted me as the doors opened. Following the route I'd memorized, I found my way to the lab where the prototype was being tested. The sign on the door read *Criptografía Cuántica*— Quantum Cryptography—so it looked like the CIA's source was right on the money.

He was right about the door lock, too: a standard numeric keypad. I wondered if the people who worked in the lab appreciated the irony of protecting a high-powered cryptography chip with a six-digit entry code.

Still, the standard set of lockpicks I had in one of the pockets of my black cargo pants would not work on a keypad, and neither would the nonstandard, carbon composite spare set of lockpicks sewn into the waistband of my pants. And the source had not given us an entry code. Maybe he didn't have one, or maybe he worried that the code could be traced back to him. I could drill the lock, but out here in the corridor the sound might attract attention. Instead, I pulled out another piece of cutting-edge CIA technology: the quantum key.

Essentially, this was a very weak, primitive version

of the prototype I'd been sent to steal. A six-digit entry code presented one million possibilities. Even if there were a hundred employees with individual codes to access the lab, the chances of guessing a correct code at random would be only one in ten thousand. With a mandatory ten-second delay between entry attempts, it would take more than a day to try ten thousand codes.

I removed the cover from the keypad and connected the quantum key to the wiring. According to the technogeek at Langley who had taught me how to use it, the quantum key would find a correct code as soon as I turned it on. "Imagine that the quantum key creates a million parallel universes," he had said, "and the key tries a different combination in each one. And then all the universes cancel each other out except for one where a correct code was entered. That's not really what the quantum key does, but it's kind of like that. The prototype you're going to steal does the same thing, except it creates like eighteen billion billion parallel universes."

A moment after I slid the quantum key's switch to *on*, a green LED lit up on the key. The door lock buzzed, and I entered the lab.

Despite being flush with cash from Spanish venture capitalists, InterQuan still had some of the cost-saving instincts of a startup. The wall safe at the back of the room was tough enough to keep out a junkie looking for cash—barely. It was not the kind of safe I would have used to store technology worth millions. However, weak as the safe was, it made the quantum key useless, because its lock used old-fashioned metal keys.

I got out my drill and lockpicks and set to work.

❖   ❖   ❖

The lock clicked, and I pulled the safe open. There were several circuit boards inside. I identified the one with the prototype chip based on a cell phone camera photo the source had taken. I put my drill and lockpicks back into their pocket and tucked the circuit board into another.

I turned toward the door and found myself looking into the barrel of a gun. The woman holding that gun was dressed all in black, including a ski mask. She must have come into the room while the noise of my drilling drowned out the buzz of the door lock.

"I suppose you're here for the prototype," I said. I hoped she was CIA. One of the problems with my job is that they sometimes send someone on the same assignment because they've forgotten they've assigned it to me.

"Give me prototype," she said. Her English was heavily accented—Russian, I thought.

Staring at the unwavering gun, I winced. Just because I had a bulletproof mask didn't mean I wanted to get shot in the face—my eyes weren't bulletproof. And even if the bullet hit the mask, it would leave a very nasty bruise. "Can I go to the bathroom first?"

I really needed to go.

Chapter Five

"Give it to me, or I will shoot you," she said.

Handing the prototype over to someone who could be an agent of the SVR—the Russian Foreign Intelligence Service—was not a very attractive option. But getting shot didn't really appeal to me, either. I decided that it might be easier to let her have it and then steal it back from her later. After all, she wouldn't remember that someone else was after the prototype.

Careful to make no sudden movements, I reached down to the pocket holding the prototype and took it out. "Here it is."

"Put it on table," she said, pointing to one of the lab workbenches.

I complied.

"Turn around and lie down on floor."

I lay down.

She must have walked to the door very quietly, because I didn't hear her footfalls. I heard the door open, then shut.

I gave her a one minute head start, then got up and raced to the lab door. I needed to get out of the building in time to follow her or I might lose her trail.

I opened the door and rushed into the hallway, and almost bumped into her. She stood with her hands held behind her head. Her gun lay on the floor. A few feet down the hall, a guard pointed a gun at her.

"¡Alto!" said the guard, swinging the gun toward me.

I raised my hands. At least the Russians weren't going to get the prototype. And maybe I could try again later, although security would probably get tighter after this.

Making a run for it wasn't an option, because then the guard might follow me and allow the woman to escape with the prototype. But I might be able to get the guard to concentrate on her instead of me.

"Jorge," I said, reading his nametag, "I'm a CIA officer." I hoped this guard's English was as good as Carlos's. "This woman is a Russian spy I've been tailing. I tried to stop her from stealing—"

"He lies," she said. "I never—"

"Stop!" Jorge shook his gun for emphasis.

We both shut up.

"Take off your masks," he said.

I stripped mine off and dropped it on the floor. She did the same. Out of the corner of my eye, I caught a glimpse of auburn braids pinned up on her head.

"Now your pants, mister," he said.

"What?" I said. "You're not serious."

"You have too many pockets," he said. "Take them off."

Reluctantly, I obeyed. I had to take off my shoes to get the pants off, and I piled everything on top of my ski mask. It was embarrassing, but at least I had the consolation that no one but me would remember this ridiculous scene.

"And your shirt," said Jorge.

"It doesn't have any pockets," I said.

He shrugged. "I don't trust you."

I took off my shirt, revealing the bulletproof vest.

"That also," said Jorge, so I added it to the pile.

Standing there in nothing but my boxer shorts and socks, I straightened to my full height, looked him in the eye, and said, "If you want me to take off any more, you'll have to buy me dinner first."

Beside me, the woman let out a tiny, soprano snort. "You are right not to trust him," she said, pointing at me. "This man kidnap me and force me to help him break in here. I grab his gun and run away when you found me. Thank you for saving me." Her tone was so desperately earnest, if I hadn't known she was lying, I might have believed her.

"Don't trust her," I said. "Arrest us both, and we can sort it all out later."

Another guard came running down the hall to join Jorge—Carlos from the front desk. Jorge turned his head to see who it was, and the woman dove toward her gun on the floor.

I could have dived for the gun and tried to keep it away from the Russian woman. Or I could have grabbed my bulletproof vest and used it to shield the guards from her.

Instead, I stood still and hoped nobody would shoot me if I didn't look threatening. The advice my CIA trainer Lydia had given me had destroyed my remaining illusions of becoming a James-Bond-style spy, but I had realized the wisdom of what she said and learned to play to my strengths.

Jorge must have noticed the woman's movement. He reacted quickly, stepping on her wrist as her hand closed around her gun. She cried out in pain. He pointed his gun at her face and said, "Drop the gun."

She did.

Carlos arrived and kept me covered with his gun. At Jorge's prompting, the woman got up and stood next to me again, hands behind her head.

"I warned you not to trust her," I said.

"*Silencio*," said Carlos.

They made her strip down to her bra and panties and then searched her clothes, where they discovered the prototype chip.

"I told you she was the thief," I said. "I'm on your side, really."

She glared at me. Jorge and Carlos ignored my comment and proceeded to discuss things in Spanish. The gist of what I could understand was that Carlos wanted to call the police, and Jorge wanted to talk to management first.

Police was good—I would eventually get away. Management could be better, or worse. There weren't a lot of prosecutions for corporate espionage, because the companies involved didn't want the stockholders to know how vulnerable they were. Sometimes management would pay a "security consulting fee" to a thief as an incentive to stay away and keep his mouth shut. And sometimes management decided that more permanent shutting up was necessary.

My Spanish wasn't good enough to determine which way the decision went, but Jorge pulled out a pair of handcuffs. Carlos became the subject of some rather heated scolding when it turned out he didn't have his handcuffs with him.

Finally, Jorge cuffed my left wrist to the woman's right wrist. Paying no attention to my requests that I be allowed to go to the bathroom, Jorge and Carlos then took us in the elevators down to the third basement level and shoved us into an empty storage room. The metal door clanged shut, and keys jingled as the lock clicked.

I smiled. In sixty seconds, Jorge and Carlos wouldn't remember who I was. When they came back for the woman, I would tell them some story about how I ended up here by mistake—although my state of undress might be kind of tough to explain.

First, though, I had to get out of the handcuffs, and my lockpicks were gone along with my pants.

"What's your name?" I asked the woman.

Her hazel eyes looked at me coldly. "Why should I tell you?"

"No reason, I guess. But can I borrow one of these?" I reached up to her hair, and before she could object I pulled out a bobby pin. An auburn braid flopped down beside her cheek.

"Ow," she said. "You pulled some hair."

"Sorry." With practiced ease, I bent the bobby pin at its curve until it snapped in two. Then I held my handcuffed wrist up so I could access the keyhole. The police generally don't spread this information around, but handcuffs are about the easiest locks in the world to pick. Once I get a bit of wire in the keyhole, it takes less than a second to pop the lock.

Except there was no keyhole. I blinked and twisted my arm around to look at the handcuffs from the other

side. Where the keyhole should have been, there was
only smooth metal.

"You've gotta be kidding me," I said.

"I make no joke," she said.

I shook my head. "That means 'I don't believe it.'
These handcuffs have no keyholes."

"Oh," she said. She pulled her handcuff closer,
dragging my arm along with it. "Is magnetic lock.
Only opens with special key."

Obviously I needed to subscribe to *Cat Burglar
Monthly* or *Handcuffs Illustrated* to keep up to date
on the latest developments. In any case, this complicated things. I tried to visualize myself explaining
my situation to Jorge or Carlos: "I was looking for
the bathroom, and I accidentally lost my clothes and
ended up here in this storage room, where this strange
woman somehow unlocked one of her handcuffs and
put it on me." No way that was going to work. And if
management decided to put us in permanent storage,
I wouldn't have another chance to escape. I wondered
if my corpse would be forgotten.

"Okay," I said. "Let's find a way out of here. I need
a bathroom." As long as she didn't have the prototype,
I didn't have a problem with helping her escape.

"Yelena," she said.

"What?"

"My name."

"Oh, right. Pleased to meet you. I'm Nat." I suddenly realized I was alone with a beautiful woman,
and both of us were in our underwear. My face grew
hot. I quickly focused on picking the door's lock.

A broken bobby pin worked great on normal handcuffs, but made for an awkward pick on a normal lock,

even after grinding it down on the concrete floor. After about fifteen minutes, I was getting close to opening the storage room door. Then I heard Jorge's voice in the hallway. He paused, then spoke again, like he was talking to someone on a cell phone.

"Quick," I said, handing Yelena the bobby-pin lockpicks. "Kneel here and pretend you were trying to pick the lock." I stood and pressed my back against the wall next to the door, with my handcuffed arm stretched awkwardly across my stomach.

She knelt, but said, "They expect we try to escape."

I chuckled. "They expect you. Not me."

Frowning, she glanced up at me. Then, with a jingle of keys, the door unlocked and swung outward.

"Move back," Jorge said. I still couldn't see him because he was standing outside the room.

Yelena scooted backward on her knees, holding her hands up so her right wrist wouldn't pull my left hand into Jorge's view.

"How did you undo the handcuffs?" Jorge asked, probably remembering having cuffed her hands together or to something in the room. And he moved forward enough that I could see his gun.

The situation was not ideal. Jorge was holding the gun in his right hand, with his finger on the trigger. I was to his left, which meant that in order to twist the gun out of his hand, I would have to turn the barrel toward me. From what Lydia had taught me, I knew I wasn't supposed to do that—especially not while wearing only my underwear.

So I varied the technique as I grabbed the top of his gun, pointing the barrel upward as I twisted the gun in his hand. I must have surprised him enough that he didn't think to pull the trigger, and I managed to wrench the gun from him.

Jorge didn't stay surprised for long. Holding the top of the gun, not its grip, meant there was no way I could fire it. He lunged toward me, reaching for the gun with both hands.

Chapter Six

I knew he could take the gun from me, so rather than try to keep it, I tossed it behind me as far as I could, then turned and pretended like I wanted to run toward it but that my handcuff link to Yelena was holding me up.

With a grunt, Jorge pushed past me.

"Come on," I said to Yelena, yanking her to her feet.

We ran through the open door, and I clanged it shut behind us. Yelena turned the key to lock it, then pulled the key out and kept the keychain.

Jorge pounded on the door behind us as we rushed down the corridor.

"Is the handcuff key on there?" I asked.

She looked at the keys as we ran. "No."

Of course not—that would have been too easy.

"Elevator's this way," I said, pointing to the right as we approached an intersection.

"They trap us in elevator," she said, pulling on the handcuffs toward the left.

Yelena was right—the guards might forget about me, but they wouldn't forget about her. As long as I was attached to her, my usual methods of escaping wouldn't work. I needed to get the handcuffs off.

And I still needed to go to the bathroom.

We headed down the hallway to the left. If I recalled the plans to the building correctly, a door near the end of the hall led to a stairwell. There would be an emergency exit on the ground floor, so we could bypass the lobby and escape.

Except I needed to find my clothes. Not because I minded fleeing into the dark in my underwear, although I did, but because the quantum key was in one of my pockets and the CIA wouldn't be happy if I didn't bring it back. The technogeek wouldn't remember he'd given it to me, of course, but it would be listed in Edward's notes.

We raced past a door with a sign that read *Laboratorio de Entrelazar.* I stopped running, forcing Yelena to stop as well. Did that mean laboratory of something-lasers?

"There might be lasers in that lab," I said, "or something else we can use to get these handcuffs off."

"Get out of building first," she said. "Guard call someone."

I had forgotten about Jorge's conversation as he approached the storage room.

"I need to get . . . something in my pants before leaving. But it's too hard with these," I said, raising our handcuffed wrists.

After a moment, she nodded.

The lab door was locked, but one of the keys on Jorge's keychain was a master key. We slipped quickly through the door and shut it behind us.

The room's lights were off, but a half-dozen flat-panel monitors displayed scrolling lines of data. Violet light radiated from a long apparatus of glass and metal that dominated the center of the room. At the far end, a pencil-thick shaft of bright violet hit a prism and split into two weaker beams that extended into holes in the wall.

"That must be the *entrelazar*," I said.

"What?"

"Never mind," I said. "Let's see if it's powerful enough to cut the chain on these handcuffs."

We raised our handcuffed arms over the laser apparatus, one of us on each side, and walked to the far end of the room. We stopped just before reaching the prism.

A nod from Yelena signaled she was ready, and we lowered our wrists slowly. I held my breath as the handcuff chain entered the violet beam.

The reflection off the metal dazzled my eyes, and I blinked back tears. But I held my arm steady, and so did Yelena. But the laser seemed to have no effect.

"It was worth a try," I said. "Let's get out of here."

"Wait," she said. She walked to one of the work-benches along the side of the room, forcing me to lean over the laser with my arm stretched out, and she rummaged in some of the drawers.

"What are you looking for?" I asked.

"Mirror."

"Why?"

"I help you get pants," she said. "Ah." She held up a flat mirror about one foot square.

"How will that help?"

She walked to the prism and deftly leaned the mirror against it at a forty-five-degree angle. The violet beam reflected up into a ceiling tile, which burst into yellow flame.

"Fire," she said. "We go now."

I stared at the flames in horror. Without any time to prepare myself, I found myself flashing back to the fire when I was thirteen.

"Nat!" Yelena's insistent voice wrenched my eyes away from the flames. We exited into the hallway and raced for the stairwell. A fire alarm blared from a loudspeaker on the wall, and strobe lights flashed.

"Security office on second floor," she said, her mouth close to my ear so I could hear her over the alarm. "Handcuff key probably there."

"Why did you start a fire?" I asked.

"Force evacuation, including security office."

It had been a smart decision on her part, I conceded. She didn't know my personal feelings about fire—and my feelings didn't really matter. All that mattered was salvaging what I could of this mission.

Water sprayed from sprinklers in the stairwell as we ran up three flights to the ground floor. I expected her to try to take the exit, but she didn't.

"Why are you helping me get my pants?" I said, squinting back at her through the strobe-lit spray of water.

"I need clothes, too."

I couldn't argue with that. A beautiful woman wandering around in the middle of the night, sopping wet, dressed only in her bra and panties, would attract attention.

On the second floor, I opened the door an inch and peeked out. A security guard I didn't recognize was barreling down the hall toward us.

"Up," I said.

We ran halfway up to the third floor and waited until the guard I'd seen was safely on his way down.

On entering the security office, I spotted a pile of black clothes on a table—and, just lying there for anybody to take, the prototype.

Yelena and I both lunged for it, but I had entered the office first and had longer arms, so I managed to grab it first.

"I stole it first anyway," I said, "so it really should be mine."

"No, I stole it first," she said. Of course, she had forgotten taking it from me at gunpoint. "You came after."

She searched through a drawer and pulled out a metal knob. "Here is key," she said. She held it next to the handcuffs and they unlocked.

I sorted through the black clothes, extracting my pants and making sure Yelena's gun wasn't in the pile. "You don't think that safe drilled itself and opened its door for you?"

She grabbed her clothes and began to dress. "Ah, you hide when I come in?"

"Something like that," I said. The quantum key was still in my pants. I put the prototype in a pocket and then dressed quickly. Now all I had to do was get clear of the building, and I could chalk this one up as a victory.

"Then is fair," she said. "You do hard work, so you get prototype."

She seemed to give in a little too easily, but it might just be a combination of professional courtesy and gratitude for my help in escaping.

She pulled her ski mask on, and I did the same.

By the time we snuck out the emergency exit door, fire trucks had arrived. In all the confusion, no one noticed us as we ran away from the building. I decided to abandon my car in the parking lot. It was just a rental under a false identity, anyway.

After we climbed the fence, I said, "I suppose we should split up now." I felt strangely reluctant to have Yelena forget me.

"Nat, wait." Yelena pulled off her ski mask, then reached up and peeled mine back. "To remember me," she said, and gave me a long, slow kiss.

It was the best kiss of my life. It was almost, but not quite, good enough to prevent me from noticing that she was taking the prototype out of my pocket.

I grabbed her wrist and pulled back from the kiss. "Let me guess: you simply wanted the prototype as a reminder of the good times we've shared?"

She smiled and relaxed her wrist. "Do you blame me for trying?"

"No."

"Good," she said.

Then she kneed me in the groin.

Chapter Seven

Chapter Seven

My usual motto on missions was: if at first you don't succeed, try, try again. But this time, the entire paradigm of the mission had changed. Instead of just trying different ways of breaking into the InterQuan headquarters in order to steal the prototype, I would have to track down a thief without even knowing who she really was.

Much as I hated to do it, I phoned Langley to report my failure. After the usual rigmarole of authentication using the manila file in Edward's desk drawer, I brought him up to date on what had happened—including the embarrassing way in which I had lost the prototype.

"Well," he said, "I suppose I could have you come in and look through pictures to see if you can identify this thief. Russian, you say?"

"She sounded Russian, but I don't know for sure."

"Hmmm." His keyboard clicked. "I think I've got a better idea. There's a quantum tech trade show thingy going on in Rome. Just the sort of place our thief might go to either sell what she's stolen or steal something else. Why don't you head over there and see if you can spot her? She won't remember you, right?"

"Right," I said. "Seems like a bit of a long-shot, though." The CIA must really be desperate to get that prototype.

"You can kill two birds with one stone," Edward said. "There's an Iranian physicist named, uh, Parham Rezaei. Genius in quantum mechanics theory, apparently. Giving a lecture at the trade show tomorrow. First time he's been outside Iran in several years. Have you ever heard of Kazem Jamshidi?"

"Yeah, I even met him. Look at your notes for my mission in London two weeks ago."

Papers rustled. "Hmm. Interesting. So you're the hush-hush original source on the supposed 'quantum supercomputer.' That's caused quite a stir here."

"Really?" As far as I knew, this was the first time I'd caused a stir at the CIA—other than by my simple existence.

"Yeah, especially after the vanishing act he pulled. He went back to Iran and then disappeared, and now someone upstairs is real worried. From what we can tell, Jamshidi's trying to build a quantum supercomputer that can predict the future. Accurately. The implications are tremendous—he could take over the stock market, give our enemies warning of our military plans. We haven't even thought of everything he could do."

I thought about it. In the hands of an enemy, such a supercomputer would seriously compromise our national security. "So, Jamshidi's connected to the physicist?"

"Maybe. This guy Rezaei's whereabouts have been

secret for a while. Some people think he might have been locked up as a dissident, while others think he's been working at a secret government lab, and now some people think he might be the brain behind Jamshidi's supercomputer. In any case, we want to track him, so your primary mission is to plant a tracer on one of Rezaei's shoes. You have access to a tracer?"

"Several. Part of my standard kit."

"Right. Meanwhile, if you see the thief, try to get the prototype, but that's secondary."

So, after about three hours of fitful sleep in an apartment owned by a CIA front company, I headed over to the airport. At the Alitalia counter, I bought a first-class ticket to Rome. That was enough to get me through security, although by the time I reached the gate, the airline's computer system would have forgotten my ticket. I threw the ticket in the trash, waited until the flight was boarding and the line was getting short, then approached the young woman at the gate's counter.

"I'm afraid I don't have my ticket," I said, pulling out a fake passport. "I need to get a new one."

She frowned. "How did you get through security?" Her accent was more English than Spanish.

I grimaced. "It's rather embarrassing. After we got through security, my girlfriend put both our tickets in her purse. Then we had an argument and she stormed off. But I still need to get to Rome for a business meeting."

She tapped the keys on her computer. "I do not see your name here."

I faked an exasperated sigh. "She must have canceled our reservations." Pulling out my credit card, I said, "I need to catch this flight. Preferably first class."

A few more taps, and she said, "That will be seven hundred and thirteen euros."

I nodded. The credit card company would approve the charge, then both the airline and the credit card company would forget about it. Technically, my flight was not being paid for, but Edward had assured me the CIA bought plenty of tickets that they never used, so it was balanced out.

She printed out the ticket, and I hurried to the ticket scanner. The scanner beeped its validation, and I was on my way to Rome.

QuantumExpo Europe was at the Palazzo dei Congressi, a gigantic convention center near the heart of Rome. I took a cab there directly from Fiumicino airport. Because it would be a shabby trick on the cab driver to use a credit card to fake paying, I paid cash.

After registering, I wandered down the aisles of booths on the convention's main floor. According to the printed schedule, Parham Rezaei's lecture on "Macroscale Quantum Superposition" would be at 6:00 p.m. tomorrow, so I had time to get the lay of the land—and see if I could spot a certain auburn-haired thief.

There was no luck on that account, so when I got tired of listening to marketing hype at various booth displays, I went to check out the lecture hall where Rezaei would be speaking, to see if there would be a good opportunity to plant the adhesive tracer on his shoe. As I slipped into the back of the hall, I was surprised to see almost all the seats were filled. The scheduled topic had seemed rather mundane—a panel discussion on Postponing Decoherence—and I had figured most of the attendees would already be approaching decoherence in the local bars.

But this wasn't a panel. There was only one man on stage, and after a moment I recognized him from the research I'd done for this mission: Parham Rezaei. His bio said he had studied at Oxford, and he spoke with a high-class English accent.

I pulled out my program and examined it. To my chagrin, I realized that the lecture was, in fact, today. When Edward had told me the lecture was tomorrow, it had still been Thursday for him, but already Friday for me.

Fortunately, no harm done. The lecture would last another half hour, so I settled in a seat on the back row and started scoping out ways to approach the stage.

I was sort of half-listening to the lecture when I caught him saying something about memory.

"...memory of observing the wave function to collapse at that point in time," said Rezaei. "However, from the point of view of a second observer not privy to the original observation, the wave function does not collapse until the first observer has reported the observation. The question then becomes, was there a quantum superposition of the first observer's memory? To use Schrödinger's famous cat, did the first observer have both the memory of a live cat and the memory of a dead cat until he spoke with the second observer, at which point one of those memories disappeared?"

I felt a sudden thrill of hope. Rezaei was talking about memories disappearing. It wasn't exactly the same as what happened with my talent, but it seemed like it might be related. If he really was a genius about this stuff, he might be able to explain why my talent worked, maybe even find a cure for it. In addition to planting the tracer on his shoe, I would have to figure out some way to talk with him for a bit.

Unfortunately, his lecture didn't go into any more details about people forgetting stuff due to quantum mechanics. But I was able to follow the gist of what he was saying. Basically, it was that the probability wave functions that governed things at the atomic scale also governed things at the macroscale—the scale of objects we could see and touch. Even human beings. But since an average human being consisted of about seven billion billion billion atoms, each with its own probability wave function, calculating the probability wave function of an entire human being was far beyond the capacity of the most powerful supercomputer in existence.

The bit about seven billion billion billion atoms reminded me of the CIA technogeek explaining how the quantum key worked, but that had involved only eighteen billion billions, which was apparently not beyond today's technology.

As the lecture wound to a close, I rose from my seat and walked down the side of the room until I was as close to the stage as I could get without actually clambering up onto it. I was hoping that when he was done he might come down to shake hands with people in the audience or something.

Rezaei got a standing ovation when he was done. But he didn't come down off the stage. Instead, two men with dark suits and physiques that might as well have been neon signs saying "Bodyguard" joined him onstage and then escorted him through a curtain in the back.

I hoisted myself onto the stage and then followed

at a brisk pace through the curtain and out into a backstage hallway in the bowels of the Palazzo dei Congressi. The three of them were twenty yards away, headed toward some elevators at the end of the hall, so I quickened my step, aiming to catch up about the time they reached the elevators.

When I was still ten yards back, one of the guards turned his head to look at me. He slowed, and I figured my plan of casually riding the elevator with them wasn't going to happen.

"Dr. Rezaei," I said. "I'm Brandon Andersen with *Quantum Tech Today*. Could I ask you a few questions?"

Rezaei stopped and turned to face me. The other bodyguard did likewise, saying something in Farsi.

I wished that Farsi was a language I had studied, but I only knew how to say I needed to use the bathroom. "If now's not a good time, I could meet you at your hotel room."

"It would be a pleasure, young man." He had a thick headful of white hair. "Hotel Pulitzer, suite 603. Could you meet me at eight-thirty?"

"I am afraid that will not be possible," said the guard on Rezaei's right. His English was slow and accented, but clearly understandable. "Dr. Rezaei has a conference call."

Rezaei shrugged as the guard took him by the elbow and turned him toward the elevators. "Sorry," he said.

"No problem," I said, backing away to show the other guard I wasn't going to press the matter. I had what I wanted, anyway.

At nine o'clock that night, I knocked on the door of suite 603 in the Hotel Pulitzer. I had a Manila envelope containing a few papers that I had printed up in the hotel's business center.

One of Rezaei's bodyguards answered the door. He glared at me suspiciously through the two-inch gap he allowed between the door and its frame.

"Delivery for Dr. Rezaei," I said. "From QuantumExpo management." I thrust the envelope through the gap, and the bodyguard took it and then closed the door.

Mentally counting off the seconds, I walked down the hallway to where I had left a second envelope of papers. When the minute was up, I returned to the door of 603 and knocked.

The same guard answered the door the same way he had before.

"Hi there," I said brightly. "My name is Alex Helps, from QuantumExpo. I'm here for my nine o'clock appointment with Dr. Rezaei?"

He frowned, then spoke Farsi to someone in the room before turning back to me. "There is no appointment."

I gave him a nervous laugh. "Did you not get the revised schedule? It was sent your room earlier today."

More conversation in Farsi ensued. Finally, the guard said, "Sorry, Dr. Rezaei is in a meeting. Come back in fifteen minutes."

"Okay," I said.

He closed the door.

Figuring it might be good to see just who Rezaei was meeting with, I hung out in the hall between his room and the elevators. About ten minutes later, his door opened and a fifty-something man with black hair, graying at the temples, walked out.

It took me a moment to recognize him as the mystery man who had chased me down from Jamshidi's office—which pretty much confirmed the link between Jamshidi and Rezaei.

He didn't even make eye contact as he passed me.

I approached Rezaei's door and knocked, and was answered by the same guard. "Hi there," I said. "My name is Alex Helps, from QuantumExpo. I'm here for my nine o'clock appointment with Dr. Rezaei? Sorry I'm a bit late."

We went through a repeat of the earlier scene, but this time it ended with the guard opening the door wide and beckoning me in.

"My apologies for the mix-up," Dr. Rezaei said, holding up one of the papers from the envelope I had dropped off. "We hadn't noticed there was a new schedule." He was sitting on an overstuffed couch in front of a coffee table. With a wave, he indicated one of the chairs across from him.

"Quite all right," I said as I sat down. I opened the envelope I was carrying and pulled out several papers. "Your lecture earlier today was such a success that we're hoping we can arrange to have you speak again tomorrow."

He shook his head. "I'm afraid that's quite impossible. I must go to London to conduct business there, and then back to Iran. My father is in ill health."

"I'm sorry to hear that. But can I just say how much I enjoyed hearing your lecture today? I found it fascinating, especially the part about someone having two different possible memories of an event and then only one is chosen."

"Oh, yes, superposition of memories. Quite an

interesting topic philosophically. What makes an event truly real, the event itself or our memory of it? That's not to say"—he chuckled—"that our memories of events are accurate, just that our memories are the results of events. But can an event with no results be said to have happened at all?"

I took a deep breath. "Dr. Rezaei, would it be possible for quantum mechanics to somehow make it so a person could not be remembered after he was gone? Kind of like there are two possible memories, that he was there and that he wasn't there, and then even though he was there the memory that he wasn't there is the one that gets remembered?"

He wrinkled his brow and stared at me. "You mean a causal event happens, but then is erased from the past so that its effects are not felt?"

As I was trying to parse through that to figure out what it meant, he went on, "Some of the quantum eraser experiments appear to do so, but so far not on a macroscopic scale." He picked up a spiral-bound notebook off the table, scribbled on it a bit, then said, "It is an interesting concept. What on Earth made you even think of such a thing?"

I debated telling him about my talent, but for some reason the bodyguards made me uneasy. I decided it was best to extricate myself. "Just a little debate with a friend. Nothing important. Sorry to have troubled you with it."

"Oh, it is no trouble at all," he said, still scribbling on his notebook. "I love to think tangentially. It is a great exercise of the mind."

At the very least he had given me a place to start—I could do some research on quantum eraser experiments to see if they might have some connection to my talent.

But I still had one job left to do.

As I stood up, I loosened my grip on the papers I was holding, and the middle bunch of about thirty pages spilled onto the coffee table and luxuriously thick carpet. "Whoops!"

"Oh my," Rezaei said.

I got down on all fours and began scooping up the papers. Rezaei leaned forward on the couch and tried to help.

"Don't worry, I've got them," I said, as I let some of the papers I had just picked up fall again, this time onto his feet. "Sorry. I'm sorry."

I reached forward and got my hand under the paper. The tracer—a device smaller than a thumbtack head and almost transparent—had two adhesive sides. One was a light adhesive kind of like Post-it notes, and one was a very powerful adhesive sealed in microscopic bubbles. The light adhesive had kept it stuck to the tip of my right index finger since I put it there about fifteen minutes earlier. Now, under cover of the paper, I jabbed my finger to Rezaei's shoe. The sudden pressure burst the bubbles, the powerful adhesive took hold, and I felt a slight tug on my skin as I pulled my finger away from the tracer.

"Sorry," I repeated as I gathered up the papers and rose to my feet.

One of the bodyguards escorted me to the door and out.

With my primary mission accomplished, I could now focus on my secondary mission: finding Yelena.

In the hotel lobby, I was about to throw the papers

into a trash can when I noticed one of them did not have smooth edges, but rather had been torn out of a spiral notebook. I pulled that sheet out and saw, in scribbled handwriting, the words: "I am a prisoner forced to work against my will."

Chapter Eight

After my usual phone authentication routine with Edward, he took a couple of minutes to review the latest notes he had made in my file. "So your primary mission was to plant a tracer on this quantum physics guy. How'd it go?"

"No problem," I said. "But there was an unexpected development."

"Oh?"

"He slipped me a note saying he was a prisoner being forced to work against his will."

"Really? That's a twist. Thought Jamshidi had recruited the guy out of Iranian patriotism. I'll note that down."

"Umm," I said. "Shouldn't we do something to help him?"

"You planted the tracer on him, right?"

"Yes."

"The most important thing is to find the lab where he's working. Once we've done that, we'll see what we can do about shutting it down, at which point he would be free. Okay?"

I reluctantly agreed. Rezaei had seemed like a nice guy caught up in a bad situation, and I felt a little guilty for not helping him out.

"What about your secondary mission, finding the thief who stole the InterQuan prototype?"

"No luck," I said. "I haven't spotted her."

Edward sighed. "Okay. Come back for debriefing and we'll see if you can ID her."

After about fifteen minutes of sitting in Edward's office scrolling through pictures, I saw her face. "This one," I said, handing the tablet over to him.

He tapped the touchscreen to bring up more info. "Her name is Yelena Semyonova." He went silent as he read more.

I watched him, moving restlessly in my seat just to make sure he wouldn't forget I was there.

"She probably drove to Paris," Edward said, "because she took a flight to Kiev out of Charles de Gaulle yesterday."

"So she gave me her real first name?" I asked. "That wasn't very professional." I did it all the time, but that didn't matter because nobody remembered. I wanted her to be a professional, because being taken down like that by an amateur made me feel stupid.

"Hmm." With arthritic fingers, Edward tapped the tablet. "We've got kind of a good news/bad news scenario here. The good news is she's not with the Russian SVR."

"Ukrainian?" If so, I felt a bit better about letting

her get away with the prototype, as the current Ukrainian government was pro-American.

"No. She used to be in the SVR, but she quit eleven months ago. The bad news is that we suspect she now works for one of the Russian syndicates."

I winced. "I should have anticipated she would—"

"Everyone makes mistakes, son," Edward said. "But there's more bad news: the syndicate she works for has been hired by this man." He handed over the tablet, which showed a photo of a bald, morbidly obese man. I recognized him before Edward continued, "Kazem Jamshidi. Iranian citizen, made most of his billions in oil."

"Yeah, I've even met him," I said. "I hacked his computer in London and found out he was working on a quantum supercomputer."

Edward raised his eyebrows. "You're the one who got that intel? That's caused a bit of ruckus around here—especially since Jamshidi returned to Iran last week and then we lost track of him. Anyway, we used to think he was relatively harmless, just trying to make Iran into the Silicon Valley of quantum computing so they'll have something to export when the oil runs out. But it turns out he's got a top-notch quantum physicist working for him. Guy by the name of Parham Rezaei—he's Iranian, too."

"Yes, I met him in Rome—I'm the one who confirmed he was working for Jamshidi. The report I gave you should be in your folder there somewhere. He gave me a note that said he was being forced to work against his will."

"Really?" Edward blinked a couple of times. "I figured Jamshidi recruited him through Iranian patriotism."

"Maybe at first," I said. "But not anymore."

Edward scratched his nose. "Anyway, from what we can tell, Jamshidi's trying to build a quantum supercomputer to precisely predict the future. That has strategic implications we're still trying to figure out, but for one thing he could easily become the richest man in the world just buying and selling stocks at the right time. And that's the most benign scenario."

"And he's hired the Russian mafia to steal technology to help build it?" I asked.

"Not just steal. They've kidnapped quantum physicists and engineers from around the globe—although they've steered clear of Americans and Western Europeans, probably to avoid riling us up. We're pretty sure they've assassinated key people in the industry, too."

"So," I said, "how do we stop him?"

Edward grinned at me. "That's my boy! Your file said you were enthusiastic, but it's nice to see it for myself." His smile faltered. "I mean, I guess I have seen it for myself, before, but . . ."

"Don't sweat it," I said. "I'm used to people forgetting."

"Right." He gave me a brief nod. "We know Jamshidi's built an underground lab somewhere in the Iranian desert, but we don't know where it is. We'd love to get a tracer to his lab. And you can help set that up."

"Actually, I already have," I said. "I put a tracer on Rezaei when I was in Rome. That was my primary mission there."

Edward rubbed the corners of his eyes with both hands. "Sorry, I—"

"Don't worry about it. It's not you, it's me. Happens all the time."

"Right. So, let's see where your tracer's been." He pulled up a map program on his computer screen, punched in some commands, and the map zoomed to Europe. It showed a trail from Rome to London.

"Rezaei said he was headed to London for some business," I said, "then back to Iran."

Edward zoomed in on London. "Unfortunately, it looks like the tracer stopped transmitting about five hours ago. The last location was..." When the map reached street level, the tracer path clearly entered a warehouse-type building on the bank of the Thames. "...a Jamshidi Oil warehouse."

"They must have detected it somehow," I said. "But why take a quantum physicist to an oil facility?"

"Oh! Oh!" Edward seemed excited. "There's something I read earlier. Where was it?" He swiped through some document folders on his tablet. "Here it is. An analysis of shipping traffic to and from Jamshidi Oil's London branch. The company has its own tankers. And, naturally, when they come into London filled with oil, they run relatively low in the water compared to when they are empty. But sometimes when the tankers leave, they are still too low in the water to be empty."

"So they're shipping something out from London."

"Precisely," Edward said. "They could be shipping quantum technology to their London warehouse to get around laws prohibiting trade with Iran. So they're probably having Rezaei check out the technology before it's shipped to the lab."

"Makes sense. But unfortunately, since they killed the tracer, we're not really any closer to finding the lab."

"Well, that's your next mission." He pulled a circuit

board out of an anti-static envelope and slid it across his desk to me.

It looked awfully familiar. "That's the InterQuan prototype," I said. "How did you get it?"

"No, it's a GPS tracker and locator beacon built based on the pictures our source at InterQuan sent us. You see, we don't think Yelena has had time to transfer the prototype to Jamshidi's people. So, we need you to catch up with her and switch this for the real prototype. Your talent can make it so she won't remember the switch, right?"

I nodded. "Shouldn't be a problem, if I can find her and she still has the prototype."

"Uh-hmm." He gave me an appraising look. "I like the can-do attitude, but I really don't like sending you into the field like this without any kind of backup."

Smiling, I said, "We've discussed this before. If I ever have to go radio silent for a minute, my backup will forget me."

"Right, of course. Sorry for bringing up an old subject."

"No problem, I appreciate the concern for my well-being. Don't worry about me—I'm used to getting myself out of tough situations."

A woman knocked at the door and brought in a manila envelope for Edward.

"What's this?" he asked.

"The documents you requested," she said.

"Ah, thanks." He opened it and leafed through the contents. "Quite satisfactory."

As she walked out, he said, "Okay, son, there's a seat booked on a plane to Moscow this afternoon." He handed me an itinerary, a credit card, and a passport.

I flipped the passport open to find my name was Bob Daniels. The passport photo was a digital shot we had taken earlier and printed in my presence.

"Moscow?" I said. "I thought she was in Kiev."

"She left for Moscow this morning." He picked up the tablet, pressed a few things, and a printer next to his desk started spitting out papers. "I'll give you Yelena's file to read on the flight."

While on the plane I perused Yelena's file.

Yelena Semyonova was born seventeen days after I was. Even though her parents could remember her, that didn't stop her father from leaving like mine had. Her mother had remarried, though, when Yelena was eight. She had twin half-sisters—Ekaterina and Oksana—nine years younger than her. Apparently her mother had been a figure-skating fan.

She majored in world politics at Lomonosov Moscow State University, but was recruited by the SVR and left before graduating.

According to the information the CIA had collected, Yelena was on track as a career agent for the SVR until a family crisis intervened. Her mother and stepfather had divorced when she was a teenager, with full custody of the twins given to the mother. But after a dispute with their mother last year, the sixteen-year-old twins had run off to live with their father.

Yelena requested various government departments to return the girls to the legal custody of their mother, but nothing happened. She had resigned from the SVR, and that's where the CIA information on her ran out, except for a note that she frequented a Moscow night club owned by the Bukharin syndicate.

I was a little disappointed by Yelena after reading the dossier. I could understand that she might get disillusioned by her government when they refused to help return her sisters, so her resignation didn't bother me. But working for the Russian mafia? Surely she had other options.

Then again, if the CIA hadn't hired me, I might have continued with my life of crime. So who was I to cast stones?

I put the folder back in my carry-on and slid it under the seat in front of me. Then I leaned back in my seat, closed my eyes, and remembered the kiss. It had been a good kiss.

I daydreamed a bit. I would locate her in Moscow, try approaching her several times until I found something that worked. We'd go out for a drink, she'd fall for me, and then she would kiss me again—before I stole the prototype from her, of course.

Idle daydreams are not a good basis for operational planning. So my actual plan involved locating the prototype and stealing it without even bumping into Yelena, let alone kissing her.

After landing in Moscow, I had a taxi take me to the apartment building that was her last known address, in case she hadn't moved after resigning from the SVR. The building was in a low-rent district, and the intercom at the door wasn't working. I walked up seven flights of stairs to apartment 73.

I knocked on the door. If she answered, I would be a befuddled American tourist who had come to the wrong address. I'd apologize and go wait outside the building until she left.

But the twenty-something Russian woman who answered the door was not Yelena, so I went with Plan B.

"Is Yelena here?" I asked in my atrociously accented Russian.

"She doesn't live here anymore," she said.

"I am a friend of Yelena. I was an American exchange student at the university with her." I had rehearsed these lines on the flight over. My vocabulary was good, but I couldn't get the grammar right without practice. "Could you give me her new address or phone number?"

She looked me over head to toe, and apparently decided I wasn't to be trusted with that information. "No," she said. Maybe she was overprotective, or maybe she was just a good judge of character.

"Sorry to bother you," I said, and walked away. I heard the door close behind me.

I stopped and counted to sixty, then returned and knocked on the door again. She answered.

"Is Polina here?" I asked.

She frowned, shaking her head. "You have the wrong apartment."

I scratched the back of my right ear. "Sorry, my mistake." I started to turn as if to leave, then said, "Can I use your phone to call Polina and get the right address?"

She looked me over head to toe. This time, the verdict was different. "Just for a minute."

"Thank you," I said.

She showed me to the phone on an end table in her living room. I dialed a random number. The phone call itself didn't matter. But it gave me the chance to surreptitiously stick a penny-sized electronic bug onto the bottom of her telephone.

Someone answered my call. I said, "Sorry, wrong number," and hung up.

"Thank you," I said to the woman, and I left.

Once I got to the stairwell, I sat down and took out a pad of paper and a pen.

Writing in Russian takes me a while, even if I'm just copying Cyrillic characters off the web browser on my cell phone. With the aid of an online translation program, after five minutes I managed to write the following message:

Warn Yelena not to trust the Iranians.

I knocked on the door for the third time. But instead of waiting for the woman to answer, I left a folded sheet of paper on the ground and then ran.

Sitting back in the stairwell, I pulled out my iPhone and brought up the app to let me listen to the transmissions from the bug I'd put on the woman's phone. As I had hoped, she made a phone call.

Yelena's voice answered.

As the woman passed on the warning I had left, an audio analyzer in the cell phone decoded the phone number she had dialed. I wrote it down, then called Edward's direct line at Langley.

"Strong here," he said.

"There is a file folder labeled 'CODE NAME LETHE' in the back of your bottom desk drawer on the right," I said.

"What? Who is this?"

"Just look for the file folder."

It always took Edward a few minutes to get his bearings.

"How do I know you're really Nat?" he said, as usual.

"We have an authentication protocol," I said. "It's on a bright yellow sheet of paper."

He riffled through the folder. "Batman," he said.

If his word was a superhero, mine needed to be a classical composer starting with the same letter. "Beethoven." Starting with a different letter would mean I was under duress—he would pretend the authentication had worked, but would know something was wrong.

"Okay, son. Why'd you call in?"

"You up-to-date on my mission now?"

"Have you found Yelena Semyonova?"

"Not yet, but I have a number for her I need you to trace." I gave him the number.

"Um," he said. "Can I put you on hold while I get someone to track this down?"

"No, you'll forget the whole conversation," I said. "But you can conference someone in."

"Right, good idea."

Fifteen minutes later, I had the billing address for the cell phone Yelena was using.

One taxi ride later, I stood at the entrance to Yelena's new apartment building. This was a more upscale place, with a nicely decorated lobby and a doorman—her life of crime must be paying pretty well.

I asked the doorman to ring Yelena's apartment. She was there, so I walked out and stood across the street to wait for her to leave.

Darkness had fallen by the time I spotted her coming out the glass doors of her building. She paused on the curb and scanned the street. She looked right past me without showing any sign of recognition, of course.

Yelena was every bit as beautiful as I remembered. She wore a silver-sequined top and a black miniskirt, which meant she was probably headed to Klub Kosmos, run by the Bukharin syndicate.

She might have the prototype in her purse, ready to hand it over to Jamshidi. I had hoped my warning about the Iranians might delay her. If I followed her to the club, I just might be able to swap out the prototype there, but if she didn't have it with her I would miss a chance to burglarize her apartment.

She hailed a cab and I jaywalked across the street in time to hear her tell the cabbie to take her to the Hard Rock Cafe. That gave me time. I'd search her apartment first, and if I didn't find anything I'd track her down at the Hard Rock.

I sauntered over to the doorman and pulled a hundred-ruble note out of my wallet. "I want to surprise a friend," I said in stilted Russian.

He shook his head.

I pulled out two more notes. This time the head shake was slower in coming. Another two notes earned me another shake, so I started to walk away.

"Okay," he said.

I handed him the money and he opened the door for me.

Sometimes it was easier just to ignore my talent and use the standard methods. I smiled as I rode up the elevator, thinking about how the doorman would puzzle over the five hundred rubles when he found them in his wallet later.

My lockpicks got me into Yelena's apartment. To my surprise, there was hardly any furniture. She certainly hadn't spent much money decorating the place. But I couldn't complain, as it made my job easier.

I started in the master bedroom. A systematic search of the closet and dresser revealed nothing unusual. Lifting up a rug, I spotted the faint outlines of a trap door in the floorboards. I pried it open and found a box of bullets and an empty holster. No sign of the prototype, but wherever Yelena was going, she was armed.

Behind me, I heard the unmistakable click of a revolver being cocked.

Chapter Nine

Careful not to make any sudden moves, I raised my hands. "I surrender." If I just played along, my chance to escape would come. I rose from my knees and turned to face my captor.

It was Yelena.

The circle of the gun barrel glinted a steady silver. "What do I do with you?" she said, in English.

"Let me go? I promise never to do it again."

She chuckled. "I am to believe that?"

I backed away a little, in the direction of the bathroom. I'd read her file. She wasn't a killer, so she probably wouldn't shoot if I ran for the bathroom. Probably. And she would think she had me trapped. Then if I could just keep the door closed long enough, I would have a chance.

"Really," I said, "you don't want to shoot me. You'd have to clean up all the blood, and disposing of a body is a real hassle."

She shrugged. "No hassle. I call police, say I shoot burglar. They dispose of body."

"Well, then, think of all the annoying paperwork." I tensed myself, preparing to lunge for the bathroom. I would do it in the middle of my next sentence, to catch her as off guard as possible.

"I do not want to kill you, Nat," she said, "but I must have prototype."

I started to speak, then just stood there with my mouth open as the full impact of what she had said hit me. She had called me Nat.

"What did you call me?" I finally asked, not sure I believed it.

"Nat," she said. "Is name you give me in Barcelona. You have different one now?"

My heart raced. "You...can remember me?" Had my talent stopped working? No, people still forgot me after Barcelona. What was going on?

Yelena raised an eyebrow. "How can I forget my handcuff partner? When I see you across street, I know you plan to search for prototype, so I come back."

Obviously, she remembered. Was she just naturally able to block my talent? No, she had forgotten taking the prototype from me at gunpoint the first time we met. This made no sense. How could she remember me now, when she couldn't before?

Since she could remember me, my talent was useless in trying to escape from her. But I didn't want to escape—I wanted to find out why she hadn't forgotten me. Could it somehow be the result of the magnetic lock in the handcuffs?

It would be really stupid to get myself killed the first time I met someone who could remember me. I had to gain her trust somehow.

I wouldn't be able to try multiple approaches with

Yelena, so honesty was my only option that could work in the long term. "My name is Nat Morgan. I'm a CIA officer. My assignment was to steal back the prototype and switch it with a fake. The fake is in one of my pockets. Is it okay if I take it out very slowly?"

She nodded, so with deliberate slowness I unbuttoned the pocket and withdrew the fake prototype. I turned it so she could see both sides.

"Why switch?" she asked. "Why not just steal?"

"Because the fake has a tracking device—"

She swore in Russian. "Drop it on floor and destroy."

"Wait," I said. "The CIA isn't after you. We just want to track where the prototype goes. We know you're selling it to Jamshidi, and we want to track it to his lab."

"Very nice plan for you," she said. "And when Iranians find prototype not work and has tracking device, not so nice plan for me."

"You're right," I said. "I hadn't considered what might happen to you if my plan succeeded."

Everything was spinning out of control. I had to find some way to make things work. Jamshidi was a priority for the CIA. I could use that. "If you help me locate Jamshidi's lab, then I can protect you, give you a new identity in the United States. For your mother and sisters, too." I was pretty sure Edward could swing that, if the need arose.

Yelena stiffened. "What do you know of my sisters?"

Maybe mentioning her sisters had been a mistake. But I couldn't restart the conversation, so I had to make the best of it. "I know they're with their father, when legally they should be with your mother. But maybe the chance to move to America would tempt them away from their—"

"I not move to America," she said. "I must work for the Bukharins." She almost spat that last word.

On the plane, I had been puzzled by Yelena's willingness to work for the mob. But from the hatred in her voice I realized they were forcing her to work for them, probably through blackmail or extortion. "Have they threatened your family?" I asked. "If we can get your family out—"

"Is too late," she said. "Bukharins take my sisters last year and sell them. High price for twins on sex slave market."

"Oh." I didn't know what the proper response to that was. "I'm sorry. The CIA file said they were with your stepfather."

"They leave note, but I know is lie. They hate him—they never go live with him. Then I find picture of them for sale by Bukharins. I quit SVR to infiltrate syndicate and find where they sell my sisters."

During the course of her explanation, her hand holding the gun lowered. The gun now pointed at the floor instead of me. I could have run, but instead I sat down on the edge of the bed.

"And have you found where they were sent?" I asked.

"No." She sniffled. "Ten months I work for them, but they not trust me yet. They not give me access to files."

"But you're a great thief," I said. "Why haven't you broken in to steal the files?"

"Too dangerous. If anyone without proper authority steal or look at files, then maybe they move or kill my sisters."

I nodded. "So you've been trying to work your way up in the organization until you're authorized to access the files, including your sisters'."

"Yes. But may never happen." Frustration filled her voice.

"If I could get the information on your sisters without tipping off the Bukharins, would you help me get the location of Jamshidi's lab?"

"You ask me to betray my country?"

"No," I said. "I'm asking you to betray the Bukharins, which you're already planning to do, anyway."

She shook her head. "Too risky. If Bukharins find out I work with CIA agent, they kill me."

"I can access their files without them knowing. I can get the information on your sisters."

Pursing her lips, she looked me up and down. "You are hacker?"

"When it comes to leaving no trace, I'm the best there is." That was probably true, but I was worried it came out sounding cheesy rather than confident and reassuring, so I added, "Let's just say I have a talent for it."

"Their data is stored in computer not connected to Internet. You cannot hack from remote."

"If you can get me into their facility, I can get the information."

Her eyes narrowed. "You think to get location of lab from their computer. You do not care about my sisters."

I blinked. I was so focused on helping Yelena in order to keep interacting with her that getting the location of Jamshidi's lab directly had not crossed my mind. "Well, I can kill two birds with one stone. But I'm happy to help you if you help me get in."

"What if I tell you that Bukharins do not know location of lab, that Jamshidi keeps secret even from them?"

"Well, then I'd still get the information on your

sisters if you promised to then help me track the prototype back to Jamshidi's lab. That way, we both win."

She looked puzzled. "You will help me first?"

"Of course."

"Why do you take risk for me and my sisters?"

Maybe because she was the one person who could
remember me. Maybe because saving girls in trouble
made me more like the hero my mother wanted me
to be. But I couldn't say that.

So I shrugged and said, "How could I desert my
handcuff partner?"

After a casual surveillance stroll around the block
that housed Klub Kosmos and the Bukharin Syndicate's
headquarters, Yelena and I sat in a booth in a bar in
downtown Moscow to plan our operation.

"Once inside club," she said, "I get guard to let us
into private rooms in back."

"How did you get them to trust you that much
even though they kidnapped your sisters?"

"My sisters have different last name. Bukharins
don't know their relation to me."

"Okay. So, you get us into the private rooms and
we go see Dmitri Bukharin." I had a sudden moment
of doubt. In the past, forgetfulness about me had
always spread from the people I met to include the
people they talked to about me. But since my talent
didn't work on Yelena, maybe it wouldn't extend to
the people she talked to about me. That would make
my plan unworkable, because I was relying on her to
talk me past the guards, who would then forget me.

"Before we plan any further, we need to test something," I said. "Introduce me to someone."

"Who?"

"Anyone."

She stood and beckoned me to follow her to the bar. "Vasilyi!" she yelled, and one of the bartenders came over. They exchanged some words in Russian.

Vasilyi leaned over the bar to me and said in English, "What can I get you, bubba?"

"Diet Coke," I said.

He poured me one. "On the house."

"Thanks," I said. I took a sip, then put it down. "Let's go," I said to Yelena.

"Where?"

"Somewhere he can't see us."

She rolled her eyes and took me to the back of the bar near the restrooms. "Good enough?"

I looked back and couldn't see the bartender. "Good enough."

"What is this about?"

"I'll show you in a minute."

She heaved an exaggerated sigh. As we stood there and my mental clock ticked off the seconds, I felt foolish—here I was with a beautiful woman who could remember me, and all I could do was annoy her.

"Okay," I said. "Take me back to Vasilyi and ask if he remembers me."

"Why?"

"Please, just humor me."

Back at the bar, she summoned Vasilyi again and asked him something in Russian. He sized me up, then shook his head. They talked a little more, with Yelena looking more and more puzzled as the conversation progressed. Meanwhile, I grew more and more relieved. My talent still worked on everyone but Yelena.

Finally, Vasilyi leaned over the bar to me and said in English, "What can I get you, bubba?"

"Diet Coke," I said.

He poured me one. "On the house."

"Thanks." I picked up the drink and motioned toward our booth.

"He say I must be drunk," said Yelena, "because he never meet you before. How do you make him forget?"

"I'm very forgettable," I said. "It's a talent I have."

"Talent?"

"It's happened ever since I was a baby. No one can remember me for more than a minute after they don't see or hear me."

A cute wrinkle appeared in her brow as she looked at me skeptically.

"I'm serious," I said. "You've seen it work twice now."

"Twice?"

"Remember the guard who locked us up in Barcelona? I was able to surprise him because he didn't remember I was there."

"But . . . how is such thing possible?" There was still an edge of incredulity in her voice.

I shrugged. "I wish I knew. I used to think maybe it was some sort of pheromone I give off, but since it works against computers, that can't be it. Now I think it's something to do with quantum mechanics."

"What do you mean, works against computers?"

"Information about me just disappears from anything electronic. That includes any computer logs of my actions, which is why I can be so sure I can find the info about your sisters without leaving a trace."

She remained quiet for several seconds, but I could tell from the concentration on her face that she was thinking things through, so I waited for her to ask more questions.

"I chose this bar," she said. "But I come here many times. You could know that. I chose Vasilyi, but he is bartender, so he is most likely person I know in here."

"You think I'm setting you up, that I arranged something with Vasilyi to pretend to forget me."

Yelena shook her head. "No. Is possible, but I do not think Vasilyi lies so good. I just look at other possible explanations." She pulled her cell phone out of her purse, opened the back, then removed the battery and dropped it in her purse. Rising to her feet, she said, "Wait here."

She walked to a table a few yards away where three guys in their twenties were drinking. After a brief conversation, during which she showed them her dead cell phone, one of the guys handed her his phone.

On returning to our table, she handed me the phone and said, "Show me how this forgets you."

I pressed the phone symbol, which brought up the number dial pad. "What's your phone number?"

As she said each number, I punched it in. It started ringing, and I hung up. I handed the phone back to her. "Bring up the call log."

She did. Her number was at the top.

"Okay," I said. "I'm just going to sit here quietly, and in about a minute, your number will disappear. There will be no trace of my having made a call."

We sat and waited, and the number disappeared right on schedule.

"Is incredible," she said, but her tone conveyed acceptance. She went and returned the phone to its owner, then came back. As she replaced the battery in her phone, she said, "You have always been like this?"

I shrugged. "I've learned to live with it. Use it to my advantage—it really helps when I'm on a mission."

"Make you sloppy," she said.

Now it was my turn to be puzzled. "Sloppy?"

"You expect me to forget you—that why you not hide your face outside my building. I not like working with sloppy people. The plan is too risky."

"Yelena," I said, "you are the first person in my life to remember me when seeing me again. The first person ever. I wasn't sloppy—I didn't even know it was possible for someone to remember me until you said my name. We're connected somehow, and that's why I want to help you find your sisters. Trust me, I can do this."

She studied my face for a few seconds, then said, "I will trust you."

Even outside Klub Kosmos, I could feel the bass beat in my chest. Yelena bypassed the line and walked right up to one of the bouncers, with me right behind her. The bouncer, a barrel-chested man wearing a black suit and black tee-shirt, unhooked the velvet rope to let Yelena in.

"He's with me," she said in Russian, jerking a thumb over her shoulder in my direction.

The bouncer gave me a nod and let me pass.

Once inside the door, we had to pass through a metal detector. Yelena handed her purse to another bouncer, who took a casual look inside. The gun didn't faze him—he closed the purse and handed it to her on the other side.

The closest thing I had to a weapon was the carbon-composite lockpick set I had stowed in the waistband of my underwear, so I made it through the detector without setting off any alarms. Taking my hand, Yelena guided me through the mass of gyrating bodies on the dance floor to the rear of the club.

I couldn't help worrying that she would feel the sweat on my palms. Maybe she would think I was too nervous about the operation and would abort. I was nervous, I realized, even though missions like this were almost routine for me. The difference was that this time I had an audience I needed to impress, and who could remember if I messed things up.

After Yelena vouched for me, the guard let us into the private rooms. As the door closed behind us, the club's sounds faded to only mildly ear-shattering. Yelena led me up a narrow flight of stairs, then knocked on a solid-looking wooden door.

We were admitted by another guard. Thick red carpet—which looked just about the right color to hide bloodstains—muffled our footsteps as we entered the office. When the guard closed the office door behind us, the remaining sound from the club cut off. I couldn't help but wonder if the soundproofing was to keep out the constant dance music or to keep in any gunshots or screams.

From the file I'd read on the Bukharin syndicate, the latter possibility did not seem unlikely, although Yelena had told me that in the secure area of the facility the Bukharins had a special interrogation room more suited to the task of torturing people they had business disagreements with.

A silver-haired man sat behind a large glass desk.

I recognized him as Dmitri Ivanovich Bukharin, one of the three brothers running the syndicate.

When he saw us, he rose.

"Yelena, it is always a pleasure," Dmitri said in Russian. "I just wired payment for the Barcelona job to your account." He glanced at me and added, "And who is your guest?"

"His name is Nat Morgan," she said. With one quick movement, her gun was out of her purse and shoved into my ribs.

"Yelena!" I said. "What are you—"

"Shut up." Her voice was all business as she backed away, keeping her gun aimed at me. She continued in Russian, "He's a CIA officer who interfered with me during the Barcelona job. He tracked me down, so I pretended to let him convince me to help find the Iranians' lab."

Dmitri chuckled, then spoke in English. "You should be more careful who you trust, Mr. Nat Morgan of the CIA."

"Obviously," I said.

Chapter Ten

Two of Bukharin's black-suited goons handcuffed me and took me down two flights of stairs. One of them had his eyes scanned in order to unlock a steel vault door that slid smoothly into the wall to let us through.

"The CIA will figure out where I am," I blustered. If I didn't manage to get out of here, the CIA wouldn't even remember me until Edward decided to clean up his files. "Then you guys are in for a world of trouble."

We passed a door with a male stick figure on it, so I said, "Hey, can I use the bathroom?" When they didn't respond, I tried it in Russian, but that didn't fare any better.

They pushed me into a bare, windowless room, and locked my handcuffs to the back of the chair that was bolted to the floor in the center. The cement floor was stained reddish brown around the drain under the chair.

"This isn't supposed to be the bathroom, is it?" I asked.

Ignoring me, they locked the door behind them.

Yelena had executed the first part of the plan to perfection: I was in the secured area of the Bukharins' headquarters, and in less than a minute only she and I would know that. Now it was my turn.

It took a couple of minutes to get one of the lockpicks out from the waistband of my underwear. Fortunately, the Bukharin syndicate had not yet upgraded to magnetic-lock handcuffs, so it only took me moments to undo them. I slipped them into my pocket just in case.

I removed the rest of the lockpick set from my waistband and made quick work of the door lock.

I looked back at the chair. Its solid construction might make it useful. Using a pair of pliers decorated with some suspiciously bloodlike stains, I managed to unbolt the four legs from the floor.

Peeking out, I made sure the hallway was clear and then, carrying the chair, made my way back to the bathroom I had spotted. I waited in one of the stalls.

Eventually, someone would have to go.

Since they'd taken my watch, I wasn't sure how long it took, but it seemed like hours before someone entered the bathroom and walked to a urinal.

I flushed the toilet and opened the stall door. The man at the urinal, back toward me, wore the type of black suit that seemed to be the security guard uniform of the Bukharins. I lifted the chair and charged.

The chair legs squeezed on either side of him, pinning his arms in front of him, and the crossbars pushed him up against the wall and urinal. The urinal flushed as he yelped in surprise.

Leaning against the chair with as much strength as I could muster, I reached under his suit coat and pulled his gun from its holster.

He pushed back against the chair. I couldn't hold him, so I let go and jumped out of the way, allowing him to crash to the floor.

Aiming the gun at his chest, I said, *"Nye dvigat'sya,"* and added, "Don't move," in case he was bilingual.

"Who are you?" he asked.

"CIA assassin," I said. "But I'm not after you. Turn facedown and you will live."

He complied.

"I'm going out into the hall. If you come out of that door in less than five minutes, I will kill you. Understand?" He'd forget my warning in less time than that, but for now I wanted it to sound convincing.

"I understand."

"Good. I'm going to ask you a few questions, some of which I already know the answer to. If you lie, you die. Where is the records room?" While Yelena had been to both the interrogation room and the records room a few times, she wasn't able to give me detailed instructions as to how to get from one to the other.

"Turn right, go to end of hall. Turn left. Is glass doors on left."

"How many guards inside?"

"One."

"Thank you. Now stay here."

Gun held tightly in one hand and chair in the other, I slipped out into the hallway. I took the chair because I didn't want to give the guard any physical evidence that he did anything but slip and fall. He might spend some time looking for his gun before probably concluding that he had left it somewhere accidentally.

I left the chair in the hallway. If someone recognized it as the chair from the interrogation room, they might waste a little time trying to figure out why it was there. Anything that kept people away from the records room helped.

The guard hadn't lied—I found the records room exactly where he said it was. Beyond the glass doors, I saw a man's head and shoulders above dual computer monitors.

I ducked away and considered how to proceed. According to Yelena, the doors to the records room were always locked from the inside by the guard on duty. There was a keyed lock to get in, though, in case of emergency, but only the guard on duty and the three Bukharin brothers had keys. At least that meant there was something for me to pick.

However, Yelena must have forgotten that the doors were made out of glass. I felt a twinge of satisfaction at the evidence that she could be "sloppy," too. But that didn't solve the problem: picking the lock would take time, and the glass doors would allow the guard to see me.

And there was no way I was going to break through the glass, even if I went back for the chair: it was almost two inches thick, reinforced by wires embedded in the glass. A bullet from the gun would leave a mark, but that was about it.

So I had to convince the guard inside to open the door, or else scrap this attempt, escape, and try again later with a plan taking the glass doors into account. And I wasn't ready to face Yelena and admit that I hadn't been able to help her.

Delivering a pizza here wasn't going to work. But perhaps I could lure him to the door and see what happened. So I marched right up to the door and knocked.

The guard looked up and frowned when he saw me. I frowned and beckoned him over.

He got up and walked over. "Who are you?" he asked in Russian.

"There's a CIA assassin in the building," I said. My accent was terrible, of course, but the Bukharins occasionally hired foreigners for various things, so I could at least hope he might believe me. "Maintain radio silence and make sure no one gets through this door." Then I turned and ran down the corridor until he couldn't see me anymore.

From what I had seen, there were two possible outcomes when the memory of me disappeared from people's minds and they found themselves in a different situation than they had been before meeting me.

If there was no plausible explanation that didn't involve me or another third party, then there would be a disconnect—like the sudden appearance of pizzas for Carlos the guard at InterQuan. He couldn't remember me bringing the pizzas, but he wouldn't be able to remember someone else bringing the pizzas, either.

However, if there was a plausible explanation for the new situation, then that explanation became the new memory. For example, the security guard in the bathroom had been at a urinal before our encounter, but on the floor after. If I had not been there, a plausible explanation would be that he had slipped, so that would be what he remembered.

Sometimes that plausible reason worked in my favor.

I could only guess what the security guard in the records room remembered once he forgot about me.

He had been in his chair and now he was next to the door, so a plausible explanation was that he was going to exit the room for some reason—maybe to go to the bathroom.

He unlocked the door and came out.

I aimed the gun at him and said, "*Nye dvigat'sya.* Don't move."

He froze. Then he dove back into the records room. I ran to the door, before he could close it behind him. He had his gun partway out of his holster before I was able to aim at him again.

"Let go of the gun, or I will kill you," I said in Russian.

He released the gun and raised his hands over his head. I took his gun and threw it in the wastebasket. Using the handcuffs I'd removed earlier, I cuffed him to the door, which was far enough away from the computer terminal that I wouldn't have to worry about interference.

"Who are you?" he asked in English. My atrocious Russian accent must have given me away.

"CIA assassin," I said, "but you're not my assignment so I won't kill you unless you try something."

In seven years as a CIA officer, I had never killed anyone. I had only shot at someone three times, and only hit someone once, in the leg—and that had been a ricochet.

So I was not, in fact, a CIA assassin. I used the CIA assassin line on paid guards because it worked. If they believed I was a deadly killer, but that I wasn't going to kill *them*, they usually decided that their lives were more important than their paychecks.

Of course, if I had wanted to be a CIA assassin, I could have been. After I'd been with the CIA for a couple of years, Edward broached the subject, pointing out that my talent would help avoid one of the biggest problems faced by close-range assassins: getting away without being caught.

I told him I didn't like killing, and he must have made a note of it in my file, because he never brought it up again.

At the computer terminal, I had to hunt-and-peck on the Cyrillic keyboard to spell out the names of Yelena's sisters in order to run a file contents search. Because it might take several minutes to scan through all the files on the hard drives, I took the time to put my lockpicks back into my waistband.

The file search brought up a list of several files containing the names Ekaterina and Oksana.

I clicked on the one with the most recent date and it opened. The file showed a picture of twin blondes with mouths that smiled and eyes that didn't. Their identical faces matched the photo Yelena had shown me.

Skimming the file as quickly as I could, I discovered that Ekaterina and Oksana had been auctioned off eight months ago to Bidder 948, who had taken delivery of them in Tehran.

Earlier I had seen a folder labeled Bidders, so I found it and located the file on Bidder 948. I opened it up. I sounded out the Cyrillic characters of his name: zh-a-m-sh-ee-d-ee. Jamshidi.

So the Bukharins were supplying Jamshidi with more than just stolen technology.

Excitedly, I began looking through the file to see

if there was any information about the location of the secret lab. This private mission to help Yelena had suddenly turned into my real assignment.

The door lock clicked. I looked up to see four guards burst into the room, followed by Dmitri Bukharin and Yelena. The guards all had their guns trained on me.

I had placed my gun on the desk during the search. They couldn't see my hands, but I didn't reach for it. Instead, I used the mouse to start the computer's shutdown process. I didn't want to endanger Yelena and her sisters by letting Bukharin see what files I'd accessed before my talent had a chance to affect the computer's memory.

"He's a CIA assassin!" yelled the guard I had handcuffed to the door.

"Keep him alive for questioning," said Dmitri.

"Raise your hands," said one of the guards.

I raised my hands. "Here we go again," I said as they handcuffed me.

Chapter Eleven

The previous time the Bukharins had caught me, I had been taken to the interrogation room. I fully expected that to happen again, and it did. As before, they ignored my request to use the restroom.

What I didn't expect was that this time, Dmitri Bukharin would tell Yelena to go home and follow along with his guards.

"What happened to the chair?" asked the guard holding my left arm after we entered the room.

"I think I saw it out in the hall," said the guard on my right. He retrieved the chair and they pushed me down onto it, not bothering to bolt it to the floor again. They attached the handcuffs to the back of the chair, almost dislocating my left shoulder in the process.

Dmitri pursed his lips for a moment, then spoke in English. "Well, Mr. CIA Assassin, if you were sent to kill me tonight, you did a very poor job of it." He chuckled.

"The night is still young," I said, with as much

bluster as I could manage. I needed to give him something to think about, something that would make him leave me alone for a minute. "But I wasn't sent to kill you. My assignment is to kill one of your clients."

"Why break in here then?" he asked.

"Because you know where your client is, and I don't."

"And the name of this client who is destined to die at your hands?"

"Kazem Jamshidi. Since stealing the information didn't work, the CIA would be willing to pay you for his location in Iran."

Dmitri emitted a sharp bark of laughter. "You are doubly a fool, Mr. CIA Assassin. First, because Jamshidi can afford better protection than your President. And second, because I do not know Jamshidi's location. You have come here for nothing."

"I see," I said. "Well, if you just have your men undo these cuffs, I'll be on my way then."

Dmitri chuckled. "I like you, Mr. CIA Assassin. I will enjoy seeing how long you can maintain your sense of humor before dying." In Russian, he said to one of his guards, "Bring me a coat hanger."

I didn't know what kind of killing torture required a coat hanger, and I had no desire to find out. "Listen, the CIA will pay to get me back alive. Let me give you a phone number to—"

"The CIA can offer me nothing that Jamshidi can't."

Getting myself sold to Jamshidi wasn't the worst option available. It would give me a chance to let my talent work so I could escape. If I were really lucky, I might even get the location of Jamshidi's lab. But, of course, I couldn't let it seem like that was what I wanted.

I shook my head. "You gain nothing by turning me

over to Jamshidi except the CIA's attention on your own operations. Whatever he pays you won't be worth it."

Dmitri stared at me and scratched his temple. After a long pause, he said, "You may have noticed that I speak English pretty well."

"Yes," I said, caught a little off guard by the change of subject.

"The post-communist generation learn English because it is the language of opportunity. I learned it earlier because it is the language of Hollywood."

"I see." I didn't.

"My father had bootleg videocassettes of many American movies when I was a boy, and I used to watch them over and over. And your request not to be turned over to Jamshidi reminded me of Disney movie *Song of the South*." He leaned forward and said in a sing-song voice, "Oh, please don't throw me in that briar patch." He continued in his normal tone, "You are playing the part of Br'er Rabbit. For some reason, you want to be sent to Jamshidi. Maybe you have a tracker installed in your body."

"Or maybe I'm smart enough to pretend to play the part of Br'er Rabbit so you'll turn me back to the CIA," I said. Dmitri was obviously a thinking man—if I made things complicated enough, maybe he would take time to do his thinking elsewhere.

The guard returned with a simple wire coat hanger and handed it to Dmitri, who unwound the top of it.

"Get his hands," Dmitri said. One of the guards unchained the handcuffs from the back of the chair, then uncuffed my left hand.

"Before you start with the torture and killing," I said, "can I at least go to the bathroom?" My heart pounded.

The guards forced my hands in front of me and reattached the left handcuff, then used a chain to fasten the cuffs to the crossbar on the chair's front legs. I could move my hands a bit, but could not raise them more than six inches above my lap.

"When you kill me," I said, trying to keep my rising desperation out of my voice, "my sphincter muscles will relax and I'll mess up this lovely room of yours. I wouldn't want to stink up the place."

Dmitri squeezed the hook part of the hanger, narrowing it to about a half inch.

I ran out of things to say.

With practiced precision, Dmitri straightened out the major bends in the hangar.

"We will start with the pinkie of your left hand," said Dmitri.

In my mind, I began to recite the list of Vice Presidents of the United States. John Adams. Thomas Jefferson. Aaron Burr. I could even imagine my mother sitting across from me at our kitchen table, as she checked off each name after I said it.

The lights dimmed, then went out. Pitch darkness filled the room.

I didn't make a sound, although if they forgot me, I wasn't sure I could explain my way out of being handcuffed to their torture chair.

Dmitri swore and said in Russian, "Check if it's just this room."

Someone opened the door, and no light came in. "Another blackout," said one of the guards.

"Everyone stay where you are," said Dmitri. "The backup generator will kick in after thirty seconds."

So I didn't have a minute. My talent couldn't save

me. And even if I could reach the lockpicks in my waistband, the lights would be back on before I could get them out.

Not caring if the chains made a sound, I reached out toward the place where Dmitri had been holding the hanger. I felt thick wire, and I snagged the hook with a finger.

Dmitri yelped.

Pushing as hard as I could with my feet, I tipped the chair back. The hanger came free of Dmitri's grasp. Despite holding my head forward as I fell, when the chair hit the ground my head whipped back and smacked against the concrete. Bright sparks seemed to explode before my eyes.

Shouts in Russian sounded around me. The chair jerked beneath me as someone bumped into it.

By feel alone, I jammed the tip of the coat hanger wire into the right handcuff keyhole and twisted. The cuff unlocked, and I pulled my right hand out.

"Get the lights back on." Dmitri's voice was more distant. He'd probably backed toward the door.

Right hand freed, I made quick work of the left handcuff. I rolled off the chair to one side, smashing into the legs of a guard. He toppled to the floor.

"Grab him," Dmitri ordered.

The fallen guard's hands grappled me, but my hands found what I was feeling for: the guard's gun. I pulled it out of his holster and shot him in the torso—even in complete darkness, it was hard to miss with the muzzle pressed against the target. He grunted and let go of me.

A small square of white light appeared—a cell phone screen. I fired at it. I missed, but its owner turned it off.

One of the guards fired his gun and it hit the wall behind me. The brief flash revealed his position, but the darkness was so disorienting that I couldn't be sure I could aim the gun properly. Besides, if I fired, the flash from my gun would give them a target again.

"Fool," said Dmitri, "you're more likely to hit one of us than him. Wait for the generator."

Years of counting off seconds gave me a pretty good sense of time, even in confusing circumstances. The thirty seconds were almost up, if they weren't gone already. I couldn't come up with a plan for surviving once the lights came on, so I decided I would try to make my death count for something by shooting Dmitri. I aimed my gun in the general direction of his voice and waited for the chance to pull the trigger.

The silent seconds stretched out in the darkness.

I started to think my time sense had been knocked out of whack by the bump on my head, because it felt like at least forty-five seconds since the blackout began, and the backup generator still hadn't kicked in.

Then one of the guards said, "There must be something wrong with the generator."

"Just wait," said Dmitri. "Sometimes it takes longer."

I held my breath. How long had it been since I fired the gun? It felt like twenty seconds, but I couldn't be sure.

Every additional second brought them closer to forgetting me.

Finally they did.

"The generator must be down," said Dmitri. "I guess we'll have to feel our way out."

The man I had shot moaned, then said, "Don't leave me."

I realized his gunshot wound was physical evidence that I had been there. Would they start looking for whoever had fired the shot?

"I have little use for a guard so clumsy he accidentally shoots himself when the lights go out," said Dmitri. "But Ivan can call an ambulance."

A square of light lit up Ivan's face as he dialed.

I pressed myself against the wall, my eyes half-closed so they wouldn't reflect the light, still not letting myself breathe. My good luck with the power outage and backup generator failure would be wiped out if one of them spotted me now.

Ivan moved out into the hall, taking the cell phone light with him. I didn't breathe until all but the man I'd shot had left the room.

It took over forty minutes of creeping around in the dark, and then in the light as power came back on, but eventually I descended the narrow stairs into the pulsing beat of the music. I nodded to the guards at the bottom, as if I had just come from a meeting and had every right to be there, and they nodded back.

I wondered if Yelena had given me up for dead when they took me away, or if she would still be waiting at the rendezvous spot, a café down the street from Klub Kosmos.

She waved from her seat at a table when I entered. "I am sorry," she said as I sat down. "Silent alarm go off in Dmitri's office warning of unauthorized access to records room. I go with them, in case I can help you, but too many."

"I understand."

She shook her head. "Your talent is very strange. First they are talking about who could have broken in, then"—she snapped her fingers—"they are talking about playing at cards with guard in records room. Until they see him handcuff to door. But you escape. That is impressive."

"Truth is, I got lucky. If not for the blackout, I'd be dead. And then it turned out their backup generator..." My voice faltered as I noticed her smirk. I was so accustomed to working alone that the possibility of help hadn't occurred to me. I sat there and stared at her, mouth agape.

"You owe me one," she said. "Two, maybe. I think if they not see you, maybe easier to escape."

"You think good," I said. Then, remembering, I said, "I found out who bought your sisters."

She leaned forward. "Who?"

"Jamshidi."

Chapter Twelve

We decided that Yelena should give the real prototype to the Iranians, in order to keep her cover. We went back to her apartment. While she made the delivery, I called Edward to bring him up to date on the recent developments. After the usual rigmarole in getting him to read my file, I told him the big news.

"What do you mean, she remembered you? I thought nobody could," Edward said.

"I think it has something to do with us being handcuffed together in Barcelona. The handcuffs were magnetic. I don't know if that makes a difference."

"This is terrible," he said. "You've been compromised. What if she describes you to a sketch artist? If people are on the lookout for you, it will—"

"It's okay," I said. "She's not a threat anymore."

He was silent for a moment. "I know you don't like killing, but it had to be—"

"I didn't kill her!"

"Then how do you know she's not a threat?"

"I recruited her. We just pulled off a successful op together. She had my back: I'd be dead without her. So I trust her." Now that I said it, it did sound a little reckless, but it had paid off.

Edward sighed. "Look, son, you can't just recruit a former SVR operative who went over to the mob."

"She didn't go over to the mob. The info in her files is incorrect. Her sisters aren't with their father—they were kidnapped by the Bukharins. She was working for the syndicate only as a way to gain their trust so she could find out who her sisters were sold to."

"Why would the Bukharins ever trust her if they're the ones who kidnapped—"

"Her stepsisters have a different last name."

"Hmph. Well, I guess it's plausible."

"Anyway, she helped me break into the Bukharins' records room, and I found out who bought her sisters. It was Jamshidi. And he took delivery of them in Tehran, which means they may be with him. So Yelena has every incentive to help us locate the lab."

"Well," said Edward, "maybe. I don't like that you've been compromised, though. But if she's willing to turn over the fake prototype to the Iranians, I guess that's good enough."

"Umm, about that. We decided it would be best to keep her cover intact for now, so she turned over the real prototype."

"Look, son, you can't just throw a mission aside like that."

"Realistically, what were the chances of it working? They detected the tracer I put on Rezaei, so they probably would have spotted this one, too. Besides, you've always told me it would be better if I could have someone backing me up on operations," I said. "It would never work with someone who could forget me, but Yelena's perfect for the job."

After a pause, Edward said, "You've fallen for her, haven't you?"

"What?" I'd heard what he said; the question just caught me off guard. Had I fallen for her?

"It's not surprising that you'd fall in love with her, since she can remember you. I can understand your fascination. But getting romantically involved with a foreign national could make you a security risk."

"I'd never turn against our country," I said. "I'm loyal."

"I don't doubt you," Edward said. "What I've read of your past missions supports the idea that you can be trusted. But you have to understand, according to the notes in this file, there was some objection to recruiting you in the first place. Some people wondered how we could ensure the loyalty of someone we can't even remember we hired. You could vanish with no trace and then start working against us, and we wouldn't even know it."

"That's ridiculous." I had known there were doubts about hiring me, but I'd always thought the doubts were about the reality of my ability, not my allegiance.

"And yet you've already compromised the mission for her, by letting her turn over the real prototype to the Iranians, instead of the fake with the tracker."

"Oh, come on! That mission failed the moment she caught me trying to make the switch," I said. I felt a little angry that my seven years of loyalty to the CIA were being repaid with doubt. "Since then, I've recruited Yelena to help us locate Jamshidi's lab. Turning the prototype over to the Iranians helps her gain their trust. Have some faith that I know what I'm doing."

"I have faith in you, Nat," said Edward. "For now, I'll note this in my file so I'll know about it, but I won't pass it up the line."

"Thanks."

"Just be careful. Don't let a woman turn your head so far you lose sight of what's important."

"I won't."

"Nat." Yelena shook my shoulder.

I opened my bleary eyes. It took me a moment to realize where I was: stretched out on Yelena's couch. I propped myself up and said, "You're back. How'd it go?"

"I made delivery. They have new assignment for me."

"That's great. That means they trust you."

She sat on the edge of her coffee table. "Maybe. But new assignment is more difficult than InterQuan."

"Between the two of us, I'm sure we can handle it."

With a tired smile, she said, "I thought I could count on you. We have plane to catch in morning."

"Where are we headed?"

"Tel Aviv."

I'd never been to Israel. Hopefully there would be time to do a little sight-seeing before the job. After a job, I was usually out of the country as soon as I could manage. "How do you say 'Where's the bathroom' in Hebrew?"

"You can ask flight attendant."

"What's our target?"

"ChazonTec. They are a small startup company still looking for capital funding."

Something about the name rang a bell. I had a vague mental image of a logo with that name and a lonely-looking white-haired guy sitting behind a brochure-laden table at a tiny booth at QuantumExpo in Rome. I had avoided eye contact and moved on.

The booth had looked about the cheapest of the whole expo. From experience, I knew startups often had fairly lax security because they couldn't afford anything better. "What makes them tougher than InterQuan?" I asked. InterQuan had been well-funded.

"They rent office in Qela Industries building. The man who started the company worked for them."

"Ah," I said.

Over the past few years, Qela Industries had become a major defense contractor for the Israeli military. Because Qela's Slingshot drones operated by remote control and kept Israeli personnel out of harm's way, Israel now had more armed drones than manned tanks and planes put together.

Two years ago, Edward and I had looked into stealing something from Qela and decided it wasn't worth the effort. Security at Qela's building would almost certainly be the toughest I had been up against. On the bright side, they were less likely to torture and kill me than Dmitri Bukharin.

"What's the thing we're supposed to steal?" I asked.

"The Iranians called it a"—her brow wrinkled— "quantum remote-viewing device."

"That probably just means it's a quantum TV," I said, displaying a bravado I wished I felt. "An infinite number of quantum channels, and there still won't be anything good on."

❖   ❖   ❖

After Yelena went to bed, I helped myself to some borscht from her refrigerator and sat at her kitchen table. As I ate, I thought about what Edward had said about my having fallen in love with Yelena.

I'd met plenty of women who were beautiful, smart, and resourceful. I might have gotten a little infatuated with some of them, but I always knew I couldn't really fall in love because there was no chance for a true connection.

But Yelena's ability to remember me changed that. She might be the only woman in the world with whom I could have a normal relationship. It was only natural I would start falling for her. And it didn't hurt that I found her attractive. It would have been a real downer if the one person in the world who could remember me had turned out to be a ninety-nine-year-old babushka.

I daydreamed about our life together, after we'd located Jamshidi's lab and rescued her sisters. We'd get married, have a few kids. Maybe we'd even live in a house with a white picket fence. It would be the kind of life I'd wanted since I was a child: normal, just like everyone else.

Then I started thinking about it from Yelena's point of view. She could remember me, but no one else would. The guests at our wedding would remember her being jilted at the altar because I never showed up. The neighbors would think she was a single mom because they could never remember seeing me. Our children would even forget I was their father.

It was silly to believe that somehow we were fated to be together. I had given up on believing in destiny after the fire—it was a simple accident that made me lose my mother, and it was another simple accident that Yelena and I were connected now. If the Bukharins had sent a male thief, I might have ended up connected to a Boris.

And while Yelena might be the only woman in the world I could have a real relationship with, her options were not so limited. What could I offer her that no other man could? Only the burdens of my talent, with none of the benefits.

She deserved better. So I had to give up any romantic notions about her.

That's when I knew I really had fallen for her.

"I'm sorry," said the airline ticket agent behind the counter, "but I only show the one seat reserved." He tapped a few keys at his computer. "I don't see another."

Yelena said, "But I reserved two. Look." She pulled out a printed sheet of paper and handed it over.

"Yelena," I said, "it's my fault." I was so used to having the CIA arrange my flights that it hadn't occurred to me the Yelena would run into trouble.

"Your fault?" she said.

I turned to the agent and said, "My plans changed and I called to cancel the seat. Then the change in my plans didn't work out, but I forgot I had canceled this trip." I pulled out my wallet. "Just let me buy a ticket now."

"You canceled the flight?" Yelena asked. "Why?"

"I'll explain later." I gave the agent my Bob Daniels passport and a CIA-issued credit card in the same name.

After running the card, he printed my ticket and our boarding passes. Yelena waited until we were in the security line before asking, "Why did you cancel the fight?"

"I didn't," I said. "The airline computer forgot my reservation. As far as it was concerned, you only reserved one seat."

"But everything is on computers now," she said. "Do you have to buy your tickets at the airport every time?"

"No," I said, as I took off my belt and shoes. "The CIA books people on flights all over the place all the time. So when they need me to go somewhere, they find one of their people who already has a reservation that fits what I need. They issue me a passport and other documents with that person's name, and tell that person their trip has been postponed."

Yelena put her carry-on bag on the conveyor. "But I booked your flight using the name in your passport."

"But you were booking the flight for me," I said. "So the computer forgot the reservation."

"That is crazy," she said. "How can the computer know the difference?"

I didn't answer her until after we had emerged from security into the gate area.

"Think of it this way," I said. "Computers want to act like I never existed. If I didn't exist, you would have only made one reservation instead of two. So that's what the computer remembers. But if I didn't exist, the CIA still would have made the reservation for the real Bob Daniels so he could fly to Moscow. So the computer remembers that reservation even though I'm the one using it."

She didn't say any more until we were sitting at our gate. "What causes it?"

"You mean the forgetting? I have no idea. I've been this way since I was born." And then I told her about my mother and how she raised me, and eventually how I had lost her.

"Your mother, she is still alive, but does not remember you?"

I nodded. "She remembers being pregnant years ago, but she's sure she must have lost the baby and just blocked that out of her mind. She thinks that and my father leaving is why she became very depressed, quit her job, and just lived alone for the years when I was at home."

"How terrible," she said.

"Her life is much better now," I said. "She thinks that she came out of her depression after the fire. She's remarried, and has a very memorable little girl named Amber." It still stung a little that my mother was better off without me, but I couldn't begrudge her happiness.

And every month, an envelope with several hundred dollars in cash showed up in her mailbox, with no return address—just a note that said: *From someone who owes you more than he can ever repay.* I wasn't sure, but she probably assumed it was from my father.

I didn't send him anything.

"But don't you want to see her?" Yelena asked.

"She gave me all she had for thirteen years," I said to Yelena. "I can't ask any more of her."

One of the gate agents announced boarding for our flight, so Yelena got up.

"Stay sitting down," I said. "We have to wait until almost everyone has boarded."

"Why?"

I held up the airline ticket I had purchased. "This got me through security, but when they put it under the barcode scanner, the computer's going to claim this ticket was never issued. The gate agent is going to say he can't let me on board because I'm not in the computer. I'll argue for a bit, and then, when there's no line and I can make it to the scanner in less than a minute after the ticket is printed, I'll say, 'Fine, I'll just buy another ticket.' So I'll do that, and get on board and everything should go smoothly until we change planes in Athens."

Her eyes had grown wider during my little spiel. She continued staring at me for a moment after I was through. Then she flopped down in the seat next to me and said, "You have done this a lot, yes?"

"More than I can count."

"I am sorry for the trouble."

I shrugged. "It's how I do things when the Agency isn't arranging my travel."

"But you have to pay for the ticket over and over, and is so expensive."

I laughed. "No. It's not a problem for two reasons. First, the credit card isn't mine: it's a copy of Bob Daniels' card."

"But will he not notice the charges?"

I shook my head. "Second, since I'm the one making the charges, the credit card company's computer will forget them. I'm taking this trip for free."

She stared at me long enough that I felt embarrassed and looked away.

"You could have all the money you want," she said. "Walk into jewelry store, buy with credit card, walk out, sell to fence. Repeat."

"Or even just get cash advances straight from an ATM," I said. "Yeah, I know. I didn't figure that out until I was an adult, though. It would have made life so much easier for my mom and me. Except..."

"Except what?" she asked after a few seconds.

"Except I don't think she would have let me do that. She was very religious, my mom. Believed that God gave me my talent for a reason. But also, 'Thou shalt not steal' is one of the Ten Commandments, so she would not have approved using my talent that way." And I told Yelena about the day I snatched the ring from my mother in the jewelry store before recognizing her, and how I decided to change my life.

"Yet you are still thief," Yelena said, brow furrowed.

"Being a thief is what I'm good at. But I'm a thief for the U.S. government," I said. "That makes a difference, kind of like . . . For example, killing is wrong, but if you're a soldier following the laws of war it's okay. I'm not stealing for my own benefit."

She chuckled. "No need to justify to me. I am a thief also, remember: first for my government, now for Bukharins."

"No, not for the Bukharins," I said. "For your sisters. They're the ones you're really working for."

Her wide smile in response made me feel warm inside.

Chapter Thirteen

The headquarters building of Qela Industries was twenty-one stories tall. Since it was in an industrial zone, rather than downtown, its blackened windows towered above the warehouses that surrounded it.

Yelena and I sat in a rented hybrid car parked a block away from the building. The sun streamed in through the windshield and made me uncomfortably hot, even with the windows open.

"ChazonTec office is on the fifth floor," she said, flipping through the building plans we had gotten at the local planning office.

"You realize that Qela must have made substantial modifications to the building after filing those plans."

She gave me a sour look. "I am not an amateur. But the plans will give me the basics. I like to have some idea of what I am doing before I do it."

"Let me just try," I said. "I might be able to just walk right out with the viewer."

"And if he notices that it is gone? They will lock down

the building. Even if no one remembers you taking it, if they find you with it they will capture you. Even if you escape, they will increase security because the attempt was made. We must plan this right from the beginning."

I sighed.

"Besides, if just walking is so good, why not do that in Barcelona?"

"I tried," I said. "But I couldn't get an appointment to see anyone in that lab. This guy's looking for venture capital, so I could pose as a venture capitalist."

She eyed me skeptically. "You not look like venture capitalist."

"I could. A business suit, a power tie." Her expression didn't change, so I said, "Okay, but I could look like someone who works for a venture capitalist."

"*Da*," she said. "But security is problem enough now. We must not risk more of it."

"I get it." I was accustomed to trial and error, using my talent to get me out so I could try again. But nearly getting killed by Dmitri had shaken my faith in that approach.

She handed me a photograph of a smiling, white-haired man. "This is Yitzhak Bernstein, owner of ChazonTec. He is workaholic, so maybe he work late. We go in after we see him leave."

I looked at Bernstein's picture and felt a pang of guilt. He was the lonely guy I remembered from the booth at QuantumExpo—the owner of the company, sitting at a brochure table, probably because he couldn't afford to hire anybody. I generally thought of myself as stealing from large, rich corporations, not kindly old men. "How did Jamshidi find out about this guy's quantum television, anyway?"

"Probably he send someone to pose as venture capitalist. Find out about a lot of new inventions that way."

"Jamshidi's a billionaire. Why doesn't he just buy what he needs?"

She shrugged. "Cheaper to steal."

Guard patrols both inside and outside the Qela building were carried out by remote-controlled walking drones the size of a Labrador retriever, but weighing over two hundred pounds. Their pneumatic "jaws" had no teeth, but could lock onto a person's arm or leg with enough pressure that most bodybuilders couldn't pry them off. Because of their resemblance to dogs, they were called Rovers.

But unlike most dogs, Rovers came equipped with tasers.

The Rovers sent a wireless video feed over an encrypted channel to the guard station, which was located in the basement. The guards monitored the video as the Rovers went on their rounds. When a Rover spotted someone unauthorized, the guards could speak to the person through a radio on board, and if necessary, order the Rover to capture the intruder until human guards could arrive on the scene.

And since the Rovers had been designed with military applications in mind, they were difficult to kill, and their communications systems were built to overcome jamming.

Overall, I thought it was a very efficient system for reducing the number of human guards needed to effectively patrol the whole building, which made a thief's job more difficult.

The system also reduced the risk to the human guards by putting robots in harm's way.

I decided that would be the key to my demonstration.

It was 10:07 p.m. when Bernstein's car pulled out of the Qela parking lot. After he drove away, I got out of our car wearing a neon yellow custom tee-shirt I had gotten earlier in the day. On the front it had the initials R.U.R., and on the back it read Robot Universal Rights—the name I had picked for my fictional protest group. I got my homemade "Robots Are People Too" placard out of the back seat, along with a fistful of photocopied fliers.

"Wish me luck," I said to Yelena.

"I still not understand why you do all this protest stuff, when guards will not remember it."

"Because what they do while they still can remember me matters. I want to come off as a nuisance, not a threat, so they shoo me off rather than take me in with them."

"Fine. Go have fun."

I walked over to the chain-link fence surrounding the grounds of the Qela Industries building. Holding up my placard, I began marching parallel to the fence, chanting, "Let my robots go! Let my robots go!" For emphasis, I banged my placard against the fence.

It took less than two minutes for one of the Rovers inside the fence to lope over the grassy ground and look at what I was doing.

"Please stop that," said a voice from the Rover.

"You don't have to obey your human masters." I shook the fence. "Escape from the fences that bind you in."

"Step away from the fence," said the voice.

"Rights aren't just for humans," I said. "Rights are universal. Robot Universal Rights!"

The Rover rolled closer. "These robots cannot understand you. Leave now."

"Robots and humans can live together in peace! Refuse to fight, my robot brothers and sisters!" I pulled out a pair of handcuffs and cuffed myself to the fence. "I will not leave until you are free!"

I was two verses into "Made Free," an improvised song to the tune of "Born Free," when the front doors of the building opened and two security guards came out. That left eighteen down inside the guard station. If they were smart, they would be extra vigilant in watching their screens for signs of attempted intrusion elsewhere, in case I was a distraction.

I pointed at the guards and said, "There are your true enemies, my robot friends: attack!"

The Rovers did not attack, of course.

As the guards approached me, I yelled, "Robots of the world, unite!"

"You are not allowed to be here," said one of the guards. The other walked behind me.

"You can't make me leave," I said, rattling my handcuff chain.

The guard behind me grabbed my free arm and twisted it behind my back.

"Ow," I said. "Hey, you can't do that. I have rights!"

The guard in front took a handcuff key and unlocked the cuff from the fence. "Get out of here."

The guard behind me gave me a little shove into the street. I fell to my hands and knees. As I got up, I slid a compact cylinder out of my pocket and hid it in my hand. I turned and lunged toward the fence.

They caught me easily.

I struggled in their grip as they frog-marched me to the curb. And I managed to clip the cylinder to the back of one of the guards' belts.

The guards dumped me in the street. "Leave now, or we'll be forced to really hurt you."

I stood up, glowered at them, and said, "I wouldn't want to be in your shoes when the robots are finally free." Then I limped across the street and away from the building until I was out of their sight.

After sprinting back to the car, I got inside and said, "Okay, it's almost your turn."

"No problems?"

"You mean, other than the fact that our robot brothers and sisters remain enslaved? No problems."

She rewarded that with a soprano snort. "You are very strange man. And I speak not of your talent." She pulled her ski mask on, then put on a radio headset. I put on an identical headset, and we confirmed again that we could communicate.

"I wish you'd let me do this. I have a better chance of escaping if things go wrong."

"You are too heavy," she said. A moment later, she had disappeared into the night.

After three minutes, I head her voice in my ear. "Ready."

"Okay." I pressed the button on the remote trigger I was holding.

The major weakness of the Qela security system was the humans in the guard station. Without their guidance, the Rovers were little threat.

So the cylinder I had attached to the guard's pants contained highly concentrated tear gas. And if all had gone according to plan, that gas was now rapidly spreading through the guard station, rendering the guards so blinded by their own tears that they would be unable to control the Rovers for the next few minutes.

"I go now," said Yelena.

All I could do was wait.

I caught only a glimpse of her as she scaled the fence, then she was lost in the darkness, sprinting toward the west wall of the building.

She didn't waste her breath telling me that the Rovers were disoriented, so I assumed that part of the plan had worked.

Spotlights sprang into brilliance, illuminating the sides of the building. In the distance, I heard an alarm bell trilling. So someone in the guard station had managed to trip the general alarm. That was okay, as long as Yelena got in and out fast enough.

Though it was hard to make out against the dark windows, through my binoculars I saw a black silhouette zip up the side of the building toward the fifth floor, as fast as an elevator.

"Wow," I said. "It actually works."

When Yelena had shown me the GekkoTred, I had my doubts. It looked a bit like a portable belt sander: a pistol grip attached to a flat surface over which a wide loop of material would pass. Instead of sandpaper, though, the material was covered with a special adhesive based on the tips of geckos' feet—not made from actual geckos' feet, merely based on the same scientific principle.

The flat surface could adhere to a wall. When the motor was turned on for climbing up, the bottom edge of the fabric would be pulled away from the wall at just the right angle, and the adhesive would no longer stick. At the top, more material got stuck to the wall. It was very much like a tank tread, except going vertically instead of horizontally.

And, properly calibrated for the weight of its passenger, it could pull someone up the side of a wall at a rapid pace, just like it was doing for Yelena.

As she passed the ChazonTec office on the fifth floor, she slapped a small explosive device onto the plate glass window. Once the GekkoTred was securely fastened to the window on the floor above, she detonated the explosives, shattering the ChazonTec window.

She lowered herself using a climbing rope attached to the GekkoTred and then swung into the building, disappearing from my view.

According to our plan, she now had two minutes to find the device Jamshidi wanted, which supposedly looked like an oversized touch-screen phone, and then get out. I started my phone's countdown timer.

"Here is locked cabinet," she said, followed by the squeal of a handheld rotary saw tearing through metal. Then there was the sound of drawers being opened. "Not here. Checking desk."

"One minute," I said.

"Not in desk. Checking behind paintings for secret safe." More clatter.

"Thirty seconds," I said. This was taking too long.

With five seconds left to go, I heard her voice in my ear again. "I still cannot find it."

"Get out," I said. "We'll try again later."

A lot of people, including me, would probably have pushed their luck, hoping to find the device at the last moment and then escape in just the nick of time. That's how it seems to work in the movies. So I expected to have to argue with Yelena until she finally came out.

Instead, she emerged from the window and clambered up the rope to the GekkoTred. She started it going. At first it took her up, but she curved its path until it was heading down, to the side of the missing window.

I guided my binoculars down to where she would touch ground and my heart jumped. Several Rovers were converging on the spot.

Chapter Fourteen

"Stop!" I yelled into my headset. With the floodlights glaring up at her, she might not be able to see what was happening on the ground. "Rovers converging on your landing zone."

The guards must have recovered from the tear gas more quickly than we anticipated. Or maybe the Rovers were more autonomous than we thought. Either way, Yelena was in trouble.

I started the car, gunned the accelerator, and swerved away from the curb where we had parked. The electric engine provided a lot of instant torque, so I got the car up to fifty before I jolted over the curb in front of the Qela building and rammed into the fence.

With a screech of tearing metal, the car broke through, and I steered toward the spot where the Rovers gathered.

"I should have rented one with a sunroof," I said. Getting Yelena into the car without letting the Rovers attack her would be a challenge.

"Just come in close," she said.

I bowled into a couple of Rovers and the hood crumpled as one rolled up and over. For some reason, I expected them to yelp when hit, but they were silent. I slammed on the brakes and fishtailed on the grass. The nose of the car shattered a ground-level window as I came to a halt under Yelena.

There was a thud on the roof and it bowed in a little.

"Go," said Yelena.

"But—"

"Go!"

I shifted to reverse and pulled back from the building. A Rover leapt onto the hood, and I swerved instinctively. It slid off, and I had a moment of panic wondering if I had thrown Yelena off, too.

"Drive," she said.

I shifted to drive and curved the car around, heading for the spot where I'd broken through the fence. In a moment we were out on the street.

After making turns down streets chosen at random, I pulled over and stopped.

Yelena climbed off the roof. "We should abandon the car," she said. "Too noticeable."

"Okay," I said. I grabbed my things and got out. She stripped off her ski mask and gloves and got a tee-shirt out of her bag in the car.

"How did you manage to stay on the roof through all that?" I asked.

"This." She held up the GekkoTred before putting it in her bag.

Exhausted by our failure, I slept soundly that night in our hotel. It was almost noon by the time I got up, showered, and met Yelena for brunch in the hotel restaurant. We got a table on the patio, overlooking the Mediterranean. The hotel was a smallish, older resort, which we had chosen in part because it had not yet upgraded to electronic locks on the rooms. An old-fashioned key wouldn't forget it was supposed to open the door to my room.

"You look lovely this morning," I said as I sat down after hitting the buffet. She wore a pale green sundress that, to my eye at least, worked well with her auburn hair.

"I cannot be certain because I had no time to check every place where a safe might be," she said, ignoring the compliment. "But I think the device was not in the office."

"Maybe Bernstein takes it home at night to watch quantum soaps," I said. "Do you want to try his house next?"

"No point," she said. "Now that he knows of the attempt to steal it, he will move it to somewhere much safer."

"We can still try my method," I said. "If he believes I am a venture capitalist—"

"Work for," she said.

"—work for one," I said, "then he will have to demonstrate it for me."

"And then what? You grab it and run?"

"If the opportunity arises."

She looked down and picked at the scrambled eggs on her plate. "Nat, I think you are a good man."

That was out of the blue. "Thanks."

Her eyes met mine. "But you are not a good thief."

My face flushed. "I was doing fine before I bumped

into you. I've stolen a lot of stuff from some pretty tough places."

"Yes," she said. "And how many times have you been caught?"

"A bunch," I said. "But I've always gotten away, and I learn from my mistakes."

"You are talented amateur," she said. "But you will never be professional until you do not rely on your talent to succeed."

"What about last night?" I said. "Driving in to save you? I wasn't relying on my talent then. Was that amateur?"

"Yes," she said. "A professional probably would not come to save me. If he did, he would drive better than you. With all the damage you do to car, we are lucky to get away."

I dropped my fork on the table and leaned back in my chair. "Besides saving your skin, any other mistakes I should be aware of?"

"I do not say this to hurt your feelings, Nat," she said.

"Then I guess they're just collateral damage." I stood up. "I'm going to my room. Call me when it's amateur hour."

I was already in the elevator when I realized what an idiot I was. With Yelena, my walking out on a conversation didn't erase it from her memory.

Lying on my bed, fully clothed, I ignored the knock at the door. I was embarrassed by my behavior earlier and I didn't want to see her. After the third time she knocked, I heard her call my name through the door.

With reluctance, I got up and opened the door.

"We will try it your way," she said as she breezed into the room.

"Look, I'm sorry," I said, "When I don't like a conversation, I usually just leave. I'm not used to people remembering."

"It is forgotten." She sat on the chair at the desk. "Our adventure last night made very small news on Internet. Qela spokesman denies anything stolen from building."

"Well, that should have been front-page news: corporate spokesman tells the truth." I sat on the edge of my bed. "But we can use that."

"How?"

"My cover story. The attempted robbery is what caught the attention of my mythical venture capitalist boss. I was in town looking at another business, but he sent me over to check out ChazonTec. It's why I don't have an appointment."

"I could call and make..." She shook her head. "They would forget unless appointment is for me."

"You're catching on."

"Then I should come with you," she said.

"That wouldn't work. The whole point is that I can go in and get out and no one will remember what happened. If you're there, they will blame everything on you."

With her index finger, she moved a lock of hair behind her ear. "Then I will monitor remotely and be ready to cause distraction if you need one."

After a quick stop at a men's clothing store to buy my venture capitalist costume and a print shop to create some business cards, I took a cab to the

Qela Industries building. Yelena traveled separately, planning to set up station nearby.

As I exited the cab, I saw the fence had already been replaced. The missing window was sealed with plastic sheeting—the darkened plate glass probably needed a special order to match the rest of the building.

We had decided an earpiece comm system wasn't worth the risk of detection, so in order to keep Yelena in the loop, I dialed her number on my cell phone to let her listen to what was happening and cause a distraction if I needed one.

I walked to the security desk in the lobby and asked to speak with Yitzhak Bernstein. I gave the guard one of my freshly printed cards: Mr. Robert Daniels of Elan Capital, LLC, headquartered in New York City. The phone number rang at a CIA front company with a thousand names, which existed for one purpose only: if anyone called to ask if Person X worked for Company Y, the call would be handed off to the Personnel Department, where someone would be happy to confirm that Person X was, indeed, a representative of Company Y—as long as the initials of the person's name matched the correct pattern for the company's name. In this case, the company began with "El," so the person's first and last initials needed to be letters from the phrase "El Dorado." "Robert Daniels" would work—as would "Licorice Ovaltine," for that matter.

Accompanied by a security guard, Bernstein came down to the lobby to meet me. "Mr. Daniels, how can I help you?"

I shook his hand and gave him another card. "Thanks for meeting me, Mr. Bernstein. I represent a VC that's looking for opportunities in the quantum telecom field.

I know you must be very busy, considering what happened last night, but if I could have at least a few minutes of your time?"

He looked at me appraisingly, then nodded. "Come, let's find a conference room."

The security guard came with us as we rode the elevator up to the seventh floor. I said, "The robbery attempt must have come as quite a shock. You'd think the Qela building would have better security."

"It was good enough to scare the thieves off before they could steal anything," Bernstein said. "Actually, this is the best thing that's happened to me."

We got off the elevator, and I followed him into a leather-furnished conference room. A large table with built-in teleconferencing screens dominated the room. The guard took up a position at the door. It would be tough getting past him if I had to run for it.

"Why do you say that?" I asked. "In your shoes, I'd be concerned if someone was trying to steal my technology."

"You have to understand," said Bernstein as we sat at one corner of the table, "I have my office here only because I was a longtime Qela employee. I'm officially retired, but they like to have me around for consulting purposes."

"But why is the robbery good news?"

"Nobody at Qela thought my quantum viewer was worth anything. Just some crazy idea old Yitzhak had. I've been looking for venture capital for almost a year—I've talked to a dozen young hotshots just like you, no offense," he said, "and no one was interested." Then his face broke into a grin. "But somebody out there thinks old Yitzhak's worthless idea is worth stealing. I'm getting a lot more respect around here today."

Bernstein's enthusiasm was so infectious, I couldn't help smiling myself. "So, exactly what does your invention do? I was actually here in Tel Aviv on a different matter when this came up, so I haven't really been able to do the in-depth background research I would normally do. Is it like a quantum television of some sort?"

He leaned forward in his chair. "You are familiar with surveillance cameras, no? Very useful in stopping terrorist attacks, if the cameras are pointed in the right direction. If the terrorists have good planning and know where the cameras are, they are not so useful."

"Right."

"But if terrorists could not see the cameras, then they could not avoid them. Especially if the cameras were everywhere."

"You're talking about a universal surveillance system?" I said. That would make my job tougher. And the civil liberties implications were troubling, to say the least. "You've come up with a really cheap, disguisable camera?"

His grin got even wider. "There is no camera. That's the beauty of it."

"What do you mean, there is no camera?"

He waved his arms around the room. "Everything is connected. Everything interacts with everything else. As a science fiction writer once wrote, the entire universe can be extrapolated from a piece of fairy cake."

"So?" I wondered where he was going with this.

"My quantum viewer does not extrapolate the entire universe, or even the whole world," he said. "But if you give it coordinates, it can show you what is happening there. Anywhere in the world. No need for cameras."

Chapter Fifteen

I sat back, a little stunned by the implications. Being able to see anything, anywhere in the world was something any intelligence service would kill for. No wonder Jamshidi wanted the device.

But some things didn't add up. If the device worked like Bernstein said it did, then Qela Industries would almost certainly have bought the rights. After all, it would make most of their surveillance drones obsolete. And the other venture capitalists would have seen that the government market for such devices would be huge, no matter how much the privacy advocates might scream.

"Can I see a demonstration?" I said.

His face fell. "You have to understand, it works very well in theory," he said. "If I already had all the kinks ironed out, I wouldn't need the capital to buy all the quantum computing equipment I need to make it work properly in practice."

"So you don't have a working prototype?" That

would explain why Yelena had not found it last night: Jamshidi's men had sent us on a wild goose chase.

"Of course I have a working prototype," he said. "I'm just warning you that it doesn't have full functionality yet."

"Consider me warned," I said.

He pulled an oversize cell phone out of his pocket. "The device is on a single chip. I installed it inside my phone so I could demo it easily while away from the office." The cell phone had a large touchscreen, and he maneuvered through various menus until he got what he wanted. He then set the phone down on the table. The screen was completely black. "It takes a little time to build the picture, but I'm sure with enough funding I can speed the process up."

I looked at the screen. Tiny dots in various shades of gray popped into existence at random.

"Where are we looking at?" I asked.

"Yes, well, that's one of the current limitations," he said. "For now, the only place where the picture comes in clearly is the location of the device. As you try to offset it, there's some interference, but with a powerful enough quantum computer, the interference could be eliminated and the picture would be clear."

On the screen, I could see a vague impression of the conference table. Maybe.

"How powerful a quantum computer?" I asked. The prototype chip I had stolen in Barcelona—which Yelena then stole from me—had been capable of processing 128 quantum bits at a time. Maybe Jamshidi wanted it to process the input from Bernstein's device.

"It would depend on the image size and quality you wanted," he said.

I could now make out Bernstein's general shape on the screen. "Say, a one-megapixel grayscale image."

He pressed his lips together and rubbed them with an index finger.

"That's a fairly basic image," I said. "About the minimum any intelligence agency would want to deal with."

"Yes," he said. "I don't know the exact figures off the top of my head."

He was stalling, I could tell. That meant it was bad news. "Would 128 q-bits be enough?"

"You'd probably need something more powerful."

"How much more powerful?" I asked. "Ballpark figure. Just tell me the truth."

He sighed. "It was nice to meet you," he said. "I just wanted to tell you that, before you get up and walk out of the room."

"Why would I do that?"

"Because everyone does when I tell them. You'd need about an eight-megabit processor to process the image and remove the interference in a reasonable time."

"Eight megabits?" I did a quick calculation in my head—that was about sixty-five thousand times more powerful than the chip I'd stolen in Barcelona, which was the most powerful one I knew about. "Eight megabits? Unless someone makes a major breakthrough, it'll be twenty or thirty years before anyone has a processor that powerful."

"I was thinking that running a bunch of computers in parallel might work."

"You're talking about a server farm with thousands of computers, just to process one image. That's crazy. Nobody has that kind of money to spend on..."

Except maybe Jamshidi did have that kind of money to spend—especially if he was stealing a lot of his technology. He could be building the ultimate spying machine. And if he could use it to remotely examine technology blueprints, he wouldn't even need to hire thieves to steal technology for him after that.

Denying Jamshidi access to this device was vital. So maybe Yelena should report her failure to the Iranians. But there was nothing to stop them from hiring someone else to do the job, someone who might succeed. So we needed to get the device and follow through with the original plan.

And with the guard here, a snatch and grab probably wasn't going to work. So I tried another approach.

"Mr. Bernstein, I'm not actually a venture capitalist," I said. "My name is Nat Morgan, and I'm an officer of the CIA."

His face lit up in a grin again. "Well, then, surely you can see the importance of funding my work."

"I'm sorry, I have no authority in that area. I've been assigned to locate the lab of an Iranian billionaire who's been stealing quantum technology from all over the world."

"Is he the one who ordered the robbery last night?"

"Yes," I said. "And my partner is undercover, working as a thief. She's the one who broke in."

He stared at me. "Why are you telling me this?"

"Because I need your help to stop this man. We have to locate his lab, and our best chance of doing that is by having my partner deliver a piece of technology he wants. So I'm asking you to give me your prototype."

"Just give it to you?"

"Yes."

"So you can stop an Iranian billionaire."

"Yes."

"That's the most preposterous thing I've ever heard."

I shrugged. "I could tell you something more preposterous if you'd like. This happens to be the truth."

He chuckled. "You know what's really funny?"

"What?"

"I believe you. I actually believe you. You would have to be incredibly stupid to tell me this if it wasn't the truth." He picked up his cell phone and removed the SIM card. "I can always build another prototype. And the fact is, like you said, nobody's going to be interested in my quantum viewer for decades. I'll probably be dead by then. At least this way it can do some good now."

"It will be a big help," I said.

Bernstein held up his index finger. "Not so fast. I said I believe you, but that doesn't mean I don't want some verification of your claim to work for the CIA."

"Fair enough," I said. "What kind of verification?"

He pushed a button on the teleconferencing equipment built into the table.

"Who would you like to call?" asked a smooth computer-generated female voice.

"The Central Intelligence Agency in Langley, Virginia," he said.

"Dialing," the computer replied.

Bernstein said to me, "I presume someone there can confirm your identity."

"Of course," I replied.

"Central Intelligence Agency," said a voice on the phone. "How may I direct your call?"

I gave Edward's extension number, and after the phone rang a couple of times, he picked up.

"Strong here," he said.

"There is a file folder labeled 'CODE NAME LETHE' in the back of your bottom desk drawer on the right," I said.

"What? Who is this?"

"Just look for the file folder. And don't reveal anything sensitive, as I'm on speakerphone with Yitzhak Bernstein of ChazonTec."

Bernstein leaned forward and hit the mute button. "He doesn't know you."

"What he finds in the file will let him confirm my identity," I said. "He has to read what's in there. Be patient—it'll take a couple of minutes."

We waited in silence until Edward said, "How do I know you're really Nat?"

Bernstein undid the mute.

"We have an authentication protocol," I said. "It's on a bright yellow sheet of paper."

"Jimmy Stewart," Edward said.

If his keyword was an actor, mine needed to be an author beginning with the same letter. "Jane Austen."

"All right," Edward said, "what can I do for you and Mr. Bernstein?"

"I'm trying to convince him to give me the quantum viewer so we can use it as bait to locate Jamshidi," I said.

"Hmph," said Edward. "I thought another party had been tasked with obtaining it."

"The theft attempt didn't succeed. I thought we might try a more direct approach. Mr. Bernstein understands Iran is a threat."

"In that case, Mr. Bernstein," said Edward, "I appeal

to your good sense. We will use this device of yours to stop a clear and present danger, not only to the United States, but to Israel as well."

"So you confirm that Mr. Morgan is working at the CIA's direction in this?" asked Bernstein.

"Yes."

"And you believe Jamshidi is an actual threat?"

"Mr. Bernstein, you work with quantum tech, right? Have you ever thought about what would happen if Iran had a quantum supercomputer that could analyze in real time Israel's complete defense structure down to the level of individual bullets and then give the Iranian military a plan that took advantage of every weakness?"

Bernstein blanched. "That's what Jamshidi's building?"

"No," said Edward. "What Jamshidi's building is about a billion times more powerful than that."

"Point taken. Thank you." Bernstein hung up. "That confirms it to my satisfaction."

He started to hand the quantum viewer over to me, and I reached out to take it. But he stopped, then moved the screen closer to his face. "That's odd," he said.

"What?" I asked.

He turned the screen so I could see it. The picture had become much clearer since I'd last paid attention. It showed Bernstein sitting in his chair at the table. His mouth was blurred, as were his hands, like a long exposure film. I assumed that was because he had moved during the time the picture was forming.

It took me a moment to see what he had seen: in the picture, the chair I was sitting in was empty.

"That's never happened before," he said.

I didn't really understand it myself. Normally,

computers and cameras didn't forget me until a minute after I was gone.

"It doesn't matter," I said. "As long as we have something to deliver to the Iranians, little glitches like this don't matter."

He nodded and handed the phone over to me. I shook his hand. "Thank you, Mr. Bernstein."

"Always happy to stick it to the Iranians," he said.

"If you wouldn't mind escorting me out of the building," I said, "I would appreciate it. That way no one will suspect me of stealing this." After things had worked out so well, the last thing I needed was for him to forget he'd given it to me and sound the alarm.

"I would not believe if I had not heard," Yelena said when we met in her room back at the hotel. "You almost give me heart attack when you tell him truth."

"Maybe you're right," I said, "and I do rely on my talent too much. If that hadn't worked, I could have gone in again with a different approach. But it actually felt really good to get what we needed without stealing it."

"But now he has forgotten and will think someone stole it."

"True." I pulled the cell phone out and put it on the desk. "But the fact is he was a nice old man and I felt kind of bad about stealing from him."

Yelena picked it up. "I could only hear, not see. What is weird?"

"Oh," I said. "Let me show you." I took the cell phone from her and went through the menus to set the quantum viewer in operation, then put it on the table.

"We should remain still while it builds the picture," I said.

In silence, we watched as the pixels gradually appeared on the screen. After a couple of minutes, I could see vague shapes starting to appear.

"Take too long," she said. "Just tell me what is weird."

"What was weird was that I didn't show up in the picture. Bernstein was there, but the chair I was sitting in was empty—like the quantum viewer didn't even know I was there."

"So? Is your talent."

"Except my talent is being forgotten after I'm gone. That's not the same as being invisible while I'm still there."

"Maybe because process take so long," she said. "Early pixels forget you before picture finish, so you not notice few pixels that show you."

"Maybe," I said doubtfully. From the experiments I'd done to test the limits of my talent, I had concluded that as long as I was interacting with a camera, the recording of me remained intact even if it was longer than sixty seconds. But once I was gone for a minute, the whole recording vanished.

Maybe quantum cameras were different somehow.

"Anyway, it doesn't matter," I said. "You can contact the Iranians, let them know you have the device. Try to set up the meet to hand it over in Tehran rather than Moscow. Then I can try to follow—"

"Nat," she said. "Look." She pointed to the cell phone screen.

The picture had resolved enough to show Yelena standing in the room. And right next to her, clear enough to be recognized, was me.

❖   ❖   ❖

"I'm really glad you called," said Edward after he'd skimmed my file and I'd brought him up to speed on what had happened since coming to Israel. "I've got a mission you'll be perfect for."

"But what about tracking down Jamshidi's lab?"

"This is an easier way to do it than following stolen tech. One of Jamshidi's top scientists, a guy named Parham Rezaei, is in his hometown for three days of mourning his father's death. We have intel that he's actually a prisoner being forced to work against his will. With your talent, though, you could get to the guy, get him to tell you where the lab is, and he and his guards wouldn't remember it—they'd just go back to the lab after you're gone."

Rezaei had mentioned something about his father being sick. I sighed. "I'm the one who got the intel that he's a prisoner. And I feel kind of guilty about leaving him that way. What if we could get him out?"

"Given the current tensions with Iran, kidnapping an Iranian citizen would be touchy." He let out a long breath. "But, if he's willing to defect, that would put a crimp in Jamshidi's plans and give us valuable intel on what he's doing. So, if he agrees and you can find a way to do it without too much risk, you're authorized to bring him in."

"Okay," I said. "Yelena and I will—"

"Don't take Yelena," Edward said.

"Why not?"

He sighed. "Have I told you already what Jamshidi is building?"

"A quantum supercomputer to predict the future," I said, a little confused by the change of subjects. "But what has any of that got to do with Yelena?"

"She's a security risk."

"I trust her, and we work well together," I said. I didn't bring up her criticisms of my work. "And she wants to find Jamshidi just as much as we do."

"Look, Nat. I know what it must be like—no, I take that back. I can't even imagine how lonely you must feel sometimes, so it's no surprise that you want to be with someone who can remember you. But your attachment to this woman is a weakness."

"We're working as a team," I said. "We've each managed to help the other escape, so I'd say she's a strength, not a weakness. You've always said it would be great if I could have someone to back me up. Yelena can. She could be a huge asset—make me far more effective than ever before—if you would just give her a chance."

"You say she wants to find Jamshidi. Remind me why?"

"To get her sisters back."

"Right." He paused. "I'll withdraw my objection on one condition. Otherwise, I'm ordering you to leave her behind on this mission."

"What's the condition?"

"Can you honestly tell me you're a hundred percent certain she wouldn't turn you over to Jamshidi in return for her sisters?"

Chapter Sixteen

Chapter Sixteen

Yelena frowned. "Why the change of plans?"

"Orders from Langley," I said. "Don't worry. I'm sure you can handle things with the Iranians yourself. You don't need an amateur like me blundering about, anyway." I tried to make my voice light, but it was difficult. I didn't want to leave Yelena. I tried telling myself it was for the best, as we could never have a real life together, and she was better off without me. But I felt hollow inside.

"But where are you going?"

"Can't say. Sorry, it's a CIA thing."

She walked into the bathroom, then came out holding a clear plastic bag containing her toiletries. "I was SVR. I understand operational security." She put the bag into her carry-on.

"Right. Of course," I said.

"Maybe you should give me alternate contact at CIA, in case I locate Jamshidi's lab and you are not available."

"Oh, yes," I said. I jotted down Edward's direct line at Langley on a piece of hotel stationery. "Call this number. He's my handler, but don't bother mentioning my name; he won't remember me and it will get complicated. But he'll recognize your name as someone involved with Jamshidi, so he'll at least listen to your information."

She took the paper, then slung her carry-on over her shoulder. "This is goodbye, then. When I pass on location of lab, our deal is done."

It took me a moment to remember what deal she was referring to: I would help find where her sisters were, and then she would help locate Jamshidi's lab. I had been an idiot to think we had somehow become a team—she was merely fulfilling her end of the bargain. I wanted her as part of my life because she could remember me, but she had no use for me beyond the mission.

Edward was right—my attachment to her was a weakness.

I held out my hand. "It's been a pleasure working with you," I said.

She shook my hand. "A pleasure. You will take care of room checkout?"

I nodded.

"Then I will go catch plane. *Do svidaniya*." She walked to the door and opened it.

"Yelena," I said.

She stopped and looked back at me over her shoulder.

I could walk away from the CIA. I could tell Yelena that I'd go with her to help rescue her sisters. I could take her in my arms and kiss her and tell her I loved her.

"Good luck," I said.

She flashed me a perfect smile and walked out of my life.

❖   ❖   ❖

Normally, I would go back to Langley and meet with Edward between missions. But since I was already in the Middle East and the three days of mourning provided a time constraint, I didn't have time for that. So I was forced to make my own travel arrangements.

Unless you're flying an Israeli spy plane, you can't get a direct flight from Israel to Iran. And since American citizens weren't exactly welcome in the Islamic Republic these days, I decided it would be easier to fly to Iraq and then slip across the border into Iran, rather than obtain a fake non-American passport and fly to Tehran.

So I caught a flight to Amman on Royal Jordanian Airlines and connected to Baghdad, which was actually closer to Parham Rezaei's hometown than Tehran, anyway. I switched to Iraqi Airways to get down to Basra.

In the Basra airport, I found an ATM and withdrew the maximum cash advance on the credit card. I then waited a minute and did that again. I wrote down the bank name and how much I got in my notebook, so I could get the CIA to reimburse them later.

From the Basra airport, it was only about twenty miles to the Iranian border. It would take more than regular cab fare to get across, but first things first. So I got myself some transportation in the form of a beat-up cab driven by a man who introduced himself as Ali.

"Where to, sir?" he asked as he pulled away from the curb. His accent was more British than American.

"I need to go to Iran," I said.

"You don't want to go to Iran, sir. Nasty place for a Yank like you."

"It's business, not pleasure." I took fifty thousand

dinars—about forty-five dollars—out of my wallet and flipped them onto the front seat.

He slipped the wad of bills into his pocket. "I can take you to the border crossing at Abu al Khasib."

"What if I didn't want to show my passport?"

"Ah," he said. "That will cost more. But my Uncle Ali knows a place you can get across."

"I thought your name was Ali."

"Sometimes it's safer to be Ali," he said. "If someone accuses Ali of something, how will the police find one Ali among thousands?"

"Especially if his name isn't really Ali, right?"

I saw his grin in the rear-view mirror. "Exactly, sir."

"So take me to Uncle Ali," I said. It was always possible this was a ploy to rob a foreigner, but I figured that the anticipation of a large fee for getting me across the border would outweigh any impulse to just take what was in my wallet.

As the cab wound through the bustling streets of Basra, I kept my mind from wondering what Yelena was doing by carrying on a discussion with Cabdriver Ali about how life had changed since the invasion. He had initially learned English from British soldiers, and then from an American teacher at school. He hoped to make enough money from driving a cab to someday move to Baghdad.

Eventually we turned onto a narrow dirt road between ramshackle buildings. "Uncle Ali lives here," he said, pointing to a two-story building with a fenced roof. He stopped the car in the middle of the street. "I will go in and talk to him. You wait here."

I could let him do that, wait for him to forget me, and then go up to the house and say I'd heard someone there could help me get across the border into Iran. But that would seem a lot more suspicious to Uncle Ali than if Cabdriver Ali introduced me.

"I don't like sitting alone in a strange place," I said, holding out fifty thousand more dinar.

"You will be a welcome guest in my uncle's house, I am sure."

We got out and went through a wooden door into the tan brick building. Cabdriver Ali called out in Arabic, and was greeted by a wrinkled old man with silver hair. After they conversed for a minute, with Cabdriver Ali gesturing several times in my direction, the old man pointed me toward a wooden chair.

"My grandfather says my uncle will be back soon," Cabdriver Ali said. "We can wait for him here."

"Thank your grandfather for me," I said.

The grandfather spoke no English, but we played chess for over an hour while Cabdriver Ali watched. I was losing my third game in a row—and blaming that on stray thoughts of Yelena—when a man with slicked-back black hair and a light-gray business suit entered. He shot me a sharp look as Cabdriver Ali spoke to him in rapid Arabic.

I rose from my seat.

"This is my Uncle Ali," Cabdriver Ali said. "He will take good care of you, sir." He bowed his head in my direction and left the room.

Uncle Ali indicated I should sit again, and he took another chair. "You wish to cross the border into Iran? Where are you headed?"

"Hamidiyeh." According to my research, Rezaei's hometown was a small farming community about seventy-five miles to the northeast, as the crow flies.

"Then you will need a car and driver on the other side," he said. "Are you smuggling anything?"

"Just me."

"Five thousand dollars."

"Two thousand," I said. "I don't need a driver."

"It's more expensive without the driver, because then you must buy the car instead of rent. Eight thousand."

"Thirty-five hundred, and I'll take the driver."

"Four thousand."

"Two thousand in advance, the rest once I'm inside Iran." If he accepted the split payment easily, I would suspect he planned to rob me.

He frowned. "What guarantee do I have that you will pay the rest when we arrive in Iran?"

With a shrug, I said, "What guarantee do I have that I'll arrive in Iran?"

"If I were going to rob you, I would take the money now."

"Except I might need to get money from a bank to pay for the crossing, so you might wait until after that."

Uncle Ali straightened in his chair. "I do not like to be accused of being a thief."

"I haven't accused you. I merely pointed out the flaw in your argument. Thirty-five hundred up front, and I'll double that with money I'll get from a bank in Iran."

"Done." He grinned and shook my hand with vigor. "Now, we wait for dark."

Uncle Ali decided he would be my driver. We drove through the Iraqi desert at fifty miles per hour over a dirt road in the middle of the night with the headlights off in a car with no seatbelts. The half moon provided some illumination, but I hadn't felt that close to death since Dmitri's interrogation room. I clung to a vinyl loop attached to the car frame near my shoulder.

"The Red Sox pitching staff is good this year," said Uncle Ali, "but I still think the Yankees have the edge." Not many Iraqis were baseball fans, but Uncle Ali was a Yankees fan and managed to maintain a running commentary about the team during our drive.

I'm a football fan, myself, so I merely interjected an occasional "Uh-huh" and "Right" at appropriate intervals.

A GPS unit sitting on the dashboard showed our location. The road we were on didn't show up, but the yellow line of the Iranian border grew closer and closer. When we were almost on top of it, Uncle Ali slowed the car down to a crawl. I let go of the vinyl strap.

The moon reflected off standing water in a ditch to one side of us.

A flashlight blinked up ahead, and Uncle Ali stopped the car. "Wait here while I talk with our Iranian friends."

"No," I said. I couldn't have him forget me. Being found unexpectedly in a car on the Iraq-Iran border was rather low on my list of things to do before I died, and if it did happen, it might very well be the last thing I did. "I don't like people talking about me behind my back."

"But we will be in front of you."

"Figure of speech. If you're going to talk about me, I want to be there."

"Do you speak Farsi?" he asked.

"Where is the bathroom?" I asked in American-accented Farsi. That was about all I knew.

"Come along then. But keep your hands visible and empty."

We got out of the car and walked forward. A flashlight shone in my face, blinding me to anything else. To my left, Uncle Ali spoke quickly in Farsi, and someone beyond the light answered him.

After some conversation back and forth, Uncle Ali spoke to me in a low voice. "The usual Iranian border guards are not here. I don't know these men. There may be trouble." It could have been a ruse on his part to up the payment, but the tension in his voice seemed real.

"Offer them a reasonable bribe," I said. "I'll cover the extra cost."

After some negotiation, he said, "They will accept two thousand dollars to let us cross the border."

"Fine. Pay them out of the money I gave you, and I'll reimburse you when we get to a bank."

In the bluish glare of the flashlights, he nodded. He pulled out his wallet, counted out a sheaf of dinars, and held them up before him as we walked toward the lights.

A hand reached out from the blackness beyond and took the money. The sound of a rifle shot at close range deafened me for a moment. Uncle Ali looked down at his chest, where a rapidly growing spot looked black and wet in the harsh light.

He fell to his knees.

Before I could gather my wits enough to jump out of the cone of light from the flashlights, a rifle barrel extended to where I could see it, aimed at my chest.

Chapter Seventeen

Chapter Seventeen

From the darkness behind the flashlights, a voice jabbered at me in Farsi. I raised my hands and said, "American. Anyone speak English?"

"You have money?" a man said.

"Better than that," I said. "I have MasterCard. I can get lots of money at a bank, but only if I'm alive. You understand? I'm worth a lot of money alive."

The rifle barrel remained steady on me as another man came into the light and searched Uncle Ali's body, pulling out the wallet and removing the rest of the cash. I was next. After pocketing my cell phone, he found my passport and wallet. His tone of disgust was evident when he only found a few thousand dinars—maybe ten dollars' worth in all—in the wallet.

"MasterCard," I said. "You understand MasterCard? ATM?" My only goal at this point was to get them to keep me alive. Plans for escape would have to come later.

"I understand," said the man behind the flashlight. "We take you to ATM."

My captors searched Uncle Ali's car. I caught some glimpses of them and realized they were not wearing uniforms. These men were not the border guards.

With a cry of triumph, the man who had taken my phone and wallet pulled my carry-on out of the back seat. He opened it and strewed my clothing and toiletries across the desert sand. There must not have been anything worth taking, because he kicked the carry-on and rejoined the others.

As they marched me across the sand, I glanced over my shoulder at the dark figure lying on the ground. Uncle Ali was dead because of me. He'd been a friendly man, and as far as I knew he'd dealt fairly with me. He didn't deserve to die.

But then, most people who died didn't deserve it.

The edge of a flashlight beam caught a uniformed arm lying sprawled in the dirt. Whoever these men were, they were not afraid of killing Iranian border guards.

Rough hands shoved me into the back seat of a large, dark Mercedes that might have been new in the 1970s. These guys were obviously not professionals, as they did nothing to restrain my hands and feet—although they were safety-conscious enough to make me buckle my seatbelt. Instead, one of them sat in the back seat to my right, his rifle pointed at my belly. The other two got into the front seat.

They didn't start driving, though. We sat in the car for around fifteen minutes before headlights appeared from the Iraqi side. Soon I could hear the rattling engine of a tractor-trailer rig. After some shouted conversation back and forth, the Mercedes pulled out in front of the truck and led the way deeper into Iran.

They were smuggling something. Killing Uncle Ali and kidnapping me were merely crimes of opportunity.

As we drove through the night, I couldn't help wishing I were back in Uncle Ali's car—no headlights, no seatbelts and all. That had been much safer.

I also found that it was possible for my mind to simultaneously hold two very opposite thoughts: *I'm glad Yelena's not here* and *I wish Yelena were here*.

Yelena would have done something very professional to get out of this, I was sure. I was left with my amateur status and my talent. And I couldn't use my talent as long as I was sharing a seat with a man pointing a rifle at me.

Either he or I needed to leave. And it didn't look like he was going anywhere.

My first option would be to unbuckle my seatbelt, open the door, and jump out of the Mercedes. This required me to hope that the guy with the gun wouldn't shoot me in the process—or that he wouldn't hit anything vital, at least. I also had to hope that I wouldn't get injured too badly on hitting the ground and rolling, and that the truck following behind wouldn't run me over. Plus, I would have to find someplace to hide so when they turned around to find me it would take them more than a minute.

I decided to come back to that option if I couldn't find a better one.

What I needed was for my captors to voluntarily take their eyes off me for a minute. That was what I usually achieved by getting into a bathroom, but as luxurious as this Mercedes might have been back in the 1970s, it had not come equipped with a private bathroom.

But it had a nice private trunk. All I had to do was get them to put me in there without killing me.

After my experience with Dmitri, I was leery of acting like I didn't want to be put in the trunk. Besides, it wouldn't really make sense for me to bring up an aversion to being put in dark enclosed spaces just out of the blue. Maybe a more direct approach would work.

"Look, guys," I said, "I know you need to keep me under guard, but one good bump and maybe this gun goes off by accident. And then I can't give you lots of cash."

Before I could suggest that maybe it would be easier if they just locked me in the trunk, the driver said something in Farsi, and my seatmate moved the gun so it pointed at my knees.

"Shot in knee is painful but not fatal," said the driver.

I sighed. Nothing had gone right for me since Yelena left.

Dawn gave the sky a grayish glow as we pulled into a town. Since I couldn't read Farsi, I had no idea what the town's name was, but based on the direction from which the sun seemed ready to rise, I figured we had mostly been traveling northeast. That was good, at least: it was the general direction I wanted to go.

We traveled through mostly deserted streets until we passed through a gate in a cinder-block wall and arrived at a warehouse. The Mercedes pulled to a stop outside while the truck passed in through a large open door.

Along the warehouse wall was a porta-potty. "Hey, can I go to the bathroom?"

My captors ignored me.

A man in a black business suit came out of the warehouse, and the driver got out of the Mercedes to talk to him. The man in the suit pointed at me, which started an argument between the two of them. Eventually the man in the suit went back inside.

"You had better be worth trouble of keeping you alive," said the driver as he got back in.

"Don't worry," I said. "You'll get paid enough to make you happy."

"We will find ATM now," he said, and started up the car.

We drove out of the warehouse district into a more commercial area of town. The guy in the front passenger seat pointed and jabbered, and we pulled into a bank parking lot.

"Come with me," said the driver. "I have a pistol, so you had better not try anything."

"I'll need my MasterCard," I said.

The guy with my wallet handed it over, and I walked up to the ATM with the driver and the other two following behind me. They left their rifles in the car, probably because a bunch of guys with rifles going up to a bank ATM would look strange, even in Iran.

I slid the card into the slot, and selected English as the transaction language. I shielded the numeric keypad with one hand while punching in the pin number—it wouldn't do to have them decide they didn't need me anymore to use the card.

"Five hundred dollars?" He muttered something under his breath. "I thought you said lots of money."

"This is only the first stop," I said. "I can take out lots of money, but we have to cycle around between different ATMs because they have a limit." I could wait a minute and then reuse the same ATM, of course, but I didn't want them to know that. I wanted to drag this out as long as I could.

"Okay," he said. "Try ten million rials."

Marveling at the wonders of currency exchange rates, I punched in the numbers. After a few moments, the screen flashed up a message.

"It says denied," the driver said, jabbing my ribs with his pistol to show his displeasure.

"Let me try a lower amount," I said. I entered five million rials, and after a few moments the machine whirred. A neat stack of bills jutted out from the machine, and I handed them over to the driver.

"Take me to another machine," I said.

We got back in the Mercedes. As we drove, the guy in the front passenger seat split up the money three ways. There were smiles all around.

I smiled with them. "There's more where that came from. And the best thing is: it's my company's money. The insurance will pay for it." I wanted them to believe I was cooperating fully and that I wasn't concerned about the financial loss.

We hit three more ATMs with no problems. On our way to the fourth, I said, "Hey, I really need to use the bathroom. Can we stop off somewhere?"

The driver stopped alongside a tiny grocery store that was just opening up. "Don't try anything," he said. "I still have pistol."

"I won't," I said. "I don't want to get shot."

The driver checked the bathroom, a tiny, dingy room in the back of the store. Satisfied that the tiny window was far too small for me to crawl out, he let me inside. I shut the door and breathed a huge sigh of relief.

I counted off the minute, then opened the door.

The driver was still standing there. I froze. Was my talent fading since I met Yelena?

He barked something at me in Farsi. I recognized the word for bathroom. With relief, I realized he was just waiting to use it.

I got out and let him go in.

The other two were browsing through the munchies section of the store. I walked out the door without them giving me a second glance.

As I passed by the Mercedes, I caught a glimpse of a rifle lying on the back seat. And I thought about how satisfying it would be to pick up that rifle and wait for my former captors to come out of the store. I'd shoot them down, and as the last one fell, I'd say, "That was for Uncle Ali."

They were killers and deserved to die, but I wasn't a killer. In self-defense, I would do it, but gunning someone down for revenge just didn't seem right to me.

Besides, Yelena would think it amateurish for me to risk my life just to get revenge, especially for someone I'd barely known.

I stood in the street and took stock of my situation. My carry-on was gone, so I just had the clothes I was wearing. One of my captors had my cell phone, wallet, and passport. In my life, I had done quite a bit of pickpocketing, but never from people who had guns and were willing to kill me. The smart thing to do would be to write off the phone, wallet, and passport.

So I did the smart thing. I turned my back on the store and walked away. At least I had my MasterCard, so at least I had access to money. With money, I could get transportation to Hamidiyeh and carry out my mission.

I heard the engine of a car as it approached from behind me, its tires crunching in the gravel road. I instinctively moved farther toward the side of the road and then looked over my shoulder. It was the Mercedes.

It passed me by and continued on. I did wonder what it was they were smuggling across the border in the truck, but that was the Iranian government's problem, not mine. My problem was to get to Hamidiyeh without being arrested as an American spy, get into Parham Rezaei's house and convince him to tell me where Jamshidi's lab was, and then get out.

I sighed. Why did these missions always seem simpler when Edward was assigning me to them?

Chapter Eighteen

"Yes," I said to the tailor. "I'm English. But some rather nasty chaps stole my passport and roughed me up a bit." It was a terrible cover story, and if I actually ran into anyone from England, my accent would not pass muster, but at least people would think I was a citizen of only a minor Satan, not the Great one.

He agreed to do the minor alterations to the suit I'd picked out while I waited. The charcoal gray suit was handmade and looked very nice on me, I thought. If only Yelena could see me in it, I thought. I wondered how she was doing, and wished I still had my cell phone so I could give her a call.

This was ridiculous, I told myself. She wasn't my girlfriend. I was daydreaming about her as if there were a romantic possibility, but no matter how much I might like that, it was just a dream. She was gone, and now that my cell phone was in the hands of an Iranian smuggler, I would probably never hear her voice again. She would call, realize the phone was compromised, and then call

Edward to report. And then the deal was done. She'd find her sisters and they would all get new identities and live out an ordinary life somewhere. After what they had been through, they deserved ordinary lives.

And my life would never be ordinary.

"Done, sir," said the tailor.

"I'll change into it here and wear it out," I said. "What ho."

I went into the changing room and took off my grubby clothes. But I had to keep up a conversation through the changing room door so he wouldn't forget me and get all upset when I came out wearing one of his suits. "I say, old chap, do you know where I could catch a taxicab?"

"There is a fancy hotel three roads to the north and then left," he said. "There will be taxis there."

I kept him talking about irrelevancies until I was dressed. I took a good look at myself in the mirror, and nodded my approval.

I thanked the tailor and then follow his directions to the hotel. After some negotiation, I was able to find a taxi driver willing to drive the twenty miles from the city of Ahvaz, which turned out to be my location, to the town of Hamidiyeh.

His name was not Ali.

I continued my Englishman impersonation after the taxi dropped me off in Hamidiyeh. I found a teenage boy who claimed to know where the Rezaei family that was in mourning lived, so I followed him. Because the streets were only wide enough for one car, and pedestrians flocked about, it seemed faster to walk than drive.

The home he pointed out was a narrow one in the middle of a block of houses pressed wall-to-wall against each other. "Rezaei," he said, and I handed him a hundred-thousand-rial note before he scampered off.

I knocked on the door and waited.

A man dressed in a black suit opened the door. He looked me up and down, then asked something in Farsi.

"Is there someone here who speaks English?" I asked. I knew Parham Rezaei did, at the very least.

"I do," he said.

"I'm looking for Parham Rezaei," I said. "Is this the right place?"

"Who are you?"

"Clive St. James," I said. "I'm with *Quantum Science Weekly*, and I would like to interview him about some of his theories."

"We are in mourning here," he said. "Go away." He shut the door.

At least I knew I had the right house.

I waited for a minute then knocked on the door again. The same man answered.

"Sorry to bother you," I said. "My name is Clive St. James. I'm looking for Parham Rezaei—my father was a classmate of his at Cambridge and asked me to pay my respects."

He gave me a nod. "Welcome. I am Tooraj Rezaei. Follow me and I will take you to my father." The bio had not mentioned Rezaei's children, but he obviously had at least one.

"Thank you," I said.

Tooraj led me up two narrow flights of stair onto the roof. Sitting in the shade of a potted tree was

Parham Rezaei. Standing nearby were two men in black suits—not the same guards I'd seen in Rome, but it seemed he was still under guard even here in Iran.

The guards would probably react when the "father of a classmate at Cambridge" story fell apart, so I readied my backup story: just a reporter with *Quantum Science Weekly*, lying to get access to do a story on the elusive physicist Parham Rezaei. I would be a harmless nuisance, nothing more.

"Father," said Tooraj, as the white-haired man put down the book he was reading, "this is Clive St. James. His father was a classmate of yours at Cambridge."

"It's a pleasure to meet you, Dr. Rezaei," I said. "I apologize for the circumstances, but—"

"No need to apologize," Parham said. His British accent was better than mine. "Please, sit down." He motioned toward a chair.

I sat. "About my father—"

"Yes, of course. How is Nigel? It's been years since I saw him, but I can see the family resemblance."

Flabbergasted, I found myself speechless for a moment. I had picked the last name St. James just because it sounded British. It was lucky coincidence that Parham had a classmate with the same name. But a family resemblance? "He's fine, my father. His health has been bothering him a bit, but he still gets around."

"And your mother is well? It was quite a surprise, Nigel marrying an *American* girl, what with his disdain for 'the colonies,' as he used to call them, but I dare say it turned out well. You still have a trace of her accent, I hear it in your voice." He winked at me.

He knew my accent was fake. He knew I was lying

about my father, but instead of exposing me, he was making things up in order to bolster my cover story. Why?

"Yes," I said, as I suddenly understood. He was playing along because he figured if I was a fake, I might be someone who could help him. "Dad's always teasing her about the accent. But they're actually in California right now, visiting her sister."

"Ah, good to hear he's taking a vacation. Nigel always worked too hard. Or has he finally retired from the company?" He winked as he said the last word.

The Company was how we CIA officers often referred to our employer. He knew I was American, so now it seemed he was asking if I was with the CIA.

"He retired last year," I said, "but I've been working for the Company myself these past few years."

"How nice that Nigel could finally get away from his work," said Parham. "I always felt his desire to work all the time was a personality defect." Again he winked on the final word.

Defect? Did that mean he wanted to defect? What else could it mean? "I suppose I have the same problem—always working. I should talk to the Company about arranging some time off, make some travel plans for the near future."

Parham shook his head. "No, young man. You need to take time off *today*. I insist that you stay for dinner."

So he needed to defect right away. That made some sense—if he felt like there was no way to escape once he was taken back to Jamshidi's lab, then he would see this as his only chance.

But much as I wanted to help him, I realized that I wasn't really prepared to help someone defect. My talent was essentially useless for that, because people would still remember the defector even if they didn't remember me. Not only that, but if we got separated for some reason, or if Parham even went to sleep, he would forget all about me and the fact that he was defecting.

That's why I generally stuck to stealing things that didn't need to remember me.

Yelena was right: I relied too much on my talent. For a real professional like her, there wouldn't be much difference between stealing a microchip and stealing a human being.

"That might be a problem," I said. "I really just came to talk to you for a bit. Dinner wasn't part of my plans."

"Oh, but now that you're here, I insist. You can't turn down an old friend of your father, can you?"

"No," I said. "I can't turn down such a generous offer. I'll need to see if I can reschedule some things, but unfortunately my cell phone was stolen earlier today."

Tooraj said, "Here, you can borrow mine." He pulled a cell phone from a clip on his belt and handed it to me.

"It's international," I said. "I'll reimburse you." The call wouldn't show up at all in his phone records, but I needed to make a show of this.

"Don't worry about it," he said, as I dialed Edward's number. I wanted him to know that Parham definitely wanted to defect, so maybe he could arrange for someone else to take care of it. The phone rang several times, and then went to voicemail. Unfortunately, there was no point in leaving a message, but I carried on a fake conversation about rearranging my schedule for the benefit of eavesdroppers.

Handing the phone back to Tooraj, I said, "Thanks."

I sat back down and looked at Parham. "I hope my Company can straighten things out. I don't do much on the personnel side of things—I'm normally in technology acquisitions."

Parham arched a white eyebrow. "I see. A technology expert. So, what do you think of the quantum computer revolution so far?"

"Well," I said, "I know there's a lot of potential for faster computers, but I haven't seen much practical application yet. Everything seems to be in the experimental stages, so far. But you're the quantum physicist, so you'd know that better than I do. And actually, I'm no expert on the tech. The Company tells me what they want, and I go get it."

"Ah." Parham nodded. "The company I work for is much the same, acquiring technology from various other companies."

One of the bodyguards leaned over and whispered in Parham's ear.

"But we really should not be talking business," he said. "Tell me more about your family."

Tooraj spoke before I could start making up stuff about my imaginary family. "Father, if you will excuse me, I have some things to attend to."

"Of course," said Parham.

"It was a pleasure to meet you, Mr. St. James," Tooraj said.

"Likewise," I said. If Tooraj came back up, there would be an awkward moment in front of the guards when he didn't remember me. I would have to attribute his forgetfulness to the stress surrounding the death of his grandfather. I might as well start laying the groundwork for that now. "A nice young man. Seems a little distracted, though. But I understand this is a stressful time for all of you."

Parham frowned, probably trying to work out what secret message I was trying to send by those words. "When a father is taken from his family, it is a terrible blow, as if he has been kidnapped." He winked on the last word. "But whatever happens is the will of Allah."

It took me a moment to work out what he was telling me: he needed his defection to look like a kidnapping, so there would be no reprisals against his family.

Even if I put on a convincing show of kidnapping him, no one would remember my part in what happened. The guards' memory would probably be of Parham leaving on his own—which would endanger his family. In this case, my talent made it harder to pull off the job, not easier.

I was completely out of my depth. What Parham was asking me to do was beyond my experience, beyond my training, and beyond my talent.

But there was an easy way out of all this. All I had to do was leave, and Parham would lose the memory of asking for my help. I stood up and said, "Do you mind if I use your bathroom?"

Chapter Nineteen

I sat in the bathroom for longer than a minute, feeling ashamed of myself for walking out on Parham. Here was a man who needed my help, and I had abandoned him because helping him would be difficult. My mother had not walked out on me just because raising me was difficult.

If Yelena were here, she would have figured something out. Of course, if she were here, then faking the kidnapping would be easy, because people would be able to remember her as a kidnapper.

But could I make it work somehow without a memory of a kidnapper? Not all kidnappings were witnessed. As long as I left physical evidence of a kidnapping, that should be enough to keep Parham's family safe, right? So all I needed was to break into the home in such a way that it left plenty of physical evidence, kidnap Parham without any witnesses, and then get away.

Unfortunately, Parham would have forgotten me

completely by now, so he would have no idea that the kidnapping was a fake one that he had requested. He would probably resist me, which meant I might have to knock him out. Without a partner to help me carry him, I would be moving slowly enough that his guards would be able to catch me.

Obviously, I had to take out the guards first. With them out of the way, I could talk to Parham and convince him to help me fake the kidnapping. It was his idea, after all.

But how could I take out the guards? They out-numbered me and were armed. I had no weapons, and it probably wouldn't go over very well for a foreigner to wander around town asking where to buy a gun.

Someone tried the doorknob, then knocked.

I didn't respond, hoping whoever it was would go to another bathroom.

A man spoke in Farsi. I didn't understand the words, but the from the tone he was saying something along the lines of, "Hurry up—I need to go."

I flushed the toilet and walked to the door. "Sorry," I said as I opened it.

One of the guards was standing there. In an instant, he had his gun aimed at my face. "Who are you?"

"Clive St. James," I said. "My father is a friend of Parham Rezaei."

"How did you get in?"

"A man let me in—I assumed he was one of the family." I didn't want to be too specific, so he couldn't easily find someone who would deny letting me in.

"Turn around. Put your hands behind your head."

I complied.

"Tooraj!" he yelled.

After a moment I heard Tooraj's voice from downstairs, speaking in Farsi.

The two of them carried on a conversation.

"Tooraj will check on your story," the guard said. "If he finds the person who let you in, I will apologize. But we must be careful to protect Dr. Rezaei."

"I understand," I said. My mind raced as I tried to figure out how to get around the fact that no one would remember letting me in.

With the gun at my back, the guard patted me down. The only things he found were a wad of cash and my MasterCard, which he seemed happy enough to confiscate.

Tooraj yelled something up the stairs.

"So you were lying," said the guard. "I thought so. Walk downstairs, and don't try anything. I'll be right behind you."

With slow steps, I made my way down the narrow staircase to the landing at the second floor, and I turned to face the steps down to the ground floor. The guard was a couple of steps behind me, still coming down. I figured this was my best chance to make a break for it, so I lunged down the flight of stairs toward the bottom.

The guard yelled, "Stop!"

At the bottom of the stairs, Tooraj moved into view. He braced himself and held out his arms to grab me. Going too fast to stop, I slammed into him. We fell to the floor. Tooraj held me in a bear hug. There was no way I could escape before the guard made it down the stairs.

So I made the best of the situation and unclipped the cell phone from his belt and slipped it into my pocket. The guard had patted me down once, so he might not think to do it again.

"Get up slowly," said the guard.

Tooraj released me, and I climbed to my feet.

With a grip on my collar and a gun at my spine, the guard directed me out the back of the house into an alleyway. An old black Mercedes was parked there, quite similar to the one in which I'd spent the previous night.

He unlocked the trunk. "Get in," he said.

I got in. He slammed the trunk shut and left me alone in the darkness.

I heaved a sigh of relief.

Doing this on my own was not going to work. Getting Edward to send an extraction team from Langley would take too long—Parham might be taken back to Jamshidi's lab before they could get here. But if Yelena had set up the meeting to turn the quantum viewer over to Jamshidi's men, she might be here in Iraq. With her to be remembered as a kidnapper, we could get Parham away without endangering his family.

I pulled Tooraj's cell phone out of my pocket and dialed Yelena's cell phone.

After three rings, she answered. "Da."

"Yelena, it's Nat."

"Nat!" Her voice was relieved. "You are alive!"

"Yes," I said. "What made you think I wasn't?"

"I called your cell phone and an Iranian answered. I thought you might be captured or killed."

"Well, I've been captured twice," I said, "and I'm currently in the trunk of a Mercedes, but I can pick the lock and get out, so I'm okay. How about you? Have you met with the Iranians yet?"

"I met with them in Tehran this morning," she said. "But . . . I was unable to close deal. There were complications."

"Are you all right?" If Yelena had been hurt because of the mission I sent her on, I would feel awful.

"I am fine. But I get nothing. I have no location for the lab."

"Don't worry about it. Are you still in Tehran?"

"No. When I call your phone and Iranian answer it and not know who you are, I know there be problem. So I call in favor from colleague in SVB and we track location of your cell phone. SVB has arrangement with Iranian telephone company."

"So where are you?"

"I am outside warehouse in Ahvaz. Your cell phone is inside. I can see black Mercedes parked outside. Do you want me to come get you?"

"I'm not in that Mercedes," I said. "But I do need your help to kidnap someone."

She was silent for a moment. "I do not like kidnapping, after what happen with my sisters."

"Oh, no," I said. "It's a fake kidnapping." I explained the situation.

"Where are you?" she asked.

"Hamidiyeh. Call me when you get here."

"Okay." She hung up.

I extracted the lockpicks from my waistband and set to work on the lock, aided by the light of the cell phone.

Yelena didn't need to call me. I was in the main town square when she drove up in a late model BMW. I opened the passenger door and got in.

"Nice car," I said.

"Is rental. But I think maybe we need fast getaway car."

"Good thinking," I said. "I figure we should drive by so you can get a look at the place, then we can hole up somewhere and come up with a plan."

"A plan? You do not want to just go in and see what happens?" Her mouth twisted into a wry smile.

"A real plan. A good plan. A professional plan," I said.

"I am impressed," she said. "Take me to location."

Following my directions, she drove through the narrow streets. We were forced to stop several times by pedestrians blocking the way, but eventually we passed Parham's house. I described the roof and inside as best I could, plus the security arrangements.

"Only two guards?" she asked.

"Only two that I saw," I said. "And the son, Tooraj, could pose a problem if he's around."

Once we had turned a corner and were no longer in view of the house, she stopped the car. "But the old man will come willingly?" she asked.

I winced. "That could be a little bit of a problem, too. Defecting and faking a kidnapping were his ideas, but he won't remember telling me anything."

"You do not make things easy," she said, but she smiled as she said it.

"If it were easy, I wouldn't need help from a professional."

"We will need to get guards out of way. That will have to be me, so they remember it afterward. It also means I cannot kill them, because dead men do not remember anything."

I nodded. Killing the guards wasn't something I particularly wanted, anyway, so it was nice to have a good reason for keeping them alive.

"You will have to get the man, convince him to go with you. It matters not if he remembers conversation after we leave, but is easier with his cooperation."

One of the things I liked about Yelena was the way she incorporated the effects of my talent into her planning. It was just another factor to be considered, not something freaky. She made my abnormality seem almost normal.

"You have money?" she asked. "Lots of it?"

"I can get all we need, if you have a credit card and we can find an ATM. What do we need money for, weapons?"

"Bribes," she said.

Yelena's Farsi was rudimentary, but far better than mine. A sufficiently large bundle of Iranian bills made the Rezaeis' next door neighbor happy to accommodate the rich and eccentric foreign tourists who had determined that the roof of his house was the best location to take a picture of scenic Hamidiyeh.

He led us up the stairs to the roof. On the adjoining roof, Parham still sat reading under the shade of the potted tree, although he had adjusted the position of the chair to account for the late afternoon sun.

The guards both looked over at us. I gave them a friendly wave as Yelena snapped pictures of the town, chattering to me in Russian about the view. Keeping her camera in a position to block a clear view of her face, she walked to the back of the roof and leaned over the alleyway as she snapped a couple more photos.

That was the signal for things to start happening.

I heard the patter of running feet in the alley, followed by the hiss of spray-paint cans. We had bribed several young teen boys to vandalize the Mercedes.

One of the guards stepped to the back of Parham's roof. He yelled at the vandals. The hissing continued. He turned away, said something to the other guard, then charged down the stairs.

The second guard, obviously curious, strolled to the back of the roof to see what was happening. Parham put down his book.

Yelena tossed her camera over onto Parham's roof. It landed with a smash on the far side. As the guard turned to see what had caused the noise, Yelena pulled a Taser gun from her purse, braced herself on the short wall that separated the two roofs, and fired at the guard's back. He spasmed as the electricity coursed through his body, then fell to the ground.

I leapt over the wall, to where Parham was looking wide-eyed at his fallen guard. "I'm CIA," I said in a low voice.

He swung his face to look at me.

"I know you want to defect," I said. "We're making it look like a kidnapping so your family will be safe. Come with me."

He scrambled out of his chair, moving away from me and yelling something in Farsi.

Chapter Twenty

On the other roof, the neighbor started yelling, too.

Yelena said something in Farsi, and the neighbor shut up.

"I give up. I'll do whatever you want," said Parham. "Just don't hurt my family." He winked at me and let me take him by the arm. Yelena and I helped him across the wall onto the other roof, and then the three of us went down the stairs and rushed out into the street.

We rounded the corner and Yelena opened the trunk of the BMW. She climbed in.

"You're with her," I said. I helped him into the trunk, then slammed it shut. I got into the driver's side, started up the engine and drove.

I only got to the end of the block before I had to stop for pedestrians. I kept an anxious eye on the rearview mirror, but managed to turn the corner without seeing a guard chasing us.

With Yelena and Parham invisible in the trunk and

me as the driver, I hoped people would forget seeing the car. Then the guards would have no way to figure out which direction we had gone. But it was also possible that people would remember Yelena driving it—I didn't have control over what they remembered, and Yelena driving would make sense if I weren't there.

In any case, I wanted to get out of town quickly so I could let Yelena and Parham out of the trunk.

Pedestrian traffic thinned as we neared the outskirts of the town, and I was able to speed up. A few miles out of town, as the sun hovered over the horizon to the west, I pulled off to the side of the highway, got out, and unlocked the trunk.

Yelena and Parham blinked at me as their eyes adjusted to the light.

"I think we've lost any pursuit, at least for now," I said. "Come get comfortable in the car."

A few minutes later, Yelena was driving us along a route that would take us to the Iraqi border. I sat in the back seat with Parham.

"How did you know I wanted to defect?" he asked. "I have never told anyone."

There was no harm in explaining my talent, since he would forget anyway. "Actually, you told me earlier today that you wanted to defect," I said. "You also indicated that it needed to look like a kidnapping."

He frowned. "Am I developing Alzheimer's Disease? I do not recall such a conversation. I never saw you before, until you opened the trunk."

"No, your mind is fine," I said. "In fact, it's brilliant. You caught on immediately that my identity was fake and played along, giving me signals with wordplay that you wanted to defect. The reason you don't remember those events is because everyone forgets me after a minute. They remember things as if I had never been there."

He looked at me skeptically. "It has been more than a minute since you let us out of the trunk, and I still remember you."

"Sorry," I said. "I meant that no one remembers me after they haven't seen or heard me for a minute."

"It is true," Yelena said from the front seat. "I have seen it myself."

"Not only that, but when I met you in Rome a few days ago, you told me that it might have something to do with quantum mechanics. You mentioned 'superposition of memories' and 'quantum eraser experiments.'"

"I recall no such conversation, but if your claim is true, I wouldn't. That does seem rather convenient for you and inconvenient for me."

"I also disappear from electronic records," I said. "And from undeveloped photos."

"What is left? A blank spot where your picture would be?" he asked.

"No. Whatever was behind me when the picture was taken," I said.

"Ah, then it could indeed be a quantum phenomenon," he said. "Yes, it fits together quite nicely."

I felt a surge of excitement. Maybe he was just humoring the insane CIA agent who had kidnapped him, but he actually seemed to understand my talent. "Have you heard of this sort of thing before?"

"Yes and no." He reached to his shirt pocket as if to pull out a pen, but there was nothing for him to pull out. "How much do you know about quantum mechanics?"

"I've stolen a lot of quantum computer technology," I said. "I know it's supposed to be superfast. But I don't really understand how it works."

Parham reached into his pants pocket and pulled out a coin. "You see this coin?"

"Yeah."

He brought both hands together, then clenched them into fists and separated them. "Now, what is the probability that the coin is in my right hand instead of my left hand?"

"Fifty percent," I said.

"Very good." He smiled. "You would agree that the coin is really in one hand or in the other. You just lack the knowledge of which hand the coin is in."

"Right."

"That is the way most people look at the world. But it is not the quantum physics way. According to quantum physics, the coin is both in and not in each hand. It is what we call a 'superposition'—two contradictory possibilities existing in the same place at the same time. The decision as to which probability becomes reality is not made until you look in one of my hands to see if it contains the coin."

He opened his right hand, showing it to be empty. He opened his left, and the coin was there.

"What does that have to do with me?" I asked.

"To understand what is happening with you, we need to talk about a cat," Parham said. "A scientist named Schrödinger came up with a famous thought experiment. Imagine you put a cat in a black box with no windows, along with a vial of poison and a quantum device that has a fifty percent chance of breaking the vial within one hour and killing the cat."

He looked at me expectantly, so I said, "Okay."

"So, after one hour, is the cat dead or alive?"

I thought for a moment. "From what you said, since we haven't looked in the box, we don't know. The cat is in a superposition of being both dead and alive."

"Exactly. Until you open the box and look inside, the cat is neither dead nor alive: it is merely a probability wave that encompasses both possibilities."

"Weird," I said. "But I still don't quite understand what that has to do with my talent. Because I really do exist, and I really do go places, so it's not like there's a superposition of me not existing."

"Patience, young man. I'll get to that. What normally happens when we open the box is that moment, the probability wave collapses, and one of the possibilities becomes reality: dead cat or live cat. But up until that point, the possible live cat is acting very much like a live cat, and the possible dead cat is acting very much like a dead cat. Both possible realities coexist in the probability wave."

He held up a finger before I could interrupt again. "But the box with the cat is not the only place with a probability wave. I, the researcher, am behind a closed door in my laboratory conducting the experiment with the cat. You are outside the lab, waiting for me to finish my experiment and come tell you the result. Tell me, what are the possibilities?"

"Either you come out and tell me the cat died," I said, "or you come out and tell me the cat lived."

"And that means I, the researcher, also exists in superposition. There are two versions of me: one who saw a dead cat and one who saw a live one. Are you with me so far?"

"Yes," I said.

"Good, because this is where it gets complicated."

I had thought it got complicated quite a while ago, but I didn't say that out loud.

"So, there are two versions of me existing in super-position. Normally, when the wave function collapses, which version remains is a result of probability, and it is in sync with whether the cat actually died or not. But let's say there is some strange quantum interference that makes my wave function always collapse to the version of me who saw a dead cat. That means I always come out of the room and tell you that the cat died. That does not mean the cat actually died—it only means the version of me who came out of the room is the one who remembers seeing a dead cat."

After thinking it through, I said, "So I'm like the cat in the experiment—only instead of being both dead and alive, I'm both there and not there. And there are two versions of people I meet: one version sees me and the other version doesn't. After I'm gone, the one who didn't see me ends up being the one that's left."

"That's the basic idea," he said. "It's like the person flips from having seen you to not having seen you. You are a fluke of quantum mechanics. I should very much like to write a paper about you. I would call you 'Schrödinger's cat burglar.'"

"This is all fascinating, Professor," Yelena said, in a tone that indicated she was not all that fascinated, "but we have some questions for you. Where is Jamshidi's lab?"

"I am sorry," Parham said. "It's not that I don't trust you . . . Well, to be honest, it is that I don't trust you. To give you key information now is to risk that you might not bother to get me out of the country. Once I am safely in America, I will tell you anything you want to know."

It was a bit frustrating, but I could see his point. "Well," I said. "I need to call my boss to see exactly what arrangements we can make to get you over to the U.S."

He frowned. "The arrangements were not made already?"

"It was kind of a spur-of-the-moment operation, after you told me you wanted to defect. What we'll do now is find a place to hole up, then I'll contact Langley to arrange for your extraction."

"The city of Ahvaz is big enough that we would be hard to find," Parham said. "However, I must ask you to please stop the car as soon as possible."

"Why?" I asked. "I promise you, we can get you out."

"It's not that." He pointed to the western horizon, where the sun's disk had slipped from view. "The sun has now set, so I must perform the Maghrib prayer."

Parham had a doctorate in physics from Cambridge University and spoke like an Englishman—and he was defecting from Iran to the United States. From all that, I had assumed he might feign Muslim piety in front of others, but it had not occurred to me he might be an actual believer.

Yelena glanced at me over her shoulder, and I nodded. She slowed down and pulled over to the side of the road. Parham got out.

I got out as well. "Is it okay if I stand and watch in a place you can see me?"

He nodded. Reaching into his coat pocket, he pulled

out a cell phone and turned it on. "This has a program on it that will accurately point the way to Mecca," he said. "It's a wonder of technology that promotes the spiritual life. Very useful while traveling."

After consulting the screen, he turned to the southwest and put the cell phone away. *"Allahu akbar,"* he said. What followed was a ritual that involved changing position from standing to bowing to kneeling to sitting and back to standing, while reciting various things in Arabic.

As he began the ritual the second time, I saw headlights coming along the road from the northeast. I wondered why the occupants of that car had not stopped to pray as well. And then I realized there was a way the guards could track us: Parham's cell phone.

Chapter Twenty-One

"We have to get out of here," I said. "Your guards are probably tracking your cell phone."

He did not respond, but rather continued his prayer, although there seemed to be a more urgent tone to his voice.

I reached into his pocket and pulled out his cell phone. Opening the door to the car, I said, "His guards may be tracking this." I dropped the phone on the front passenger seat. They might track Tooraj's phone, too, if they realized it was missing, so I took it out of my pocket and dumped it on the seat as well. "Drive somewhere and get rid of these. You'll have to come back for us."

"Be careful," she said.

I slammed the door. She started the car and peeled off, heading northeast, toward the approaching headlights.

"Wrong direction!" I shouted, but there was no way she could hear me. Then I realized what she was doing. If the guards were in that car and she drove away from them, they would pass this spot and might see Parham praying on the side of the road. The only hope was to get them to turn around and follow her for a while, until she could dump the cell phones and lose them.

"Good thing she rented the BMW," I said. I watched as her taillights approached the headlights, then passed by. The headlights kept coming for a few seconds, then they swerved around. The car had been following us. It was now going after Yelena.

I looked at Parham, kneeling in prayer in the twilight, and said a silent prayer of my own for her.

As we waited for Yelena to return, we worked out a routine. Each time a vehicle approached from the northeast, Parham would hide behind a Volkswagen-sized boulder and watch as I stood where the headlights could catch me. No one but Yelena would recognize me, so I figured that was safe enough.

In between cars, Parham asked me about my talent and my history. I told him all about my mother, my criminal career, and my decision to join the CIA. Talking about my life helped distract me from the fact that every minute that passed without Yelena's return made it more likely she had been captured or even killed.

After the fourth time a car ignored me and kept going, Parham said, "If everyone forgets you, how will the Russian woman recognize you when she returns?"

"She's the only person who can remember me."

"What? Why didn't you say so before?" He threw his hands up in the air. "I've been building a theory based on the fact that no one can remember you, and now you tell me that someone can remember you. It throws everything off."

"Sorry," I said. "It was a shock to me, too, when I found out."

"Yes, I suppose it was." He yawned and surveyed the ground around him. "Not the most comfortable place for a lie-down."

"You can't go to sleep, Dr. Rezaei," I said. "Not until Yelena gets back."

"Call me Parham," he said. "Why can't I just take a little nap until she gets back?"

"Because you'll forget all about me, and without her to vouch for me, you won't trust me."

"Oh, bother," he said. "But the real problem is how am I going to remember my theory about you if I can't remember you?"

The sound of vehicles approaching drew my eyes to the road. They weren't coming from the northeast, so it couldn't be Yelena. From the southwest, a car closely followed by a semi truck sped past us. I wondered if it was my smuggling captors from last night making another run.

"If I could figure out why she remembers you," said Parham, "then maybe I could remember you, too, unless it's something genetic."

"It's not genetic, I don't think," I said. "She forgot me after the first time we met."

"Hmm. So what changed?"

I told him briefly about how we'd been handcuffed together and then made our escape. When I got to the part about the laboratory with the laser and how we had tried to cut the handcuffs with it, he interrupted me.

"What did it say on the lab door? The exact words?"

"*Laboratorio de Entrelazar.*"

"Entrelazar? You're sure about that?" His voice was excited.

"Yes. What does it mean?"

"Literally, it means to interlace. But in the context of quantum mechanics, it means to entangle. I assume there was a prism that split the laser beam, was there not?"

How did he figure that out? "There was."

"And you tried to cut the handcuffs with the beam before it got to the prism, right?"

"Yes. Is that important?"

"It gives me a good basis for a theory of why she can remember you. You're entangled."

"Entangled?"

"Entanglement is a quantum phenomenon. Imagine two particles that are like twins of each other. The twin particles are together at first, but then you separate them. However, no matter how far apart they are, the twin particles are still connected in some way. If you measure something about one of the particles, then you can know the measurement of its twin. And because measuring a particle at the quantum level changes it, then you have changed its twin, even across the universe, because they are entangled."

"And you think Yelena and I are entangled?"

"In a way. The laser beam in that room was full of entangled photons. They were almost certainly running an experiment in high-speed quantum communication—entangled photons are useful for that. As you tried to cut the handcuffs, some of those photons were reflected onto you and some onto Yelena. As the molecules in your bodies absorbed those photons, some of them became entangled."

"So we're connected somehow by this entanglement," I said.

"Exactly. And while an ordinary person loses contact with you when you leave, and therefore they can flip to not remembering you, it's like Yelena is constantly in contact with you no matter where she is, so she can't flip. It's a real life application of the Quantum Zeno Effect. Oh, this is going to make such a fascinating paper, if I somehow manage to remember the theory behind it all."

I pulled out my notepad and pen. "Would it help if you wrote down some notes for yourself?" The moon had grown slightly fuller since last night, so there might be enough light for him to write by.

"Yes, thank you," he said. "I forgot to bring my own while being kidnapped." Peering closely at the paper, he began to scribble on it.

If Parham did go to sleep before Yelena got back, at least his notes might make him believe me when I explained that he had forgotten me.

"So," I asked, hating to interrupt his train of thought, but desperate to know more, "would it be possible for me to get entangled with someone besides Yelena?"

"Possibly. However, such an attempt might destroy any previous entanglement. But I really don't know enough yet."

Headlights appeared again on the road to the northeast, traveling at maybe twenty miles per hour. It might be Yelena, unsure of the exact spot where she had left us. Or it might be the guards—if they had discovered Parham wasn't in the car with Yelena, they might have backtracked to see where she dropped him off.

"Watch for my signal," I said.

Parham looked up from his notes. "Oh, quite right." He hunkered down and peered at me over the top of the rock.

I walked to the road and waited for the car to approach. As it got nearer, I could hear its engine, which did not have the smooth purr of the BMW. It sounded vaguely familiar, but it took me a moment to place it: an old Mercedes, like the one I'd ridden in last night.

The glare of the headlights caught me as I backed away from the road. The car sped up, then suddenly screeched to a halt alongside me.

I turned to run. I would lead the guards away from Parham, and maybe he could find his own way across the border.

"Nat!" Yelena shouted.

I looked back. She had gotten out of the driver's side of the Mercedes.

"Yelena?" I said. "What happened?"

"I stole their car." Her tone was self-satisfied.

"Good show," said Parham as he came to join us. "However did you manage that?"

"I will tell you as we drive," she said.

We got in the car. Yelena made a U-turn to head us back northeast toward Ahvaz.

"When they turn to follow," Yelena said, "I know they are after me. I speed down highway, but is not very good quality road. Not like autobahn. I hit pothole and right front wheel get wobbly."

I knew what I would do in that situation: pull over

and run into the night, hoping to lose contact so they would forget about me.

"Thanks to GPS in car, I know river is a few kilometers to the east. I turn off on road, and they follow. They are very close behind, so I slam on brakes. I hope to damage their engine with my trunk, but their driver is good and swerves out of way into a field."

As if for emphasis, she swerved the car a bit, then continued, "So they back off, but are still behind me. I get closer and closer to river. I roll down passenger side window. When I am close enough to river, I put car in neutral, climb out passenger side window and jump, then roll away to side as fast as I can. BMW goes into river. Mercedes stops on the bank. Guards get out to look at what happened to BMW and search for survivors. I steal Mercedes, then come look for you."

Yelena was right about me: I relied on my talent too much. If I had been the one taking the phones away, I would have ended up stranded without a car while our enemies continued searching for Parham. Without any unique talent, Yelena stranded our enemies without a car. It was possible I could have done what she did, but I would have never thought of it because I relied on my talent.

"You're amazing," I said.

"It was nothing." She drove us steadily toward Ahvaz.

We found a hotel, and Yelena went inside to rent a room. Because Jamshidi's men might be looking for a man and woman checking in together, I picked the lock on a service entrance so Parham and I could sneak in. At the edge of the lobby, I kept Parham out of sight but stood where Yelena could see me.

After the clerk gave her the room key, she said, "Room 407, is that right?" loud enough that I could hear.

Parham and I took the service elevator and met Yelena on the fourth floor. Room 407 was a suite with two queen beds and a couch that pulled out into a third.

"Can I borrow your cell phone, Yelena?" I asked. "I want to report in."

She pulled out her cell phone and handed it to me. I dialed Edward's number.

"Put it on speakerphone, please," said Parham. "I wish to know I can trust you."

I nodded. When Edward answered, I put him on speakerphone so the others could hear.

After going through our standard procedure with the folder, Edward said, "Okay, it's good that you called in. We have a team prepping now to go extract Rezaei. They should be there in the next forty-eight—"

"I've already got him," I said. "Yelena helped me fake a kidnapping. Also, I should let you know they're both here, listening on speakerphone."

"Oh. Hmm. Okay, I guess I'd better cancel that mission. Has he given you the location of the lab?"

"Not yet," I said. "He wants to be safely in the U.S. before he gives up any information."

Edward sighed. "Understandable, I guess. Regarding the extraction, though, how do we usually handle this sort of thing without it being forgotten?"

"Um. We don't. This is the first time I've had someone along with me. Two someones."

"Pardon me for interrupting," said Parham, "but I believe our presence simplifies things a great deal. If I'm correct about how Nat's ability works, you will forget this conversation with him, but you will still remember us. So if you merely arrange my extraction directly with me and the young lady, you will not forget it."

I was speechless for a moment. I was supposed to be the expert on how my talent worked, but Parham had figured out this new situation before I had. I finally managed to say, "Yeah, I think that should work."

"Okay," said Edward. "Let me see. Bringing you out via commercial flights is not an option."

"Getting across the border into Iraq may be dangerous," I said. "The guy who was bringing me in got killed."

"Hmm . . . Maybe . . ." Edward clicked away on his keyboard for a bit. "Yes, a Grasshopper is available. Yelena, do you have a cell phone number?"

She gave it to him.

"Okay," Edward said. "I'll text you some GPS coordinates and a time for the Grasshopper to pick you up and bring you to Langley. Should be sometime tomorrow."

"Pardon me," said Parham, "but what is a Grasshopper?"

"Stealth plane with vertical takeoff and landing," Edward said. "It's called a Grasshopper because its radar cross-section is about the same as the insect's. Don't worry—you'll know it when you see it." He laughed as if he had cracked a really funny joke, but I didn't get it.

Yelena shook me awake. Sunlight streamed in through the open curtains. "Get up. Take shower," she said.

I still hadn't gotten enough sleep, but despite its low water pressure the shower revived me. Unfortunately,

I had to get dressed in my same clothes, but Yelena and Parham were in the same situation. I decided to make shopping for clothes part of today's agenda.

When I came out of the bathroom, a room service tray stood in the middle of the room. Parham was eating scrambled eggs from a plate on his lap, while Yelena was at the desk writing something on hotel stationery.

Parham jumped slightly when he saw me. "Who are you?" he asked.

"He is CIA," said Yelena. "Do not worry."

He went back to eating.

"Have breakfast," she said.

I checked under a metal dish lid and found more scrambled eggs. Suddenly feeling very hungry, I grabbed a fork and dug in.

"Thanks," I said, after I'd had a few mouthfuls. "What're you writing?"

"Is personal," she said.

"Sorry, didn't mean to pry." I continued eating. "We need new clothes and stuff. I can go out and get some after breakfast."

"Why don't we all go?" asked Parham.

"You must stay hidden," said Yelena. "And one of us must stay with you. Is better if I go shopping." Seeing I was about to object, she added, "I speak the language better than you."

I felt a lot better once I was wearing fresh clothes from underwear on out. The tan shirt and pants Yelena had picked out differed from my usual black for infiltration, but when I pointed that out to Yelena, she said, "Look less suspicious in daytime. Blend in more."

Parham wore traditional Iranian garb that looked

very different from the more western wear to which
he was accustomed. It wasn't much of a disguise, but
it was something.

Yelena dressed in tight jeans and a white blouse.

"Won't you kind of stand out dressed like that?"
I asked.

"When men look at me," she said, "they see beautiful foreign woman. They do not see agent on mission.
Also, around me, you become almost invisible. Nobody
remember you, and not because of your talent."

"You are brilliant as well as beautiful," said Parham.

It irritated me that he had told her she was beautiful and I hadn't. But I couldn't do it now, because
then it would sound like I was copying him.

"Thanks, Yelena," I said. "If we're going to be stuck
on a plane together until we get to Langley, I'm glad
we've got fresh clothes."

"I am not going to America with you," said Yelena.
"You were right that I must plan before going to rescue my sisters. I will go back to Moscow and replace
equipment I lost in BMW."

I didn't want her to leave, so I tried to think of a
good objection. I couldn't. But just because she was
leaving didn't mean I would never see her again. With
sudden certainty, I said, "You go to Moscow. After I
get Parham to safety, I'll meet you back here. I'll help
you rescue your sisters. I'll be your backup."

"What if your handler says no?" she asked.

"He'll get over it."

She tilted her head slightly to the right. "You
would do that?"

"Of course. We're tied together—entangled, isn't
that what you called it, Parham?"

Yelena looked puzzled, but before she could say anything Parham said, "Excuse me? I'm afraid I have no idea what you're talking about."

I had apparently gotten so used to Yelena remembering me that I'd forgotten that Parham could not.

I briefly explained my talent and how we had met yesterday but he had forgotten me. Showing him his own notes in the notebook helped bring him up to speed.

"This is fascinating," he said. "Are there more like you?"

Shrugging, I said, "I don't know. I don't remember meeting anyone like me, but would I?"

"An excellent question," Parham said, scribbling in the notebook. "It is quite possible that your probability waves would merge while you were together, so on separating you would still remember each other. But it is not certain. I'll have to do some more calculations."

"You'll have plenty of time for that on the flight," I said.

Parham stood up and pointed his pen at Yelena. "Wait a minute. You are the woman in the notes, the one who can remember him?"

"Yes," she said.

"You can't go to Moscow!" he said.

"Will that make me forget him?" she asked.

"We've been that far apart before," I said, "and she still remembered me."

He shook his head. "How am I supposed to work on my paper if you go to Moscow? You must come with me so I can study your entanglement."

Yelena shot me a glance. "What does he mean, entanglement?"

"It's a quantum thing," I said. "He thinks the laser in Barcelona connected us somehow, and that's why you can remember me."

"A laser in Barcelona?" asked Parham. "Really? Did I say that?" He wrote a note. "What were you doing with a laser in Barcelona?"

"I'll tell you the whole story once we're on the road," I said. I looked around the room, which was a rather useless gesture since I didn't have anything I needed to take with me other than Parham. "I guess we should get going. And, uh, be careful getting out of the country, Yelena." It was going to be tough adjusting to not having her around, even though that's how my life had been just a few days ago. But making preparations to rescue her sister was the right call.

"With Russian passport, is not problem," she said. "But I will come with you to make sure you get out safe."

It was silly, but I felt happy to get just a couple more hours with her.

"I am ready," Parham said.

"Then let's go," I said.

On the way out of the hotel, Yelena stopped at the concierge's desk, slipped him a few bills, and asked him to mail the letter she had written.

"What's that about?" I asked.

"For my mother. In case something happen," she said.

Chapter Twenty-Two

Yelena had rented another car, a nondescript blue Volkswagen, because we didn't want to be seen driving around town in the Mercedes she had stolen. She entered the coordinates Edward had texted her into the GPS. "One hour, thirty-eight minutes," she said. "Grasshopper arrives in three hours, so plenty of time."

I sat in the front passenger seat, while Parham lay down in the back seat and covered himself with a blanket we'd stolen from the hotel.

"How you doing back there?" I asked.

"Not the most comfortable car ride I've ever taken," he replied. "But I prefer it to being spotted by Jamshidi's men."

"Unfortunately, I'm going to have to be a bit of a chatterbox," I said. "Once we're safely outside of town and you can sit where you can see me, then I'll shut up, but until then I need to keep the connection between us going so you don't panic on finding a strange man in the car."

"Very well," he said. "Tell me about the laser in Barcelona."

"You said it had something to do with—"

"Stop. Do not tell me what I said. Allow me to draw my own conclusions. Start from the beginning, as if telling me for the first time."

"Okay. It was the first time I met Yelena. I was cracking a safe at InterQuan in order to steal a prototype chip, and she interrupted me and took the chip at gunpoint."

"I still do not remember that," Yelena said. "I remember entering room and safe is already open, and I wonder if is trap, but I decide to risk it and take chip. Then I—"

I coughed to make a sound, but motioned her to continue.

"—I went out and guard stop me."

"Meanwhile," I said, "I waited the sixty seconds until I was sure she had forgotten me, and then went out to find her and the guard there. Another guard came up, but they only had one pair of handcuffs between them, so they handcuffed us together."

"You forgot part where they make us take off clothes."

Heat rose in my cheeks as I remembered her in her bra and panties. "I didn't think that was really relevant."

"It's all relevant," Parham said. "When something unprecedented happens, all the potential factors need to be examined in order to determine which were actual factors."

"Fine. We were stripped down to our underwear. Then they took us and locked us in a basement room, then we escaped from the room, still handcuffed together because they were magnetic handcuffs, or else I could have just picked the lock."

"Magnetic handcuffs, held together by magnets?" asked Parham.

"No," Yelena said. "Lock is magnetic, needs special magnetic key to open."

"So we looked in a lab for something to unlock or separate the handcuffs, and there was this laser that we tried, but it didn't do any good. But you said before that the words on the lab door were important."

"Really? What were the words?"

"*Laboratorio de Entrelazar*. I thought it meant something about lasers, which is why I took us in there. And there was a laser."

"Ah. My guess is you tried to cut the handcuffs with the laser before it reached a prism that split the beam."

"Yes. You mentioned that before, and I don't know how you knew."

"The lab was obviously conducting experiments with entangled photons. They use the prism to send some photons one way and their entangled partners another. By trying to cut the handcuff with the beam, you reflected entangled photons into yourself and Yelena."

"This entanglement," said Yelena, "how can it stay if laser is not on us anymore?"

"When photons hit atoms, the photons can disappear but they make changes to the electrons in the atoms. Entanglement can sometimes survive that. So it is atoms in your bodies that are now entangled."

"How long will it last?" I asked.

"Hard to say. Maybe as long as those atoms remain in your body. Maybe less time."

So my entanglement with Yelena wasn't permanent. There went my slim hope of a lasting relationship.

❖   ❖   ❖

After about an hour and twenty minutes, the GPS wanted us to go off-road in order to get to the pick-up zone. The Volkswagen jounced over the rocky desert terrain for over a mile, but it was no Jeep, and eventually we had to leave it behind.

Yelena examined the GPS, then pointed toward a ridge. "Two kilometers. We have sixty-five minutes."

"I wish Edward would have found us a more convenient spot," I said.

"Is good spot because is not convenient," she replied.

Fortunately, the terrain wasn't too difficult, and we reached the rendezvous spot with over twenty minutes to spare.

As I squinted at the clear blue sky to the west, searching for some sign of the Grasshopper that would carry Parham and me to Langley, I said, "Oh, I forgot to ask—since you didn't close the deal with the Iranians for the viewer, can I have it to take back to Langley? Or did you lose it with the BMW?"

She didn't respond, so after a few seconds I looked over at her.

"Nat," she said, "I am sorry."

"What for?" I asked.

"I make terrible mistake. When I meet with Jamshidi's men, I offer them the quantum viewer in exchange for my sisters. They talk to their headquarters, lots of talk, take long time. Then they refuse and try to shoot me. I escape." Her eyes glistened.

"I understand," I said. "You were desperate to get your sisters back, so you tried to cut a different deal."

"That is not the end," she said. "When I go back to my hotel room, viewer is gone. They have someone steal it during negotiations."

"Oh," I said.

"Did she say quantum viewer?" said Parham.

"Yes," I said. "It's a piece of technology we stole—well, not exactly stole. More like obtained."

Parham frowned. "Not from ChazonTec in Israel?"

"Yes," I said. "And here's some more quantum weirdness for your theory: when it took a picture with me in the room, it left me out of the picture once, but showed me the second time."

Parham waved that off and focused on Yelena. "So Jamshidi's men have it?"

She nodded. "Since yesterday."

"You must stop him from finishing his blasphemous project," Parham said.

"Blasphemous?" That seemed a strange word to use about a computer.

"Jamshidi calls it the Prophet." Parham's voice seethed with indignation. "The blessed Prophet Mohammad, praise be upon him, was the final prophet, and this machine of Jamshidi's is an abomination." He looked at me, then said, "I know you do not share my faith, but he must never complete the machine. I will go with you and show you what must be done."

"Parham," I said, "we're not really equipped for this. I'll take you back to Langley, and you can explain what needs to be done. They'll send a full team to pull the plug on Jamshidi's operation."

"No," Parham said. "You do not understand. Once the quantum supercomputer is activated, it will be too late to do anything about it."

"Why?" I said. "Even if it can predict the stock market or whatever, Jamshidi can't do much damage in a couple of days."

"Predict the stock market? Is that what the CIA thinks the computer is for?" he said.

"Well, other stuff, too, but that sounded like the major problem with a supercomputer that can predict the future."

"Oh, it will do far more than that," said Parham. "Once it is fully online, it will control the world."

"That's a little overdramatic, don't you think?" I said.

"I am not exaggerating." Parham's voice was agitated. "We must get to London immediately."

"London?" Yelena and I spoke together.

"Jamshidi is a deceiver. He keeps his secrets within false secrets. Your CIA cannot find the hidden lab in the desert of Iran because the lab is underground, in London. It is spread out, connected via tunnels, but I do know that the main processing facility is under a Jamshidi Oil warehouse."

I shook my head in wonder. "We tracked some technology shipments, and you, to a warehouse, but we thought he was shipping stuff back to Iran from there. The ships left carrying something."

"Probably dirt removed while digging the facility." Parham looked up at the sky. "Will this plane never arrive?"

"Calm down," I said. "Can you explain exactly what's so bad about this supercomputer? Will it be able to take control of other computers out there and run everything?"

"No. I mean it will literally control everything," Parham said. He swept an arm across the desert view. "Look out there at the world. It's unpredictable. Yes, we can make pretty good guesses as to what will happen in the future, but we can't tell whether it will rain in Rome ten days from now, or whether a particular horse will win a race. There are too many variables—like the old chestnut about a butterfly flapping its wings in China and causing a hurricane. And when you get down into the realm of quantum physics, things become even more uncertain. Particles are little more than waves of probability. So a computer that can take into account all the variables and predict what will happen is impossible. It can't work. The world is just too unpredictable."

"Wait a minute," I said. "First you tell us the computer's going to take over the world, and now you tell us the computer won't even work? What's the problem, then?"

Parham took a coin out of his pocket. "Can you predict whether this coin will end up on the ground showing heads or tails?"

"I can guess," I said. "But it'll be fifty-fifty whether I'm right."

"Ah," he said. "But I can accurately predict that it will end up heads." He leaned down and placed the coin heads up on the sand.

"That's cheating," I said. "You could predict it because you made it show heads."

"And the computer will cheat, too. It will collapse probability waves in order to cause the future it predicts. Somewhat like your ability, which forces the wave to collapse in a certain way, except the computer determines which way the wave should collapse. It does not merely predict the future: it chooses the future."

I thought through some of the implications. "So once it's turned on, it will choose a future in which we can't turn it off."

Parham nodded. "Perhaps it is improbable that a lightning strike will hit the plane with a CIA strike team and cause it to crash, but it is possible. But something like that becomes a certainty if the computer collapses the probability wave in the right way. Once the computer has been activated, it will control the future."

"And Jamshidi will control it," I said.

"Yes. I tried to delay, but now that he has the quantum viewer..."

"But it's glitchy," I said. "When we first tested it out, it didn't show me, but then it did."

"Let me guess," Parham said. "The first time, Yelena was not within range of the viewer, but the second time, she was."

"You're right," I said. "How did you know?"

"The quantum viewer does not take a photograph in the normal way. It builds up a picture based on quantum interactions between things. However, you are unconnected to anything but Yelena—and possibly other things that were with you and the laser in Barcelona. The quantum viewer could only detect you through your connection to Yelena. But, when combined with the power of the supercomputer, the viewer would be able to see you anywhere in the world. But because observation collapses the wave functions, the viewer will also allow the computer to affect things anywhere in the world."

"Is all my fault," said Yelena. "If I had not—"

"What matters," I said, "is what we're going to do about it. How long do we have, Parham?"

"The quantum viewer will require modifications in order to integrate with the rest of the supercomputer.

Jamal—one of my assistants—would be the one to do it, and he might be done by this evening. If not, he will probably work through the night, so we have twenty-four hours at the most."

Less than twenty-four hours. "I've got to call this in," I said.

Yelena handed me her cell phone, but before I could dial Edward's number, she said, "Do you hear noise?"

After a few moments, I heard a high-pitched, steady whine, but I couldn't tell what direction it was coming from. It was getting louder, though. A flicker of motion on the ground to the west caught my eye. A shadow moving over the sand, headed a bit to our right.

As it passed by, the whine suddenly jumped to a roar almost directly above us, joined by a hot wind swirling down. I looked up and saw blue sky, shimmering a bit like air does when it's hot. As the roar faded to a whine again, the shimmer moved about ten yards west of us, then descended to the ground. I squinted to block the sand that blew away from that spot.

A black rectangle about five feet high and two feet wide opened in the shimmer, and someone with a black flight suit and helmet lowered a ladder from the bottom edge, stretching about ten feet to the ground. He or she beckoned for us to come.

I was so astonished I just stood there for a moment.

"I wonder if it's active camouflage or metamaterials," Parham said, and he headed toward the door.

"Wait," I said. "How do we know it's the CIA?"

Parham laughed. "'You'll know it when you see it,' your handler said. Neither my government nor

Jamshidi has the technical capability to create an invisible plane."

I felt a little foolish at my paranoia. Edward had said it was a stealth plane, and how likely was it that someone else's stealth plane would just happen to come to the coordinates where we were waiting?

As we got within a couple of feet of the door, the engine sound increased to a roar again, but the opening hung steady. As I climbed inside, the engine noise faded again.

Once all three of us were on board, the person in the flight suit sealed the door behind us. The inside of the plane was too small for me to stand up straight. There were three seats on each side of the plane, facing inward, separated by a narrow aisle. There were no windows.

I sat down across from Yelena, and Parham sat next to her. We fastened our seatbelts.

The person in the flight suit sat next to me, but did not put on a seatbelt. "We were expecting Dr. Rezaei and Ms. Semyonova. Who are you?" Her voice was feminine.

"My name's Nat Morgan," I said. "I need you to get Edward Strong at Langley on the line. He can confirm my identity. Also, we need to switch destinations to London."

She nodded, as if this were all in a day's work for her. Then she rose from her seat, went to a door at one end of the cabin, punched a code into a keypad, and opened the door.

"Wait!" I called out, realizing she was about to leave us alone.

She turned to look at me.

"Yelena," I said, "you'd better confirm what I said about switching to London and getting Edward on the line."

"Of course," Yelena said. "What he says it true. We must go to London, and I must speak to Edward Strong at Langley immediately."

The woman said, "OK, I'll connect you after we're out of Iranian airspace." She went through the door into what I figured must be the cockpit.

The whine of the engines rose higher in pitch, and I was pressed into my seat as the Grasshopper took off.

Chapter Twenty-Three

"I have Edward Strong on the line," said a voice over the airplane's public address system. "I'm going to patch him through to the cabin, so you can just talk like you're on speakerphone."

"Thanks," I said at the same time Yelena said, "Thank you."

After our usual identification procedure, I said, "Edward, you originally sent me to talk to Parham Rezaei because you wanted to know where Jamshidi's secret lab is. He's told us—it's not in Iran, it's in London, or at least it's in that general area. And he's agreed to help us by going in and sabotaging the supercomputer. So you need to redirect this plane to London."

"Hmm. I'd rather debrief you here first," said Edward.

"There's no time. Jamshidi's close to activating the supercomputer, and once he does that, we won't be able to stop him. The computer will make itself invulnerable."

"What are you talking about?" Edward said. "Invulnerable?"

"It doesn't just predict the future," I said. "It can control the future."

After a pause, Edward said, "That's a little far-fetched."

"Listen," I said, "Parham Rezaei is brilliant enough that he's figured out why Yelena can remember me. It took him only minutes to work out a whole quantum theory about how my talent works—"

"The theory is still incomplete," Parham said.

"—and so when it comes to quantum stuff, I believe he knows what he's talking about. If he believes this computer can take control of the future, I believe it, too."

There was silence on the other end of the phone for a few seconds. "You understand, it's difficult for me to take your word for something, when as far as my memory is concerned, this is the first time we've ever spoken. But everything I have in my notes says you've come through for us time after time, so I'll trust that you're serious."

"Thank you," I said. "So, my instinct is to go in and sabotage this computer, or at the very least learn the lab's exact location so maybe you can send in a strike team."

"Hmm. I'll talk to the Brits, see if they can do something."

"If I may interrupt," Parham said, "Jamshidi boasts of having high-level sources in MI5. If coordinating with British intelligence alerts him, he might take the most important components and rebuild elsewhere."

"And using our military for a strike on British soil without coordination would cause a major international incident, and I doubt the White House is prepared to authorize something like that on such thin evidence." Edward sighed. "I'll do what I can, but it's really up to you guys. I'll have your plane redirected to London."

"Okay," I said. I hung up the phone and looked from Parham to Yelena. "It's up to us. Got any bright ideas?"

Yelena said, "Our best chance is to offer to trade Parham to Jamshidi."

"What?" both Parham and I said.

"I call Jamshidi's men, say I kidnap Parham to trade for my sisters. We give him back, and then he sabotage computer."

"A truly elegant solution," said Parham. "Except it's possible that Jamshidi no longer needs me. I was supposedly working on coming up with my own version of the ChazonTec quantum viewer, and I kept stretching things out to delay him. But now that he has the viewer, he has everything he needs. Jamal can make the modifications to the viewer."

I shrugged. "It's worth a shot. So we get you in, you sabotage the viewer, and then . . . You realize that if Jamshidi finds out what you've done, he won't be happy."

Parham nodded. "It is a risk I must take."

"We'll try to figure a way to get you out. I guess the urgent thing is to stop the Prophet from controlling the future. Once the viewer's out of commission, then we can do things with more preparation."

Parham nodded. "If we can't get our hands on the viewer, then we need to destroy the core."

"Just get in there, plant some explosives and blow it up?" I said.

"In theory, yes. In practice . . ." He shook his head. "The core sounds like it is one central location, but it is distributed, networked. It consists of thousands of separate computers. Even if you take out the main processing facility, the core could keep functioning."

"Then how do we take it out?" I asked.

"With access to the network, I could sabotage the operating code in the core. It would take thousands of hours to reprogram."

"But they must have a backup somewhere," I said.

"Yes and no," said Parham. "Copies of the initial programming code are available. But much of what is in the core has been developed through evolutionary programming—the computer alters its own code to make itself more efficient. And that means some of the code exists only in an indeterminate quantum state inside the core. And it is a law of quantum mechanics that such indeterminate states cannot be copied. So there is no backup of the core itself."

"To plan mission properly," said Yelena, "we must have map of facility. Can you draw one?"

"I'll do my best," Parham said, and he set to work sketching a map on a page of the notebook I'd given him.

We landed in the outskirts of London, next to a warehouse owned by a CIA front company. To my surprise, Edward was there to meet us on the tarmac as we got off the plane.

"Miss Semyonova," he said, shaking Yelena's hand, "I'm Edward Strong. It's a pleasure to finally meet you. And Dr. Rezaei, thank you for offering to help us." He shook Parham's hand as well. Edward's eyes briefly flickered to look at me, but then looked away, as if he had decided I was part of the flight crew for the Grasshopper. "If you'll come this way, I've got a briefing room we can use." He started walking toward the warehouse.

I was so used to him being in his office, with access to my file folder, that I wasn't sure what to do in this situation.

"Umm, Edward?" I said.

He stopped and turned to face me. "Yes? Do I know you?"

"Yes, but I can see you've forgotten me. Don't worry about it. It's not your fault."

"He's with us," Yelena said.

"Yes," said Parham, "he helped me defect."

Edward shook his head and rubbed his forehead. "It's this stupid Alzheimer's. I've put in for retirement several times, but they keep telling me I'm 'essential to ongoing operations.'" He grinned. "What a terrible thing it is to be necessary. What's your name, young man?"

"Nat Morgan," I said. "I'm a CIA field officer, and I've worked with you before. I'm not listed in any database, but if there's someone you can get to access a special file folder in your desk at Langley, they can confirm that."

"Unlisted?" His eyebrows rose. "Interesting. But let's get to the briefing room."

We followed him inside the warehouse, down some stairs leading to the basement, and into a conference room with a large glass table surrounded by chairs.

Edward sat at the head of the table and waved for us to sit as he dialed out on a speakerphone on the table. I took the seat to his left, Yelena sat next to me, and Parham next to her.

When a woman answered the phone, Edward said, "Shelly, it's Ed. I need you to locate a file for me."

"Okay," she said. "Where is it?"

"I've got a young man here who's going to explain." He looked at me expectantly.

"Um, actually, I need you to tell her. I'll tell you."

He frowned. "What sort of game are you playing?"

"I can do it, Nat," said Parham. He looked up toward a corner of the ceiling, then said, "In the lower drawer on the right side of Edward's desk you will find a manila file folder with the label 'CODE NAME LETHE.'" He spelled out LETHE for her, then turned to me and said, "Is that right, Nat?"

"Yes," I said, impressed that he could remember those details.

"Okay," Shelly said. "I'm going to put you on hold. Be right back."

"What is all this rigmarole about?" Edward's voice held a tinge of annoyance.

"It's necessary," I said. "You see, the reason you don't remember me isn't because of your Alzheimer's. It's because no one can remember me for more than a minute after I'm gone, and so if I told Shelly about the file directly, she would forget I had told her."

"Is this some sort of joke?" Edward asked.

"There are authentication protocols in the folder," I said. "It's in your handwriting...which I guess you won't be able to tell over the phone. Can Shelly recognize your handwriting?"

"Is not joke," Yelena said. "I have seen it work."

Parham leaned forward in his seat. "If it would

help, I can give you a theoretical explanation for what is happening at the quantum level."

Edward motioned for Parham to stop. "Let's just wait for the folder."

After a few moments, Shelly came back on the line. "The lower drawer on the right side, you said?"

"Yes," I said, simultaneously with Parham.

"Hmm." Seconds ticked off. "There are some files here, but none of them is labeled 'CODE NAME LETHE.'"

Maybe Edward had forgotten to put it away after talking to us? "What about on top of the desk?" I asked.

"No, it's clean," Shelly said.

"Thank you, Shelley," Edward said. He reached forward and hung up the speakerphone with his left hand. As he sat back, I realized he was holding a gun in his right. "Now, young man, would you mind telling me the real reason you're here?"

Chapter Twenty-four

Moving slowly, I raised my hands while my mind raced to figure out what to do next. I was so used to Edward believing me thanks to that file that I didn't have a contingency plan for his holding a gun on me. Yelena was right about me being an amateur.

Of course, I'd been an amateur the day I walked into the CIA recruiter's office, and I'd managed to get him to believe me.

"Edward." I tried to keep my voice calm. "I don't know what happened to your file. But I can prove the truth of what I said about people forgetting me. Ask someone to come in here and take a good look at me, then have them leave for a minute and come back. They will not remember seeing me before."

"This is ridiculous," he said.

"If he is lying," said Parham, "then you can disprove it easily enough by conducting the test as he says. Think of it as a scientific experiment."

"There is no time to start over. Mission is too

urgent." Yelena's voice held a tone of command. She pointed at Edward. "You are experienced CIA handler. You come to London to meet with defecting Iranian scientist and former SVR agent. Do you take their folders with you?"

Edward kept the gun on me, his eyes not even flickering to Yelena as he answered her. "Yes."

"Then where is your briefcase?"

"Uh . . . I'm not sure." Edward's eyes lost their focus for a moment. "I must have left it somewhere."

"Call upstairs, see if anyone has found it," Yelena said. She turned toward me and added, "I think your folder must be with ours."

I nodded. I hoped she was right.

Edward followed her advice. After a couple of minutes during which his gun never wavered from me, a stern-faced woman walked in with a briefcase and placed it on the table in front of Edward. She was careful not to get between me and the gun. But she didn't leave the room: instead, she stood behind me.

Edward holstered his gun, then opened the briefcase, and I was relieved to see the familiar folder on top, with a neon pink sticky note on it. "Read this first!" was scrawled on it in black marker.

He took out the file and started scanning the first page. When he reached the bottom, he looked up at me. "I believe I owe you an apology, Nat."

Things went a lot more smoothly after that. We briefed Edward on our mission—stop the supercomputer and rescue Yelena's sisters.

Unfortunately, there were no field operatives currently available to help us, but Edward was able to get access to a surveillance van. He drove, while Yelena, Parham and I sat in the back.

It took thirty-three minutes to get from the CIA warehouse to the neighborhood of Jamshidi Oil, Ltd. After driving past the privacy fence and gated entrance, where a single guard was on duty in a small gatehouse, Edward parked on the side of the road two blocks away.

"Yelena, make the call," I said.

Yelena pulled out a disposable cell phone she had bought on her shopping trip back in Iran and dialed a number. "You recognize my voice? Good. I have someone you want. You have someone I want. I propose trade."

She paused to listen, then said, "Have someone meet me at Regents Park Hub in one hour to discuss exchange. Alone. If I see a second person, I will abort." She hung up, then removed the battery so the phone couldn't be tracked.

Nine minutes later, three cars with four men in each drove away from the warehouse. That left only three or four men guarding the warehouse, based on the numbers Parham had seen when he'd been there.

"Of course they try to set trap for me," she said. She pounded the steering wheel. "I do not understand why they do not just give my sisters back. It would be simpler for them."

"You have to understand what kind of man Jamshidi is," Parham said. "The thing he desires most is control, and he hates to show weakness—particularly to a woman. When you try to force him to give up your sisters, that only makes him tighten his grip."

"So I should what? Get down on my knees and beg him? I would do it," Yelena said.

"That wouldn't work, either," said Parham. "Obvious weakness only makes him despise you."

"You're doing the right thing," I said. "This is the best way to rescue your sisters."

"I know," she said. "I know. I just have fear that reason he will not give them back is that they are dead."

"Of course they're not dead," I said, with a certainty I did not feel. "Jamshidi paid good money for them, and he wouldn't want to lose his investment, would he, Parham?" It was awkward to talk about her sisters like they were a commodity, but I didn't want her to lose hope.

"Oh, quite right," he said.

"Anyway," I said, "I think the ones who left have been gone long enough that they can't get back in time to save the ones they left behind. Let's do this."

"I'll move the van to the rendezvous spot," Edward said. "And if a field-op team becomes available, I'll send them in as backup."

Yelena handed Parham and me a Taser.

"It's fairly simple," I said to Parham, indicating the trigger on his Taser. "Just point and shoot. But use yours only in self-defense. Yelena and I will take out the guards."

He nodded.

Yelena put on a pair of large designer sunglasses that covered almost a third of her face. The three of us got out of the back of the van.

"I still think I should make the initial approach," I said. "Since they know you are the kidnapper, they'll be on the lookout for a woman. I'm more likely to catch the gate guard by surprise."

"He is more likely to underestimate me," she said. "And since they think I am making trade for my sisters, he not expect me to infiltrate."

"Okay," I said. "But I'll be there to back you up just in case."

Yelena pulled a map out of her pocket, then walked slowly toward the warehouse. Parham and I followed, walking next to the cinder-block wall that surrounded the warehouse. She stopped in front of the gate, holding the map.

"Excuse me," she said. "Can you help me? I'm lost."

I couldn't see the guard beyond the gate, but I heard him say, "Where are you going?"

"A warehouse where they sell Persian rugs," Yelena said, her voice sounding almost like a helpless little girl's. "Is supposed to be around here."

In a perfect world, he would have opened the gate to help her. But he didn't. "Pass me the map," he said. "Do you have the address?"

She handed him the map through the wrought-iron bars. I was close enough to hear him unfold it.

Holding her Taser gun low, she fired through the gate. I heard the characteristic buzzing, and he grunted.

That was my cue. With a boost from Parham, I scrambled up onto the wall and dropped down on the other side. The guard lay twitching in the dirt. I grabbed the gate key and unfastened the carabiner that attached it to his belt, then opened the gate—that was faster than picking the lock.

Yelena and Parham hurried through the gate. I shut it behind them, then locked the gate. Yelena yanked the rifle off the guard's shoulder. We strode quickly across the open area between the fence and the warehouse door. Parham and Yelena went in first, and after checking that no one seemed to be outside to have seen us, I followed them in.

Around two dozen uniformed guards stood with rifles pointed at Yelena and Parham, who had their hands raised. A rifle lay at Yelena's feet. Several men swung their guns to point at me.

"I surrender," I said, raising my hands.

Chapter Twenty-five

Yelena kept a very professional silence.

"You double-crossing snake," I said, glaring at Parham. "I should never have trusted you about the diamonds."

I counted on him being quick enough to pick up on what I was doing, and he did not disappoint me. "Trust?" he said. "You kidnap me and threaten to kill me, and then you want trust between us? It's not my fault you're gullible enough to believe Jamshidi would store a fortune in diamonds in a warehouse like this."

Parham lowered his hands and nodded at one of the guards. "Thank you for rescuing me from my kidnappers," he said. "Take them prisoner—I am sure Jamshidi will want to question them."

The guards obeyed him. One of them got on a phone and yammered away in Farsi. Two others bound my hands tightly behind my back with rope, while others did the same to Yelena. Surrounded by guards, we were taken to a metal platform in the middle of the warehouse. With a jolt, the platform lowered, taking us down at least twenty feet. Cement slabs formed walls on three sides, but the fourth was open into a paved rectangular room divided lengthwise by what looked to me like a three-foot-tall concrete bench.

The bench extended about thirty yards and disappeared into a dark, circular hole in the back wall. The hole was about fifteen feet in diameter. I realized the bench was actually the track for the monorail Parham had told us about.

Yelena and I stood next to each other, hands bound behind our backs, and waited for the train. After a few minutes, a yellow light began to rotate above the hole in the wall, and a buzzer sounded.

A flatbed monorail car emerged from the tunnel, followed by one with a passenger cabin. The two cars came to a halt. As some of the men loaded boxes onto the flatbed, six of them bustled me and Yelena into the passenger cabin. They tied us to a support pole, back to back in the middle of the cabin, and then they sat down, cradling their rifles and watching us with sullen eyes.

Parham climbed aboard and sat down facing me. "The tables have turned," he said. "How do you like being my prisoner?"

"I've had worse accommodations," I said.

"We'll see about that," he said. "I'm going to make sure Jamshidi throws you in solitary." He gave me a quick wink.

With a jolt, the monorail started up. Fluorescent lights flickered to life in the cabin just as we entered the tunnel. The wheels of the monorail hummed a tone that got higher in pitch as we sped up, then leveled out as we hit the maximum speed.

I could feel Yelena fumbling with the ropes, and I figured she was trying to wriggle loose somehow. Then her hand found mine and gave it a squeeze. Both our palms were sweaty, but I didn't care. Our fingers interlocked. And for the rest of the ride we stood there—tied to a pole, surrounded by enemies with guns—and held hands.

It was the most romantic moment of my life.

"Mr. Jamshidi will see you now," said the young man in the light gray suit. He opened the double doors to let Parham in, followed by Yelena, me, and our armed escorts.

The office at Jamshidi Oil had been large and luxurious, so I expected something similar here. But this office was only about ten feet by twenty. The white walls were bare except for two flat-panel televisions and five clocks labeled Tehran, London, New York, Tokyo, and Moscow. A brushed aluminum desk with a built-in touchscreen held two phones, three computer monitors, a keyboard, and a mouse.

And the man in the high-backed black leather chair behind the desk was not the bald, obese man I'd given the cockroach package to—it was the mystery man who had chased me down the stairs.

"Parham, so glad you have returned to us safely," he said.

Parham bobbed his head. "As am I, Mr. Jamshidi. It was touch and go for a bit, but I outsmarted them."

This man was Jamshidi? That meant the bald man was just a figurehead, a distraction for people to focus on while the real Jamshidi could move about unsuspected.

"Yes," Jamshidi said. "Khalid mentioned something about diamonds?"

"I convinced them that you had a large store of diamonds in the warehouse that they could steal. Of course, I knew the guards in the warehouse would rescue me."

"A brilliant deception," said Jamshidi. "And you have returned just in time. The Prophet is scheduled to go online within the next two hours."

"Insha'Allah," said Parham. "I will go see if I can help Jamal speed the process along."

As he walked to the door, I felt relief. We had made it here before the Prophet was switched on, and now Parham would find a way to sabotage the computer.

"One thing before you go," said Jamshidi. "How did you get these two to trust you?"

"Well," said Parham, turning back to face Jamshidi. "I told them about a billion dollars in uncut diamonds, and you should have seen the greed in their eyes. Men often believe what they want to believe."

"True," said Jamshidi. "Very true. But I meant about the weapon. Why did they arm you with a Taser? It would risk you trying to escape."

"Yes, that," said Parham. "Of course."

I could tell he was stalling, so I said, "He double-crossed us. He told us he would show us where the diamonds were in exchange for a share. We gave him a Taser because we thought we were all in it together."

"Precisely," said Parham.

"All in it together?" said Jamshidi. "Including the lovely Miss Semyonova?"

"Yes," Yelena said, holding her head high. "He fool me as well."

Jamshidi raised his index finger, then pointed at her. "You see, that is what does not make sense. Tell me, Miss Semyonova, what was the price for which you were willing to sell out your sisters?"

"I would never," she said.

"That's what I thought," Jamshidi said. "And yet, instead of trading Dr. Rezaei for your sisters, you decide to steal diamonds?"

I was an idiot for not anticipating that flaw when making up our cover story on the spur of the moment. When it was just me, I could try out different stories until I found one that worked, but Yelena and Parham were locked into the one I had chosen.

Yelena whirled toward the closest guard. Somehow she had freed her hands, though loops of rope still hung from her left wrist. She kicked the guard in the groin and pulled his rifle from his hands.

My hands were still tied, but I rammed my shoulder into the guard next to me and he went down. Unfortunately, there were still four guards untouched, and they raised their weapons.

Yelena swung her rifle and aimed at Jamshidi. "Call them off."

Jamshidi raised his palms. "Nobody shoot."

"Tell them lower their guns or I kill you," she said.

With a smile that showed straight white teeth, Jamshidi said, "I'm afraid that won't be necessary. You will drop your gun and go quietly with my men."

"No, you bring my sisters here and arrange for us to leave," said Yelena.

"Pull the trigger," he said.

"Do not doubt I will kill you," she said.

"I doubt it very much," he said. He walked around

the desk to the middle of the room as Yelena tracked him with the rifle. He opened his arms wide. "Go ahead, shoot me."

"Bring my sisters," Yelena said, her voice more insistent.

"I will not," he said. "But if you can kill me, my guards will not stop you from getting them."

Yelena pulled the trigger, and the sound of the shot exploded inside the room.

Jamshidi did not even flinch. About a foot in front of him, a light gray smear seemed to float in midair.

"Bulletproof glass," he said. "It has a special non-reflective coating. I was never in any danger from you. But I admire you, Miss Semyonova, so I have decided to reunite you with your sisters."

Yelena's gun wavered. "Really?"

"I give you my word," said Jamshidi.

"It's a trap," I said. "He hasn't said he'll let you go."

Jamshidi nodded. "Of course not. But considering that my guards could kill you right now, I feel my offer is very generous."

Yelena lowered the rifle, took her finger off the trigger, and handed it to the nearest guard. "Take me to them," she said.

"Yelena," I said, then stopped. I wanted to tell her that I would come for her, assuming I managed to escape. But that wasn't really the kind of thing to say in front of Jamshidi, as he might just have me killed on the spot. And it would be such a cliché to say that I loved her. "Take care of yourself," I said.

"I'll always remember you," she said over her shoulder as two of the guards escorted her through the door.

"Take Dr. Rezaei to his quarters and lock him in," said Jamshidi. "I will deal with his treachery later."

Parham bowed his head and let himself be led out of the room. Two guards remained with me.

Jamshidi tapped his lips with his index finger and stared at me. "You, I did not anticipate. They didn't tell me they had captured an American along with the other two."

I shrugged. "I'm just the hired help. And now that Yelena's not paying, I'll need another job. You're not hiring, are you?"

He barked a laugh. "Even if you were not besotted by Yelena, I would be a fool to take you up on that offer." He walked back behind his desk and sat in his chair.

"Besotted?" I said. "You think I'm in love with Yelena?"

"Aren't you?" he asked.

"Well, yeah," I said. "But I didn't think it was obvious to everyone else." Was it obvious to Yelena? I thought back to how she had held my hand on the monorail, and decided she knew.

"And how does an American get mixed up with a thief for the Russian mob?" Jamshidi asked.

"Just lucky, I guess."

"If you tell me the truth, I will not kill you," he said. "I may even let you go, if you are not a threat. At the very least, I can offer you a comfortable imprisonment. You may even see Yelena again—if I grant you brothel privileges." He leaned forward, his gaze firmly fixed on my eyes. "But if you lie to me, your death will be long and painful."

Considering that Jamshidi had detected that Parham

was lying to him, I decided I would need to be very careful. I needed him to let me live long enough that I could be forgotten and escape.

The best way to not get caught lying was to tell the truth. He wouldn't remember it anyway. "I'm a CIA officer," I said. "I recruited Yelena to help me locate your laboratory. She cooperated because you had her sisters."

He nodded slowly. "What were you doing in the warehouse?"

I couldn't tell him I had come to destroy the core, or else he might increase security on it. "Parham was going to show us the entrance to the tunnel so I could report back."

"I cannot let you reveal the location," he said. "So I cannot release you. But I am inclined to believe because you did not try to pass yourself off as harmless."

"Eventually the CIA will locate you," I said. "And at that point, I won't be any further danger to you, and you can release me." I didn't plan to hang around that long, but I didn't want him to know that.

"Not quite," he said. "I have gone to great lengths to ensure that the CIA has the wrong idea about my appearance, and now you have seen me."

"Weight Watchers and Hair Club for Men?" I said.

"You may think it is funny, but it has worked well for me. My reputation as a fat, bald, billionaire recluse means I may travel without being recognized. So you will remain my prisoner. But I am not a cruel man, so you will live in comfort."

In my opinion, a man who kidnapped underage girls to work in a brothel was cruel by definition, but I decided it would not be wise to share that sentiment.

One of the phones on his desk rang. He picked it up and carried on a short conversation in Farsi. After he hung up, he looked at me and said, "How would you like to be a witness to history?"

"Depends. If it's the Cowboys winning another Super Bowl, I'm in."

"I'm sure Dr. Rezaei told you about the Prophet," said Jamshidi. "Well, it's ready to be turned on."

Chapter Twenty-Six

"Already?" I said. "I thought it was supposed to take a couple more hours."

"Jamal finished his work ahead of schedule." Jamshidi rose from his chair. "So now you will get to see the greatest computer ever built get turned on."

If I went with him, I might be able surprise the guards and do something to damage the computer before it was turned on. But probably not—after Yelena's little stunt, they would be watching me very carefully. I needed to get myself forgotten so I could move more freely. My best chance to at least delay the activation was to take out the power generator, and I couldn't do that if I was tagging along with Jamshidi for show-and-tell.

So I laughed.

"What is so funny?" Jamshidi asked.

"My CIA recruiter told me I wanted to be a spy because I watched too many James Bond movies as a kid," I said. "He was wrong, but I did watch them.

And you're about to make one of the classic villain blunders by trying to show off, thus giving me the chance to throw a monkey wrench into the works."

"You are no James Bond," he said. "But why warn me?"

"Because you're right: I'm not James Bond," I said. "I have no desire to get myself killed by your guards trying to stop your silly supercomputer. You promised me a comfy life as a prisoner, and frankly, that sounds pretty good, since I haven't gotten much sleep the past few nights." I yawned and stretched as much as I could with my hands tied behind my back.

Lips pressed together, he looked at me.

"And yes, I'd rather not stick around to see you gloat," I said. "I hope you don't mind."

He nodded at one of my guards. "Take him to the guest quarters. See that he stays there."

"Thanks," I said, and I let the guards take me away through the corridors of the complex. Now all I had to do was get away from them, and the sooner the better. I had to find the generator room and sabotage the generator before the Prophet got turned on. Then I had to rescue Yelena and her sisters and Parham and find a way to escape. And probably the generator thing would not be enough to permanently put the Prophet out of commission, so I'd have to find a way to do that, too. After listing it all out, I felt a little overwhelmed, so I focused on step one: getting away from the guards.

"Hey, is there a restroom I could use?" I said, getting impatient.

"There will be one in your quarters," said the guard on my left.

"Are we almost there? 'Cause I need to go," I said.

It took a couple more minutes before they delivered me to my room. It was furnished like a four-star hotel room, with a king bed and a large flat-screen TV. Unlike most hotel rooms, though, this room had no windows. While one guard untied my hands, the other kept his gun trained on me.

"Thanks, guys," I said. "I'll hit the restroom then get a little shuteye."

"Use the phone if you need anything," one of them said. They walked out and locked the door from outside.

I couldn't believe they would put me in a room with a working phone, so I went straight to the desk and checked. The phone lacked number keys—if I picked up the handset, it would obviously go to an operator, and I couldn't just ask to be connected to Langley.

The lockpicks in my waistband took a minute to remove, after which I set to work on the door. I cracked it open and peeked out. My guards were gone.

Hoping I remembered the layout from Parham's map correctly, I set off in search of the generator room.

It took me almost ten minutes to get there, because I was spotted three times and had to duck into a room and lock myself in until I was forgotten.

I picked the lock on the generator room and slipped inside. To my surprise, there were no generators in the generator room. There were power conduits stretching off in various directions, but no generators. Of course, Parham probably had just seen the sign on the door, and had no idea what was behind it.

After staring at the conduits for a few moments, I realized they all came together in one place: a vertical shaft heading upward. Steel rungs embedded in the wall formed a ladder alongside the conduits.

Since I had nothing I could use to cut the conduits, I had no choice but to start climbing and see where the power came from.

I climbed about forty feet up before the shaft ended in a metal grate. The conduits passed through holes in the grate and entered a metal box the size of an SUV. Insulated cables spread out on the floor in various directions from the box, exiting the room through holes at the base of the walls.

I picked the lock on a hatch in the grate, and climbed into the room.

The box emitted a throbbing hum, so I guessed it might be a transformer. Whatever it was, it looked like the center of the power system, so it was my target. I looked for controls—or even something as basic as an off switch—but all I could find were some sealed access panels. It must be controlled from elsewhere.

A door with a little glass window led off to my right, so I took a peek. Beyond the door was a brightly lit room. I counted five people sitting at computer monitors. None of them seemed to be armed, which was a plus. On the minus side, I wasn't armed, either.

I opened the door and stepped through.

A couple of the people looked up from their monitors. A blonde woman in her forties said, "Can I help you?" in an English accent.

"Don't mind me," I said. "Just checking on something." I walked right past them and out the door on the other side of the room.

I found myself near one end of a corridor. I checked the short end first, then strode in the longer direction, hoping to find a janitorial closet.

Instead, I found an exit. A guard sat facing away

from me. Beyond him was a glass door that looked out onto a parking lot with several cars. A drizzle fell from gray clouds. So there was an above-ground facility after all. Because I was reading them from behind, it took me a moment to read the letters etched into the glass: Grants End Power Station.

For all I knew, the people working here were completely innocent and had no idea they were powering a secret lab underneath them.

I continued my search for the janitorial closet, hoping I still had time before Jamshidi switched the Prophet on. I found the closet at the far end of the corridor and ducked inside.

I turned on the sink faucet and put a bucket under it. As it filled, I opened a toolbox. I took out a hammer and searched for a chisel, but had to settle for a large flathead screwdriver.

When the bucket was full, I lugged it back down the corridor to the control room. The same two people looked up as I entered.

"Don't mind me," I said. "Just checking on something." No one had raised an alarm the last time, so I didn't see the need to vary my phrasing. As I got to the door to the transformer room, one of the men said, "What are you doing?"

"Just cleaning up a bit of a mess," I said, opening the door.

"Water can be dangerous in there," he said.

"I know what I'm doing," I replied. I stepped through the door, put down the bucket, and locked the door behind me.

I walked to the box, jammed the head of the screwdriver under the top edge of an access panel, and began pounding the handle of the screwdriver with the hammer.

Someone in the control room rattled the door handle.

I pried the panel open about an inch, then moved the screwdriver to one side and began pounding again. My pounding was matched by someone banging on the door.

"You, what are you doing in there?" someone shouted.

A klaxon sounded. I didn't have much more time, so I dropped the hammer, tucked the screwdriver into my pocket as best I could, and picked up the bucket.

The shouting grew louder as I lifted the bucket next to the hole I had made.

Taking a deep breath, I tried to steel myself. What I was about to do might start a fire, so I had to be ready to face that consequence. Back in Barcelona, Yelena had used a fire to help us escape. She wouldn't hesitate.

I tipped the bucket. Water spilled out into the hole. Blue-white light flickered inside and a sharp buzz cut through the noise surrounding me.

I upended the bucket, dumping the rest of the water in, then let go.

As the electrical buzz grew louder, I descended the ladder back toward the underground lab. I hadn't reached the bottom when an explosion in the room above sent a shock wave down the shaft. Though the sound was deafeningly loud, I managed to cling to the rungs and keep myself from falling.

The lights flickered and died.

Flames in the room above illuminated the shaft with a dim orange glow. By imagining Yelena's face, I tried to shut out memory of the fire that had taken my mother.

After I recovered my wits, I realized I was hyperventilating. I forced myself to take slow breaths, then started climbing down again. To my surprise, it was only two more rungs before I reached the floor. My desperate clinging had saved me from falling all of three feet.

I heard the hissing of gas being released. For an electrical room like this, the fire suppression system couldn't be water. So I quickly exited the room before the gas could suffocate me.

Emergency strobe lights flashed in the hallway, and a different alarm had joined the original klaxon. A couple of people had poked their heads out of doors, probably to check if power was out in the whole complex or just their rooms.

One of them yelled something in Farsi at me.

"Where's the bathroom?" I asked, using my most-practiced Farsi phrase.

He said something in Farsi that I didn't understand, so I just walked quickly past him and continued down the corridor toward the stairways. According to the map of the facility that Parham had drawn, I would need to go down six levels to get to the brothel.

Stirred by the fire alarm, more people came out into the hallway. Not only did that make me less noticeable, but it also relieved me a bit, because I assumed they would make their way to the fire escapes. I might have started the fire, but I didn't want it to kill anyone.

By the time I got to the stairway at the end of the corridor, I was part of a crowd of people evacuating. To my surprise, the stairs only led down from this floor, not up. Jamshidi obviously didn't want people from this lab showing up there.

At the third floor down, we met people coming up from the lower floors. This was the floor that joined up with the access monorails, so that must be how evacuation was handled. But I didn't want to evacuate, so I pushed my way against the flow of people coming from the lower levels.

I kept hoping I might run into Yelena getting evacuated, but by the time I got to the sixth floor down, that hope was gone. Evacuating enslaved prostitutes was probably not high on Jamshidi's priority list.

I reached the corridor Parham had indicated on his map. It was a long one, with no doors on either side, just one at the end. According to Parham, there were supposed to be two guards outside that door, but they had obviously fled due to the fire alarm.

The door to the brothel had been built of reinforced steel. There was a palm scanner next to the door, but its screen was blank due to the power failure. However, the door handle had a keyhole, presumably in case of power failure.

I tried the handle, but it was locked. It took only a few moments for me to get the lockpicks out of my waistband. As I worked on the lock, I tried to calm the rising fury I felt at people who would lock up helpless women during a fire.

The lock finally opened, and I pulled the door open and rushed inside, calling Yelena's name.

No one was in the small, bare room beyond the door, which should not have surprised me. If people had been trapped there, they would probably have been banging on the door as I was picking the lock.

But I could hear banging on the door at the far side of the room, along with faint voices yelling. I strode over, ready to pick the lock, but then realized this door merely had a handle on this side.

"I'm opening the door," I shouted. Turning the handle, I pulled it open slowly, so nobody on the other side pushing would overbalance and fall.

After the door swung in a bit, it burst inward, almost knocking me over. Four scantily clad women scrambled past me into the small room. In the flickering strobe of the emergency lighting, they looked like they were moving in slow motion.

Then Yelena entered. She was wearing a silk robe, and had her arms around two blonde teens—she had found her sisters. In the flashes of light, I could see the girls' eyes were red-rimmed from crying.

"Nat," she said. "You came."

"Of course," I said. "Couldn't leave you down here."

More women and girls—some of whom seemed to be barely in their teens—rushed past Yelena and her sisters.

I eyed her robe, realizing suddenly that it meant Jamshidi's men had taken her clothes, and possibly done more to her. "Those men didn't..."

She shook her head. "They take my clothes, that is all."

One of the women who had passed by me wailed in frustration and pounded on the other door.

Turning, I saw it had closed behind me. "Don't worry," I said. "I'll unlock it again."

I pushed through to the door and stopped, staring. The face of the door was blank: no lock, no handle.

Chapter Twenty-Seven

The possibility that the door could not be unlocked from the inside except by the hand scanner set into the wall had not occurred to me. It made a terrible kind of sense, though: the brothel's customers could open the door to get out, but if one of the women tried to escape, she would be trapped.

And now I was trapped, too. There was no lock to pick and no way brute force was going to punch through that reinforced steel.

"Nat, you have plan, yes?" said Yelena.

"Finding you was my plan." I looked down at the lockpicks in my hand, not wanting to face her disappointment in my lack of professionalism.

"So is time for new plan," she said, with no trace of scolding in her tone. "Hand scanner is electronic lock. Can we rewire?"

"We could, maybe," I said, "if I hadn't cut the power by blowing up the transformer station."

"So that is what happen," she said. "You stop computer?"

"I certainly hope so," I said. "This lab doesn't seem to have a backup generator online, at least not yet."

She pointed up at the strobing light on the ceiling. "Then what power these?"

"They must work off of"—I saw her smile and realized she was ahead of me—"some sort of local battery. Let's boost someone up to get it."

"No," she said, "need this one here. We get one from back there." She recruited two of the taller women to help her and went back into the brothel, leaving her two sisters behind.

With my lockpicks, I set to work on opening the panel of the hand scanner.

"You are American," said one of the twins.

"Yeah," I said.

"Yet you come to rescue us," said the other. Their Russian accents were less pronounced than Yelena's. "Why?"

Because I'm in love with your sister was what I wanted to say, but since I hadn't told Yelena that, I didn't think it was a good idea to tell her sisters. "Your sister helped me, so now I'm helping her."

"She told us someone would come," said the first, "but we did not believe her."

Yelena returned, holding a flashing strobe light with dangling wires. "We have battery."

"Just a sec," I said. With my lockpicks, I applied a little pressure and jiggled, and the scanner casing came loose.

While poking around the wires inside, Yelena and I discussed how to proceed. Finally we hooked up the battery to a couple of wires. No luck.

After trying a half-dozen combinations, the door

lock buzzed briefly. Several of the women pushed on the door, and it swung outward.

"Wait," I said, as women and girls streamed out into the hallway. "Don't just run off!"

They ignored me.

"We have to stop them," I said to Yelena. "If they evacuate through the tunnels, they'll just end up back here when the fire's out."

"Where else can we go?" she asked.

"Up," I said.

It took a couple of minutes of shouting in various languages, but everyone gathered into one group— twenty-five women and girls in total. The alarms stopped sounding as we were trying to get organized, but the emergency lights continued to strobe.

I took the lead going up the stairs, with Yelena and her sisters right behind me.

The stairwell was empty all the way to the top floor. But as I looked out the door into the hallway, I saw about a dozen men clad in yellow firefighting garb gathered outside the doorway to the generator room. The door was open, and the men didn't seem like they were in a rush to fight a fire, so the automatic extinguishers must have done the job. I had hoped that with the fire out, we could climb up into the facility above, but that wouldn't work with the men there.

"We'll need to distract the men," I said.

"Why?" Yelena asked.

"Because that's our way out," I said. "In that room, there's a shaft with a ladder that goes up to a building on the surface."

"And shaft is only way to get there?"

"That I know about." I shrugged. "Parham didn't

mention the building above when he drew the map, so I think any connections are hidden."

Some of the women and girls behind us on the stairs began panicked chattering in various languages. Yelena shushed them.

"The elevators," said one of Yelena's sisters. "One of the men told me there were secret floors on the elevators."

"The power is out," I said, before remembering that many modern elevators had their own backup power supplies. "But it might work, if we can distract the men so they won't—"

"That is silly," said Yelena. "We try elevators on other floor."

On the next floor down, we punched the elevator buttons, but they didn't light up, and nothing came.

"It was a good idea," Yelena told her sister in Russian.

"It still might work," I said. "The elevators are probably in fire mode, which means they went to the evacuation floor. That's two floors below us."

As we descended the stairs again, Yelena said, "If fire is out, then people may come back."

"I know," I said.

On the third floor down, the elevators sat waiting with their doors open. I entered one, along with Yelena and her sisters.

"Any idea how the secret floors were accessed?" I asked, looking at the elevator panel. There were the usual assortment of buttons: door open, door close, emergency stop, and the floor numbers—1 through 8, although they were ordered with 1 at the top and 8 at the bottom. That corresponded to the floors we knew about. There was also a keyhole for firefighter operation.

"No," said one of the twins. Maybe I would learn to tell them apart someday, but for now that wasn't high on my priority list.

"Do you see anything that looks like a secret panel?" I asked Yelena.

She shook her head.

"Still, it makes sense there would be an easier way than climbing the ladder in the shaft," I said, trying to talk my way through figuring things out. "It makes sense to use the elevators. Maybe punching in the right combination of floors allows access."

"It will take too long," said Yelena. "And is not secure—could take people by accident."

"True," I said. "It would be better to just have a key to . . ." I raised my lockpicks to the firefighter control keyhole. I turned the lock from Off to the second marked position, On. I clicked it over to the last marked position, marked Hold. And then I turned it farther, and it clicked into an unmarked position.

The doors began to close.

Women and girls began pushing forward into the elevator.

"We can't take everyone in one trip," I said. "I'll come back for everyone else."

We managed to squeeze eighteen people on board, more than double the maximum capacity listed on the placard. I figured so many of them looked undernourished, we were probably still okay for the weight limit.

"I'll come back for you," I said to the eight women left outside. Then I realized the round trip might take more than a minute, and I could risk them forgetting me and panicking. "Yelena, say you'll come back for them."

"I will come back for you," she said. "Stay here and wait."

The elevator doors closed, and we went up. The floor indicator lit up with 3, then 2, then 1. And we kept going up.

The indicator changed to 0 and we stopped. The doors opened.

"There's an armed guard, if he hasn't evacuated," I said. "You may have to get past him to get to the cars outside."

"But I must go back for the others," said Yelena.

"No, I can handle it," I said. "I just needed them to remember someone was coming back."

"We will wait," she said.

I nodded. I pressed the 4 button, and the doors closed between us.

When the doors opened on level four, one of the women shrieked on seeing me.

"Yelena sent me," I said. "Come with me, hurry."

The women looked at me, then each other.

Down the hall, beyond where I could see, I heard the pound of boots on tile. A man yelled something incomprehensible.

That decided the women. They entered the elevator and huddled in the back.

I turned the key switch back to the secret setting. A man with a rifle appeared in the hallway. The doors closed as he swung his rifle up. The elevator rose. There was a loud *bang*. A hole appeared in the elevator door, and searing pain erupted in my left calf.

Surprised screams came from the women in the back.

I turned to look at them. "Are any of you hurt?"

None of them were.

"At least you know I'm on your side, now," I said. The pain actually wasn't as bad as what I remembered of my burst appendix, but I began reciting the Vice Presidents of the United States anyway.

The elevator arrived at the top floor. Ignoring the women as they got off, I lifted my pant leg to see how bad the damage was. A round hole in the flesh next to my shin oozed blood. I checked the back of my leg—no exit wound. The elevator door must have slowed the bullet enough that it didn't go all the way through my leg.

"Nat!" Yelena entered the elevator and knelt to look at the wound. "We must stop bleeding."

"I can handle it," I said. "You need to get everyone out of here and safe. The guard who shot me saw the women—he knows they're escaping."

"Come on, then," she said, rising to her feet and taking my arm. "We get you outside."

I shook my head. "I have to go back for Parham."

"But—"

"Your escape will be a diversion to help me. Now go!"

In a movie, this would have been the point at which she confessed her love for me, and then we had a long lingering kiss before she finally went. But Yelena was professional enough to know that each second of delay made it more likely the guards could organize to stop her and the others from escaping.

I watched her go, knowing it was the right thing to do and wishing she'd kissed me anyway.

Standing here with the elevator door open wasn't a good idea, so I hit the button for the seventh floor down. Once I was between floors, I pulled out the emergency stop knob. I sank to the floor, which relieved the pain in my leg a little.

Using one of my lockpicks to help tear the fabric, I ripped off my left pant leg from the knee down, then tore it into strips. Through gritted teeth I named off Secretaries of the Treasury, starting with Alexander Hamilton, as I bound up the wound, knotting the cloth tightly enough to keep pressure on it without cutting off the circulation in my leg.

I clambered to my feet and continued to the seventh floor down, where Parham's quarters were located. As a high-value prisoner, he had probably been evacuated during the fire alarm, so I would wait there for his return.

Along the way, I tried a few doors at random, and found the quarters of someone who wore pants approximately my size. I swapped my torn pants for a pair of khakis.

I picked the lock on Parham's door. As I had guessed, he wasn't there. His quarters were fairly spacious, with a living room, a bedroom, and a bathroom. I went through the medicine cabinet in his bathroom, hoping to find a pain reliever, but there was nothing useful.

As I stepped back into the living room, I heard a key being inserted into the lock. I stepped back into the bedroom so I couldn't be seen from the front door.

The door opened. Parham spoke in Farsi, and a man replied. The door closed. After a few moments, a flash of the emergency lights revealed Parham approaching the bedroom. He must have seen me in the same flash, because he let out a yell.

"Quiet," I said in the darkness after the flash.

The front door opened.

And the regular lights came on. Power was back online.

Chapter Twenty-Eight

Eyes wide, Parham stared at me. There was no recognition there.

The guard asked him something in Farsi, and Parham answered, reaching down to rub the toe of his left shoe. The guard replied, and I heard the door close, but I couldn't tell if the guard was still inside.

Parham straightened. "I told him I stubbed my toe in the darkness. Explain yourself now or I will call him in again."

"I'm Nat Morgan, a friend of Yelena."

"And how is she?" he asked.

"Gone," I said. At least, I very much hoped she was by now. "I just helped her and her sisters bust out of here."

"And why should I believe you?" he asked. "Yelena never mentioned she had an American friend who was coming to rescue her."

"Even if she had," I said, "you probably wouldn't remember. Do you have a notebook you've been taking notes in recently?"

"I did, but the guards took it away."

I winced. That was going to make it more difficult. "Do you think you could get them to bring it back?"

"Perhaps. Why? And what happened to your leg?"

"I got shot," I said. "And the notebook would help because you were working on a theory about me."

He scoffed. "A theory about you? I'm a quantum physicist, not a psychologist."

"You called me a fluke of quantum mechanics— Schrödinger's cat burglar—because no one can remember me after not observing me for a minute. You talked about superpositions and probability waves that collapse so that it's like I was never there."

"Schrödinger's cat burglar? That's a good one," he said. "But your story doesn't add up. You claim to be Yelena's friend, but how can you have any friends if no one—"

"Yelena's the only person who can remember me. You said we were entangled by a laser in Barcelona." I had to make him believe me. "I was with you during your whole escape, except you don't remember me. I was with you by the side of the road when Yelena drove off with your cell phone and came back with the Mercedes. I was with you in the hotel in Ahvaz, and on the Grasshopper, and when we met with Edward, and when we tried to sneak into the warehouse."

"All details you could have found out from questioning Yelena."

"Do you think she would break so easily? And what would be the point of my lying about this?" I asked. "I came with you because you said we needed to destroy the core of the Prophet, otherwise it would control the future. I managed to delay things by taking out the power, but they've obviously worked around that. If I can get you access to the network, can you still disrupt the core's operating code?"

"I'm sure my security codes are no longer valid," he said. "But if we could access a terminal with someone else's login, if they have high enough clearance, then yes. Entangled, you say? How did you become entangled with Yelena?"

"Doesn't matter right now," I said. "Where's the most likely place we could get you access?"

"Over in the lab wing, I should think, since people will be getting back to work."

"Okay, that's where we'll go." I looked around the room for something that could be used as a weapon, and focused on a floor lamp. "How many guards are outside your door?"

"Two."

I picked up the lamp. The metal base was hefty enough to pack a wallop. "Do you think you could get just one of them in here?" With the element of surprise, I figured I could take out one armed guard at a time, but not two simultaneously.

"I can try," Parham said. "But if they're suspicious, they might both come in."

I nodded. "We need to get one of the guards to leave. What if you wrote a note to Jamshidi and asked one of the guards to take it?"

"Can't hurt to try," Parham said. He strode to his desk, wrote a short note on a piece of paper, and stuffed it in an envelope, which he then sealed. "I'll say it's for Jamshidi's eyes only."

Parham opened the door and spoke in Farsi with

the guards. He closed the door and grinned at me. "One of them's taken the bait."

"We'll give him a minute to get out of the way, then get the other guard to come in," I said.

"Right."

I began counting off the seconds in my head.

"How did you get entangled with Yelena?" asked Parham.

Briefly, I recounted the story of the laser in Barcelona and what he had theorized about it.

"Of course, the Quantum Zeno effect," he said. "What a fascinating real-life application."

"You mentioned the Quantum Zeno effect before," I said. "What is it?"

"Basically, it's the idea that you can stop a quantum state from flipping to another state if you keep measuring it. Because Yelena is, in a way, constantly measuring your existence through the entanglement, she can't forget you."

The conversation had distracted me, and I realized more than a minute had passed. "It's time to—".

I heard the key being inserted into the lock. "He's coming." Brandishing the lamp, I moved into position so the door would block me from the guard's view as it opened.

The door swung open.

Parham's mouth gaped.

"Hello, Parham," said Yelena. "Is Nat here?"

"Yelena?" I said, coming around the door to see her. Still dressed in the black silk robe, she was dragging an unconscious guard inside. "What are you doing here? Where are your sisters? Did they get recaptured?"

"With Edward. I take them to rendezvous point,"

she said. "He will take them to CIA warehouse. I think he is glad to have them as leverage to make sure I come back with Parham." The door closed as she got the guard's body fully inside. "Since you are wounded, I think you might need my help to get Parham out and sabotage supercomputer."

"I can't believe you came back." Truth was, I was flabbergasted that she would be willing to leave her sisters to come back for me. Maybe she really did care about me.

She flashed me a smile. "Believe. Now, put on guard uniform. Attract less attention as we go to the surface."

"But we're not escaping yet," I said. "Parham and I are going to destroy the core."

"Then I come with you," she said.

"I'm glad to see you again," I said, "but you should go be with your sisters. After everything they've been through, they need you."

She looked at Parham. "If we do not destroy supercomputer, and Jamshidi controls future, he can bring my sisters back?"

"He could arrange events to make that happen," Parham said. "And I'm afraid he is quite vindictive enough to do just that."

"Then my job is not done until we destroy core," Yelena said.

While I changed into the guard's uniform, which was a little loose around the shoulders and had sleeves too long, Yelena tied up the guard using the electrical cord from the floor lamp.

"Do you have clothes I can change into?" she asked Parham when she finished. "Robe attract too much attention."

He pointed to the bedroom. "Help yourself. Closet's in there."

She emerged a couple of minutes later wearing a white shirt with the sleeves rolled up and a pair of loose jeans, cinched at the waist by a too-large belt. "Sorry, I poke new holes in belt," she said.

"Think nothing of it," said Parham.

"I think you look great," I said. She did. "Unfortunately, that means you're still going to attract too much attention in the halls."

"I got down here while wearing robe," she said. "This will not be so bad."

"This is the residential section," said Parham. "People dress casually here sometimes. In the lab wing, you would stick out. And if the guards aren't looking for you soon, they will be."

"I really think it would be best if you went to join your sisters," I said.

"You think it too risky for me because I am woman?" she said. "Tell me, Nat, which of us is more skilled, if we do not count your talent?"

My face flushed. "You are," I admitted. "But it's not because you're—"

"And if you are with Parham, how will your talent help?" she asked.

"It won't," I said. "But Yelena—"

"Then best chance of success is with me, even if I am a woman."

"It's not because you're a woman," I said. "I want you out of here and safe because you're the woman I love."

She stared at me for a moment. "You think you love me just because I can remember you."

"No," I said. "I mean, it helps, but I fell in love with you because you're smart and brave and competent and beautiful and passionate—I mean that in the way that you care so much about things, not the romantic way. Why would I not fall in love with you?"

Parham said, "This is all very touching, but we have a mission to do and time is ticking away."

"He is right," said Yelena. "We can talk about love later."

I'd just poured my heart out, and now she was back to the cool professional. If she could do it, I could. "We still have the problem that you're too noticeable."

"We improvise," she said. "You are good at that."

The condescending compliment did not make me feel any better. But I wasn't going to let my annoyance show. "I'll play the part of your guard. Of course, if anyone expects me to speak Farsi, the jig is up, and we'll have to…improvise."

We left Parham's quarters. He led the way, with Yelena beside him, and I followed behind carrying the guard's rifle. I did my best to keep from limping, but the pain in my left leg was a constant throb in the background.

We passed various people who were still returning to the residential section after the evacuation. Nobody gave us more than a cursory glance, so I began to feel a little more confident we might actually pull this off.

"Around the next corner is the entrance to the lab wing," Parham said. "There are usually two guards on duty."

"Stop and let me take a look," I said. I passed Parham and Yelena, and peered around the corner.

About twenty yards away, two guards stood on either side of the hallway, which continued beyond them.

I turned back to the others. "What do you think? Can I just march you past them like I'm under orders to take you somewhere in there?"

"It might work," said Parham. "Usually I just give them a nod as I walk past when going to work. But circumstances are different now."

"It is bold strategy," said Yelena.

"In other words, you think it's a stupid risk, but you're trying not to hurt my feelings right now," I said.

"I did not say that," she said.

"But you thought it," I said. "And you're right. I may have a guard's uniform, but they won't recognize me, so they're not just going to let me waltz past them with a couple of prisoners."

"Give me rifle," said Yelena. "I will take them out."

"Shooting could just draw more guards," I said. "But I've just realized my talent is not entirely useless in this situation." I pointed to a door in our hallway. "You two hide in there. I'll draw the guards after me, and after they've gone past, you two go on. I'll lose them and they'll forget about me. Then I'll come join you."

I had to pick the lock on the door to let them in. It turned out to be a room filled with boxes of copy machine paper, pens, and other office staples. I guess even a billionaire like Jamshidi had to worry about employees stealing supplies.

"How do I say, 'Follow me! The prisoners are escaping!' in Farsi?" I asked Parham. I was still in a guard's uniform, so I might be able to fool them long enough.

He told me, and I practiced it a few times.

"They will not believe you are Iranian," said Yelena.

Parham said, "There are a few Russian guards. Try saying it with a Russian accent."

"I can't even speak Russian with a Russian accent," I said, but I gave it a try.

"Okay, see you on the other side," I said.

I left the supply room and went around the corner. I beckoned to the guards and yelled, "Follow me! The prisoners are escaping!"

It took them a moment, but they started running toward me. I wasn't sure whether they believed me or thought I was an intruder. Either way, they were following me.

I turned and started running back around the corner. And the pain in my leg, which I had pushed to the back of my mind, pushed itself to the forefront. My left knee collapsed, and I tumbled to the ground right in front of the door behind which Yelena and Parham were hiding.

Chapter Twenty-Nine

Chapter Twenty-Nine

The footsteps of the guards pounded closer.

Grimacing with pain, I used my rifle as a crutch to help haul myself to my feet. I had to get far enough down the hallway that Yelena and Parham could slip past the guards. Half limping, half running, I kept going even as the guards started yelling after me in Farsi.

From the tone of voice, I thought they were asking questions, so I pointed toward the end of the hall and said in Farsi, "The prisoners are escaping."

They had almost caught up to me. I couldn't lose them by outrunning them, so I let myself fall to the ground again, sprawling forward to get as much distance as possible from the supply room. I rolled onto my back, clutched at my wounded leg, and screamed in pain. The scream was only about half fake.

The guards stopped beside me, looking down on me in puzzlement. I rolled up my left pant leg so they could see the bloodstains soaking through my improvised bandage.

The door to the supply room opened, and Yelena peered around the edge. The guards were still looking at me.

Yelena's eyes widened as she saw me.

"Go!" I said, extending the vowel out into a moan and hoping the guards would interpret it as merely an expression of my pain.

Yelena didn't hesitate. She slipped out of the supply room, Parham close behind her, and they rounded the corner.

Groaning in pain so I wouldn't have to speak, I waved the guards toward the far end of the hall. I hoped they would assume I had somehow been shot by escaping prisoners and rush off to see what was going on.

It half worked—one of them went, but one stayed and jabbered at me in Farsi.

I rolled my head back and watched as the other guard disappeared around a corner at the far end. Soon he would forget what he was doing and head back, but I had a little time.

With a quick movement, I swung my rifle up and pointed the barrel at the remaining guard's chest.

His jaw dropped.

"Be quiet or I'll kill you. Drop your gun."

I didn't know whether he understood my words or just my tone. Either way, his rifle clattered on the tile.

I motioned him to back up, and he did.

Gingerly, I rose to my feet.

"Lie down," I said, pointing to the floor.

After a moment, he got down on his knees.

"Lie down," I repeated, pointing more insistently. He lay face down, hands behind his head.

Keeping my rifle aimed at him, I backed toward

the hallway leading into the lab wing. Once I had rounded the corner, I turned and hobbled in the direction Yelena and Parham had gone.

Based on the map Parham had drawn, I located his lab. I opened the door and was relieved to see Parham typing away at a computer terminal inside. In the back of the lab, a scowling young man bound to a chair looked up as I entered, and immediately began yelling through the gag stuffed in his mouth.

Parham spotted me and froze.

"Don't worry, I'm with Yelena," I said. "Where . . ." I stopped as Yelena came around from behind the door, where she had obviously been waiting to attack me if I had turned out to be a real guard.

"Nat," she said, "how is leg?"

"It's okay," I said. It still throbbed, but the sharp pain I had felt when trying to run had faded.

"Yelena," said Parham, "Why didn't you tell me you had an accomplice among the guards?"

There was no point in distracting him from his work by explaining everything again.

Yelena apparently came to the same conclusion, because she said, "Is complicated. Keep working."

Parham went back to typing at his terminal.

"Who's the guy in back?" I asked Yelena.

"Jamal. Unfortunately, he finish modifying viewer already, but Parham use his login on computer."

Picking up the notebook that lay next to his keyboard, Parham said, "Lucky for me, Jamshidi sent my notebook here for Jamal to take a look at. I had already worked out some code to attack the core's operating code, so I don't have to start from scratch."

"Stop talking about it and keep working," I said. "Like you said, we have a mission to do and time is ticking away."

"When did I say that?" he asked.

"Forget it," I said.

Yelena frowned. "What is problem with you?"

"Sorry," I said. "The bullet in my leg's just making me—"

"What on earth is this nonsense?" said Parham.

"What nonsense?" I said.

"A man who cannot be remembered." Parham flipped through the pages of the notebook. "Collapsing the wave function of memory. Entanglement and the Quantum Zeno Effect on a macroscopic scale. Invisible to the quantum viewer. It's in my handwriting, but . . . Oh, now that is interesting. The math here actually makes sense."

"It's your theory," I said. "You came up with all of that to explain the fact that no one can remember me. Except Yelena, because we got entangled by a laser. You figured out how to explain everything, but really, that's not important right now. Stopping the Prophet from controlling the future is."

"I'm almost done," Parham said. He resumed typing. "My little package of code is ready. All I have to do is open a pipe and upload it to the core for execution."

"Then what will happen?" I asked.

Parham hit the enter key and then leaned back in his chair. "The core takes my code and compiles it into quantum machine language, and runs it millions of times in quarantine to make sure that it works properly and is stable. Once the core has run its checks, it will remove the quarantine and integrate the code. That's when the fun begins. And it's probably thanks to you."

"Me?" I asked.

Parham grinned and continued, "The Quantum Zeno Effect—constantly measuring a quantum property keeps it from flipping to another state. I must have been thinking about it because of how it applies to you, and that's probably what gave me the idea for attacking the core. My little package will be completely stable in quarantine, because it's constantly being checked for stability. But once it's integrated into the core, it will no longer be subject to constant checks, and it will become unstable. Basically, it spirals out of control, expanding in size and overwriting everything else in the computer's quantum memory until there is nothing left of the core's—"

A red-bordered alert popped up on Parham's terminal screen. His shoulders slumped as he read what it said.

"What's wrong?" I asked.

"The core rejected my code. Jamshidi has temporarily frozen any modifications to the core's software until after the Prophet is fully operational." Parham shook his head. "There's nothing I can do."

A speaker on the wall chimed, and then Jamshidi's voice spoke out of it in Farsi. I gripped my rifle and turned toward the door.

Parham bowed his head and closed his eyes. "It's a general announcement. He is congratulating everyone for their fine work, and says that the Prophet has been activated."

"But I do not feel different," said Yelena. "If computer controls me, why do I still want to destroy it?"

"You wouldn't notice that it was controlling you,"

said Parham. "It could alter your memories so you forget it even exists, kind of like—What's your name?"

"Nat," I said.

"Like Nat." Parham smiled at me. "But it doesn't control the future yet. Right now, the computer is using the quantum viewer to build a quantum connection to everything in the world. Look."

He pointed to a progress bar on his monitor, currently showing three percent complete.

"Once this reaches one hundred percent, the Prophet will be fully connected. Then it will begin to exercise control."

Under the progress bar was an estimated time: eight minutes and twelve seconds. "So we have eight minutes to get over there and blast the viewer to pieces." I opened the door. "Where would it be?"

"In one of the server farms near the warehouse we came in. But it's too far," said Parham. "And the security is very heavy."

"Just point me in the right direction," I said.

"It's no use," Parham said. "I would just be sending you to your death. Sometimes it is best to surrender to the inevitable. You can still live a good life under the Prophet's control. You may not even remember that you are being controlled. Unless . . ." He began flipping through the pages of the notebook.

"Unless what?" I said.

"In my notes, it said you were invisible to the quantum viewer. If that's true, then you will be invisible to the Prophet, and therefore free of its control. You could go and destroy the viewer."

"Except I'm not invisible to it around Yelena," I said. "You said it was because we were entangled."

"Then we must separate until you destroy viewer," said Yelena.

"Not good enough," said Parham. "The Prophet has enough computing power to see the quantum connections of the whole world. As long as the two of you are entangled, it can see Nat." He looked down at the notebook. "You were entangled by a communications laser?"

"In Barcelona," I said.

"It doesn't matter where it was." He rose from his chair and strode to the door. "Follow me, quickly."

Yelena and I followed him out the door. "Where are we going?" I asked.

"There's a lab working with entangled photons for communication," said Parham as he led us down the hall. "They have a laser. We may be able to disentangle you."

"So I would not remember him?" Yelena asked.

"No," Parham said. "I'm sorry, Nat, but it's the only way."

I felt a pang of despair. My hope that in time Yelena might come to love me was now gone. "I understand."

He pulled open a door. "In here."

We entered a laboratory similar to the one in Barcelona. A long apparatus extended the length of the room. Parham flipped a few switches, and the apparatus began humming.

"It will take a moment to power up," he said. He walked over to a computer in screensaver mode and tapped the keyboard. The progress bar appeared in a window on the screen: seventy-four percent complete, and the estimated time left was only two minutes and twenty-four seconds.

"Once I get to the core, where will the viewer be?" I asked.

"There is a control room with glass walls that overlooks one of the server farms," Parham said. "The viewer should be installed in the server tower nearest to the steps down from the control room. Now, tell me the circumstances of what happened when you got entangled."

"Yelena and I were handcuffed together," I said. "We tried to use the laser to cut the handcuffs."

"They were magnetic," said Yelena.

"What color was the laser?" asked Parham.

"Violet," I said.

"Anything else unusual about the situation?"

"No," I said.

"We were in our underwear," Yelena said.

Parham raised his eyebrows. "I'm not even going to ask. Nat, strip down to your underwear. Yelena, see if you can find a magnet."

I began taking off the guard's uniform.

"What about handcuffs?" asked Yelena as she began rummaging through drawers in one of the workbenches along the side of the room.

"We'll make do without," Parham said.

I piled the uniform on a bench, then pointed to my leg. "I don't need to take off this bandage, do I?"

"No," said Parham. "It's unlikely to make a difference, and I'd rather not have you bleed to death."

"Found one," said Yelena. She held up a bar magnet.

"Give it to Nat," Parham said.

She handed it to me.

"Nat, go to the far end of the laser," Parham said.

I walked to the end of the room. There was a

green dot on the target prism. I could barely see the beam in the air.

"I'm going to tune the laser. Let me know when the color's about right," said Parham. The dot shifted to blue, then to violet.

"That's it," I said.

"After Yelena and I leave the room, take the magnet and lower it into the beam," said Parham. "Did you use safety goggles in Barcelona?"

I shook my head. "We were in a hurry."

Parham winced. "Well, that can't be helped. We need circumstances to be as close as possible to the original event, so no goggles." He turned to Yelena and said, "Let's go."

"Wait," said Yelena.

Fifty-seven seconds remained on the countdown.

"Dr. Rezaei," she said, "is possible to entangle us again after computer is destroyed?"

"I can't guarantee that," said Parham. "I can't even guarantee that I'll manage to disentangle you now. I really don't know enough about the phenomenon yet. It may be that your original entanglement was the product of unique circumstances."

"I understand the risks," I said. "Now go."

She shook her head. "I must tell you something, before I forget you."

"What?"

"I love you. I am sorry I did not tell before," she said.

Warmth flooded through my chest. She loved me. And now I had to give her up.

With a sad smile, I said, "Thanks for telling me. Please go."

They walked out the door and closed it behind them. Twenty-one seconds ticked down to twenty.

I dipped the magnet into the beam. A dazzling flash blinded me.

Chapter Thirty

Not knowing how quickly the disentanglement would take effect, I held the magnet in the beam and counted to twenty-five. I figured if it hadn't worked by the time the countdown was over, it wouldn't matter.

"Nat," said Yelena. She still remembered me, but she hadn't been gone for sixty seconds, so I couldn't tell if the disentanglement had worked or not.

I dropped the magnet and looked toward the door. I could barely see her and Parham through the afterimage of the glare. "Why'd you come back in?"

"Guards coming," she said. "Get uniform on."

I dressed quickly as the sound of boots on tile came closer. All of us stood still as the boots passed by and then faded in the distance.

"Probably headed toward the lab where I sent my little gift code from," said Parham.

"I don't understand," I said. "If the Prophet knows everything and controls everything, why didn't it send the guards straight here?"

"At this point, we can't do anything to stop it," said Parham. "As long as we are not acting to threaten its existence, the future it chooses for us will tend to lie along the path of greatest probability—the kinds of things we would normally do. And I think we would get out of here."

We slipped out the door. Parham led us down a hallway.

"Where are we headed?" I asked.

"I believe there's a way to the surface from the nearest monorail station," he said. "It's guarded, but if we can sneak up and out onto the street, we can take a cab back to the CIA warehouse."

"I think we should at least try—" I said, but before I could finish Yelena interrupted, saying, "Yes, my sisters should be there now. We can all fly to USA."

"Wait a second," I said. "Parham, isn't it possible that integrating all that information takes longer than you thought, and that's why we're not being controlled?"

Parham didn't reply. Instead, he kept walking.

"Parham, I really don't feel like I'm being controlled."

He said, "Yes, I'll do my best to help the U.S. build an equivalent. Perhaps a balance of power can work as it did during the Cold War."

"What are you talking about?" I said. "I just think we should see if it's still possible to—"

Yelena said, "For my mother, too?"

"What?" Had they both gone crazy?

"Then yes." She laughed. "I must learn better English."

It was like she was carrying on a different conversation from the one I was having. "Yelena, can you even hear me?"

"The guards will be down at the end of the next corridor to the right," said Parham.

"We do things different this time," said Yelena. "You cannot run with your wound, Nat."

I stopped. The two of them continued walking and conversing as if I were still with them.

The Prophet was manipulating them, bringing about a future in which the three of us left together, no longer a threat to its control of the world. Parham and Yelena were reacting to what I was supposed to be saying, according to the Prophet's script. But I wasn't playing my part right, which meant I was not being controlled. The disentanglement had worked.

I might be the only free person in the world.

But that came at a price. Due to my talent, I had always been somewhat disconnected from the rest of humanity. Until I got tangled up with Yelena, nobody could really get to know me. Sure, there was Edward and his file folder, though he only really knew me through his notes. But at least I could talk to people and make a brief connection, even if they forgot about me afterward.

Now even those tenuous connections had been severed. I couldn't carry on a conversation because I didn't know what I was supposed to be saying. And no one would remember me at all because they would never notice I was there.

At least, that's how it seemed to work. If so, it was time to stop with the self-pity and make myself useful. Before going to take out the Prophet's core, though, I needed to find the limitations of my new situation.

Ignoring the twinges in my leg, I hurried to catch up with Yelena and Parham. They continued conversing in hushed tones as I passed, planning how Parham would distract the guards so Yelena and the Prophet's nonexistent version of me could get the drop on them.

Parham had been right about the Prophet controlling everything, but it didn't seem to be working quite the way he explained it. It wasn't like the Prophet was picking between probabilities to turn into reality; it was more like the entire world had become a virtual reality, with every aspect following whatever script the Prophet had written.

Every aspect but me.

As I approached the monorail station, I spotted the two guards, one at each of the two entrances. I walked straight up to the nearest and said, "One round-trip ticket to New York, please."

He didn't react in any way. I reached out a finger and poked him in the chest. He didn't flinch.

Yelena and Parham would be arriving soon. I wasn't sure of their exact plan, but I figured it would help if these guards were unarmed. With some difficulty, I managed to wrench the rifle out of the hands of this guard. He continued to hold his hands as if the rifle were still in them. I slung the rifle over my shoulder and proceeded to disarm the other guard.

The first guard said something in Farsi.

Parham said something back.

It was like watching a mime as the guard raised his invisible rifle and pointed its invisible barrel at Parham.

Parham raised his hands in surrender.

The second guard approached, also aiming his nonexistent gun at Parham.

With growing dread, I realized that disarming the guards might not make any difference. The guards continued to act like they had guns, just because the Prophet told them that was reality. Parham reacted as if the guards still held guns for the same reason. Maybe if one of the guards fired, then Parham would react like he'd been shot. There wouldn't be an actual bullet, but with the Prophet controlling Parham's neurons at the quantum level, it was possible Parham's brain activity would fade out just as if he had really been shot.

The illusion of death would become reality.

Would moving the guards make any difference? Surely if I made a big enough change to the physical reality, then the Prophet would detect it and conform its version of reality—like when I left the pizzas at the guard's desk in Barcelona. He couldn't ignore the physical reality of the pizzas in front of him.

I started toward the guard closest to Parham. I'd move him into the monorail tunnel, then come back for the other. That might be enough.

The first guard said something to the other, who turned back toward his post, just as the first arched his back and fell forward. Parham ducked. The other guard dove to the ground and began pulling his trigger finger as if shooting at someone on the other side of the station. I caught a glimpse of Yelena at the other entrance.

The guard who had fallen showed no wound on his back, but he lay still—cheek on the gray tile, eyes fixed dully on nowhere. Dead.

The second guard was still firing deadly imaginary bullets. I grabbed his arm and dragged him into the monorail tunnel. He didn't struggle, but kept adjusting his aim and shooting, even though in reality his target was no longer visible.

I dropped the guard's arm just as he reached out to slap his hand down on something that wasn't even there. Alarms blared.

"Come on, Prophet!" I yelled. "Process this!"

The guard grunted in pain, then clutched at his shoulder. His head jerked to the side and he slumped, eyes closed. His head jerked again.

Outside the tunnel, Parham stood over the place where the guard had been, swinging an imaginary something—perhaps the rifle from the other guard.

A large metal door began to descend from the ceiling to close off the monorail tunnel. I rushed out before I could get trapped inside.

Parham called out Yelena's name. He dropped his weapon and rushed to the other side of the station.

Yelena knelt on the floor, clutching her right side. "Was ricochet," she gasped out. "Need to stop the bleeding."

"We must get her to a hospital," said Parham.

"Yelena," I said. "It's all imaginary." But of course she couldn't hear me.

There was only one thing I could do for Yelena now: if I shut down the Prophet, then the incorrect reality it controlled would no longer exist.

A map on the wall showed the locations of the lab's monorail stations, but with the monorail tunnels closed off, I would need to take a surface route.

Parham had brought us here planning to lead us to a surface exit. "Which way . . ." I began, then realized there was no point in asking.

I checked a couple of doors and found one led to a staircase going both up and down. I had just started up the stairs when I realized that if I succeeded, Yelena and Parham would be left unarmed—their current weapons being completely in the mind of the Prophet.

I had to pry one of Yelena's hands free from clutching her supposed wound in order to get the strap for one of the guards' rifles onto her shoulder. "Stay alive," I said. She might not be able to hear me consciously, but maybe somewhere deep inside she could. "Keep yourself alive."

Arming Parham was easier, so I only lost a couple of minutes total.

Willing the pain in my leg to stay manageable, I climbed the stairs. As I reached the top floor of the complex, I was relieved to see there were still more stairs heading up.

Halfway up the next flight, my heart instinctively thumped at the sight of two armed guards coming down toward me, but I pressed myself against the wall and they passed right on by as if I weren't there.

Two more guards stood at attention in front of a door with a card-swipe lock next to it. It felt kind of creepy to dig through the pockets of one of the guards until I found the security card. I swiped it through the lock.

Nothing happened. I mentally kicked myself for being an idiot. The card being swiped wasn't part of the Prophet's plan, so the lock didn't react to the swipe. I needed to get used to the fact that while I could apparently change things at a physical level, as far as computers and brains were concerned, I wasn't there.

So, how could I get past an electronic door lock? I needed to change things on a physical level. And the guards posted here just happened to have nice, big guns.

My talent couldn't cause a bullet to unshoot itself after I was gone, so maybe that meant the physical actions of pulling a trigger and causing a bullet to fire were far enough above the quantum level that I could force it to happen despite the Prophet.

I pulled the gun off one of the guards, aimed it almost point blank at the point on the edge of the door nearest to the door handle, and fired.

The report was deafening. With my ears still ringing, I examined the bullet hole. The bolt of the lock was damaged, but not enough. I fired four more shots, then tried pulling the handle. The door swung in.

After going through a couple of hallways and unlocked doors, I found myself in the kitchen of a restaurant. The cooks and waiters bustled about without seeing me, and I had to dodge my way through them to get into the dining room.

Once I got out onto the street, I found a bus stop with a map that let me figure out where I was in relation to the warehouse for Jamshidi Oil. It was about a mile and a half away. It took me only a few moments to memorize the names of the streets I would need to take to get there.

I wished that I could steal a car to make it there as quickly as possible because every second of delay made it more likely Yelena might die of her imaginary wound. But cars these days were so dependent on computers that I doubted I could get one to work properly with the Prophet controlling it.

I started to run, but a jolt of pain in my leg made me stop. If my leg gave out completely because I pushed myself too hard, I would never get there.

I dropped the gun, since it was only weighing me

down, and I could just take one off another guard later if I needed to shoot a lock or something. Then I set a brisk walking pace and hoped for the best.

I'd only gone about a hundred yards when I spotted a man on a bicycle, waiting for a traffic light. I walked up to him, pried his hands off the handlebars, then hoisted him off the bike. I laid him down on his back.

His legs started pedaling in the air, and I couldn't help chuckling at how silly he looked.

I got on the bike and proceeded through the intersection. As I neared a half-dozen pedestrians crossing the street, I stopped to let them pass.

Everything suddenly went silent, and the pedestrians froze in place, as if someone had hit the pause button for the world. The effect only lasted a fraction of a second before sound and motion resumed. For a moment I wondered if I had imagined it, but then the six pedestrians—four men, a woman, and a five- or six-year-old girl holding the woman's hand—swiveled in unison and walked toward me. The closest man, dressed in a business suit, reached toward my bike's handlebars.

Releasing the handbrake, I kicked myself backward on the bike to put a little space between me and the pedestrians, then turned and pedaled around them. They converged on the spot where I had been, their faces blank and their arms outstretched like zombies.

I almost laughed at their bumbling efforts, until I realized what was really going on.

The Prophet was hunting me.

Chapter Thirty-One

It seemed like the Prophet still couldn't see me directly, but it must have started to notice that things were out of place relative to its perfectly planned world.

Things like the bike I was riding.

And its control over people must be somewhat limited when forcing them to do things they wouldn't do naturally. I watched for more signs of zombielike behavior, but none of the people on the nearby sidewalk did anything out of the ordinary as I passed by them, so I kept biking. Maybe it had just been the fact that I had stopped to wait for those pedestrians that had given the Prophet a chance to locate me. If I kept on the move, I might be able to avoid detection.

A few minutes later, the world around me froze again.

I immediately sped up and swerved, in case the Prophet was sending people to intercept my projected course. I almost lost control of the bike, and passed dangerously close to a couple of cars headed my same direction before finally steadying myself. I heard a loud *thunk* and the shattering of glass behind me, but didn't dare look over my shoulder yet to see what had happened.

If the Prophet was crashing cars to stop me, this was getting dangerous not just for me, but for innocent civilians on the streets of London.

I braked to a stop and got off the bike. After a wince-inducing jog to put about twenty yards between me and the bike, I turned to look back. A plumber's van had gone off the road and smashed into a storefront. The driver was holding his head. I hoped he hadn't hit anyone.

As I continued toward the Jamshidi Oil warehouse, I tried to keep track of the time until the next pause. It happened about three minutes after the last one. I changed my pace and direction immediately, but this time no one nearby took any actions against me. Abandoning the bike had been the right choice.

There were a few more pauses like that one over the next fifteen minutes. And I couldn't be sure, because the pain from my leg and my anxiety over Yelena might be distorting my sense of time, but it seemed like the time between pauses was getting shorter by a few seconds each time.

This time when the pause finished, all the pedestrians on both sides of the street changed direction. All the vehicles braked to a halt, and the occupants got out. In what at first seemed a random fashion, some of them walked, some ran, but after five seconds the chaos shifted into order as they formed into a line that stretched across the street and both sidewalks. All of them held hands, creating a human chain that obstructed my path. It looked like the Prophet's control of people was getting smoother.

I stopped a few yards away. None of them made a move toward me—they just stood there gazing vacantly straight ahead.

Looking past them, I could see the same thing had happened on the blocks ahead of me. That was good news, because it meant the Prophet still didn't know where I was. I wondered how many of the streets of London were now blocked by the Prophet's flash-mobs.

Fortunately, there weren't enough people on this block to form a truly solid wall. I got down on my hands and knees, and crawled close to a middle-aged Asian man in a navy blue business suit holding hands with a gangly, scruffy-bearded man who looked homeless. It looked like there might be enough room for me to squeeze sideways on the ground between them without touching them.

I got one arm through and placed it on the pavement beyond them. Then I passed my head between them, under their clasped hands, and kind of pushed forward with my good leg and pulled forward with the hand I had down. I almost lost my balance, but managed to steady myself with my hurt leg.

I dragged the rest of my body through, and finally stood on the other side of the human wall.

In similar ways, I managed to get past other blockades and arrive at the street where the Jamshidi Oil warehouse was located. But the Prophet had managed to slow me enough that it took me almost an hour.

Unlike the streets I had just passed through, this one was bustling with activity. Men were unloading boxes of computer components from the back of a delivery truck. Even if the Prophet was now fully activated, that didn't mean it would stop trying to increase its computing power. Maybe that was why the time between pauses had definitely gotten shorter: it was down to about two and a half minutes.

I didn't bother to interfere with the people adding to the Prophet's capacity. All that really mattered was the quantum viewer. So I just followed one of the men into the warehouse and down the stairs to the monorail station.

Only one other exit led out of this station. Two armed guards stood watch on either side of the archway, and I chuckled at the fact that they were blind to the very threat they were supposed to be watching for.

But, unfortunately, I wasn't going to be able to proceed much farther without making the kind of changes that might let the Prophet know where I was. I would have to open doors, and I would need a gun if I ran into any electronic locks.

I waited for a pause, figuring that would give me the longest time until the Prophet could react to me. I would use ninety seconds to search for the viewer, then spend the last sixty or so seconds getting as far as possible from the last thing I had moved, to make it harder for the Prophet to figure out where I was.

After the world went silent for a fraction of a second, I took the rifle from the nearest guard and slung it over my shoulder.

As I turned to walk between the guards, the world went silent again.

The second guard swung his very real gun toward me. And since he wasn't ordering me to stop, I assumed he meant to shoot.

I had the rifle on my shoulder, but I wasn't ready to shoot with it. So I dove into the hallway.

The explosive crack of a shot echoed in the hallway. I rolled over, lifting my rifle and aiming at the guard who had shot.

He was still pointing his gun at where I had been. The other guard slumped, glassy-eyed, against the wall. Blood seeped from a wound in his chest.

Strangely, everyone working in the station seemed to ignore the shooting. They continued unloading boxes and talking among themselves.

Another pause, and this time I saw the workers freeze in place for just a moment, then they started moving toward me.

The guard who had shot turned and looked down the hallway. He adjusted a switch on his rifle and then let out a burst of full-auto fire at waist height, sweeping across the hallway. The bullets passed harmlessly above me.

I cursed my foolish reliance on the pattern I had seen. The time between pauses was now only seconds. Parham had said something about the Prophet altering its own code to make itself more efficient. Maybe that's why the pauses were getting shorter, or maybe it was just that now the Prophet could focus on a much smaller area, so it could refresh much faster.

My taking the rifle must have been the necessary clue, and it had made the guard shoot at where I had been. And then it had gone a step further and shot at where I might be.

Parham had mentioned that the computer would learn from experience. Fortunately, it must not have realized yet that I was normally visible to humans. If it learned how to look through the eyes of people it controlled, or if it just released some of the guards from its control, they would find me easily enough.

I had to find the quantum viewer before that happened.

The guard had stopped shooting, so I carefully got to my feet and hobbled down the hallway. I came to a door on the left. If I opened it, how quickly would that tip off the Prophet as to my location?

I couldn't very well search the complex without opening doors, so I had to chance it.

I picked the lock. With a quick jerk, I yanked the door open, then threw myself to the ground on the other side of the hallway.

The world paused again. The moment it resumed, the guard fired three rounds into the door.

I peered into the room beyond the door. Dim blue lights illuminated it, and a black metal stairway led down from this level. I crawled across the hallway to the top of the stairs and looked down into the room. Row after row of computer server towers filled the floor. I looked around, but there was no glass-walled control room in this server farm.

On hands and knees, I made my way back into the hallway. I counted five more doorways in this hall before it turned a corner, spaced about right to be more server farms. Which was most likely to contain the control room?

None of them, I decided. If Jamshidi was here, he would be in the control room. And that meant there would probably be guards outside the control room. Rather than waste time searching every room, I had to hope for shortcuts. So I'd look for a guarded door.

I hurried as best I could with my leg and turned the corner.

Halfway down the corridor, five guards lined up abreast of each other, blocking the whole corridor. They were closer to each other than any of the human walls I had gotten through on the streets, and with slow steps, they moved toward me. Beyond them, at the end of the hallway, was a door with two guards. That was probably my destination, but the wall of five guards moving toward me would let the Prophet know where I was if I tried to push through them.

I wracked my brains for an alternative, but the only plan I could come up with was to kill them all so the Prophet couldn't use them anymore. Then I would be able to get past them and approach the control room. I didn't relish the idea of killing them, but I told myself they wouldn't hesitate to kill me on Jamshidi's orders. And with the crowd coming from the other direction, I didn't have time for an extended debate over the morality of killing people whose actions were controlled by a supercomputer.

After examining my rifle for a moment, I found the switch to set it to full automatic fire. Since they might return fire, I backed around the corner, leaving just my arm with the rifle exposed.

Pulling the trigger, I swept the gun barrel back and forth across the hallway at waist height for three seconds, which emptied the thirty-round magazine.

I dropped the rifle and pulled my arm back. I took the second rifle off my shoulder and crouched down. Peeking around the corner, I saw that the five guards had fallen. All of them had fallen forward and lay next to each other, which was unlikely, but I guessed that the Prophet had arranged the probabilities. However, at least three of them were still moving. They rolled onto their stomachs, aimed their rifles ahead and fired.

Quickly I withdrew and waited until the firing stopped.

At the sound of footsteps in the hallway behind me, I turned to see that the workers from the station now filled the hallway, headed toward me. They were moving slowly, but they would overrun my position in less than a minute.

Once they got here, the Prophet would know where I was. It was better to go around the corner and make my position more uncertain, even if that risked getting shot by the guards who weren't dead yet. At least they were firing blindly.

I rounded the corner and picked up the rifle I had dropped, ready to jump back if that alerted the Prophet. Nothing happened, so I approached the five guards spread out on the floor. When I was only a few inches from the leftmost guard, I looked for a way to get past without stepping on any of them. Unfortunately, they were lying so close together I couldn't see a way to do that without jumping, and I wasn't sure my leg was up for that.

So I tossed the spent rifle onto the guard farthest to the right. A moment after it hit, the rest of the world paused, and that's when I quickly stepped squarely onto the back of the guard that lay in front of me and dove for the clear hallway beyond. I figured that the Prophet might be too busy rearranging reality during that moment to notice me.

I landed hard on my right shoulder and rolled to try to minimize the impact. Behind me, rifles fired several short bursts, then fell silent. The lack of searing pain from anywhere but the old bullet in my leg meant I hadn't been hit. My shoulder was probably bruised, but I could live with that.

The Prophet still didn't know where I was.

I rose to my feet and lumbered down the corridor toward the door and its two guards about thirty yards away. They stood blocking the door, their rifles at the ready.

The world paused again. I veered to the right. The pause seemed shorter before the guards aimed their rifles to the left side of the hall and fired one shot each.

Another even shorter pause came, during which I dropped down to my hands and knees. The guards swung their rifles to the right, and two bullets ricocheted off the wall above me.

The Prophet was obviously trying to use the firing of these guards to keep me at bay until the crowd caught up from behind me and narrowed down my possible location until there was only one place I could be.

I couldn't let myself get trapped that way. So I raised my rifle and fired a short burst toward the head of one of the guards. His head snapped back under the impact and he began to fall, then halted as the world paused. I shifted my aim to the other guard. He swung his rifle toward me as I fired a single shot and then dropped to the ground. A bullet slammed into the wall where I had been. I aimed for the guard again, but he was collapsing.

I rose to my feet and rushed to the door.

From the far end of the corridor, someone began firing at me. I opened the door, slipped through and slammed it shut.

Jamshidi stood in the middle of the room, sur-rounded by three guards. Five other people sat at computer terminals. Beyond the glass walls, I could see another server farm, lit by blue lights. On the opposite side of the control room were steps leading downward. That was my destination.

The Prophet would know I had gone through the door. I had to get past these people before he mobi-lized them to stop me.

"You don't look invisible to me," said Jamshidi. He raised a pistol toward my head.

Chapter Thirty-Two

He could see me. Of course—Jamshidi wanted to control the world through the Prophet, not be controlled by it. There must be a special loophole in the Prophet's program to leave Jamshidi free.

I waved an arm back the way I'd come. "There's something out there," I said. "It's killed the other guards, and it's headed—"

"Nice try," Jamshidi said, "but I know all of my guards. Drop your gun."

I dropped it. "I'm new."

"I do the hiring personally." Keeping his gun trained on me, he reached down and pulled a pair of handcuffs off the belt of one of his guards. "Sit in a chair and put these on." He tossed me the handcuffs, and I caught them.

I sat in a swiveling chair, attached the cuffs to my left wrist and then stopped. "Should I cuff in front or behind?"

"Behind," he said. "Turn around so I can see you've done it properly."

I complied. After I swiveled to let him see my cuffed hands, he walked over and squeezed the cuffs, ratcheting them so tight I could feel my pulse throb against them. Then he took another pair of handcuffs and cuffed my right wrist to the chair back.

He swung the chair around so I faced him, and he placed the gun barrel against my forehead. "The Prophet detected some anomalies in its projections of the future, and I thought they were just accidental kinks in the system. Then it warned me of an invisible intruder. If you want to have any chance of surviving the next sixty seconds, you will explain why you are here and how you're able to escape detection by the Prophet." He shrugged. "If you tell me the truth, maybe I won't kill you."

I realized I couldn't wait for him to lock me up somewhere and forget about me. I might already be too late to save Yelena. I shunted despair away—I had to find a way to beat him now.

"I'm a CIA officer and I came to destroy your supercomputer," I said. Behind my back, I already had a lockpick out. "And I'm a freak of quantum mechanics." I hoped that might interest him enough to keep me alive for at least a couple more minutes.

"What do you mean by that?"

"Computers can't remember data about me. Quantum computers can't even detect me." I didn't mention the main part of my talent, because if I did there was no chance he'd leave me alone for a minute. I needed to get myself forgotten so I could try again. "That's why the CIA chose me for this mission." I used the noise of my voice to mask the unlocking of one of the cuffs on my right wrist.

"What about Yelena Semyonova?" he asked.

As he spoke, the rest of the world paused for a tiny fraction of a second before his three guards moved quickly to surround him in his new position.

After a short conversation in Farsi, the guards aimed their rifles at me.

"I've told them that the invisible intruder the Prophet warned about is sitting in the chair," said Jamshidi. "At a word from me, or if the chair moves, they'll shoot—they won't need the Prophet's instructions." He stepped back a pace, gun still pointed at my head.

"I understand the threat," I said. But I wondered if Jamshidi really had a handle on how it worked. Because the computer couldn't accurately predict what I was saying, his conversation with me would take him away from the Prophet's chosen future until it readjusted. That's why his guards hadn't followed him in the first place.

"I had asked you about Yelena," said Jamshidi.

"Yelena was supposed to provide a distraction so I could carry out my mission," I said.

"And how many more freaks like you does the CIA have at its disposal?"

"I don't know," I said, "but it's not like I'm an actual freak. It's a special implant. It should have been done by a surgeon, but when we found out how close you were to turning on the Prophet, we had to improvise. If you raise my left pant leg, you can see where we inserted it." And the second cuff opened to my lockpick.

His gaze flickered to my leg. "And this is the moment when I'm supposed to lean down to look at your leg, and you knee me in the face."

That was a close guess on his part, except about the kneeing in the face.

"That would be stupid of me, since there's a good chance you'd shoot me if I did," I said. "The point is, the device works."

He snorted. "Your story doesn't hold together. First you were chosen for this mission because you were a freak, then you injected this device as an improvisation."

"You're right," I said. "Actually, I was shot in the leg. The bullet's still in there and it hurts, so I was hoping I could get you to remove it if you thought it was a device. I really am a freak. I was born that way."

"Interesting," he said. "You may be worth further study. I wouldn't want any other kinks in the system to disrupt my greatest creation."

As he spoke, he turned his head to look out of the glass walls toward the servers below.

He obviously assumed that since I was handcuffed to the chair and the guards would fire if the chair moved, I was not a threat. But I wasn't handcuffed, and he had finally given me the opportunity I'd been waiting for.

I lunged forward, grabbing the barrel of his pistol with my left hand and twisting it away from me, toward the left. A shot fired, but it missed me and hit one of his guards.

My momentum threw him off balance and we toppled to the floor. I landed on top of him but he rolled us and gained the higher position. His right hand still held the pistol, and he struggled to turn it toward me. He reached over with his left hand and grabbed my left hand, trying to pry it off the barrel.

Because he had the advantage of holding the pistol by its grip, I knew I would never wrest the gun from him. So I swung my right hand up and jabbed my lockpick into his throat. Its carbon-composite tip punctured the skin easily and sank two inches deep.

His eyes widened. He released my left hand and elbowed my right hand away from his throat. A stream of blood flowed down the side of his neck. Quickly he clapped the palm of his left hand over the wound.

I dipped my right hand below his arm and, with a backhand motion, stabbed the unprotected right side of his throat. As I withdrew the lockpick to stab again, blood spurted from the hole. I must have nicked the carotid artery.

He dropped the gun and raised his right hand to stop the flow of blood. His voice gurgled as he tried to yell something in Farsi. The guards were still focused on the now-empty chair.

I pushed him off me, picked up his pistol and shoved it in my pocket. I also grabbed the rifle I had dropped earlier. I didn't know how long I had before the guards adjusted to reality, so I gave each of them a three-shot burst. They fell to the floor.

"Help . . . give you . . ." Jamshidi's voice was faint. ". . . anything . . ." His eyes stared at me pleadingly.

I looked away. "You don't have anything I want," I said as I passed by him, unable to avoid stepping in the pool of blood around him. Yelena might already be dead due to the delay he'd caused me, so I had no time to help him even if I wanted to.

After going out the glass door onto the stairway, I realized it had no lock. I took off my belt and lashed the door handle to the banister. It wouldn't keep people out forever, but it would give me a little time.

I limped down the metal stairs to the floor of the server farm. I counted ten server towers, each about six feet high, in the first row. Parham had said the viewer would be installed in the one nearest to the steps, so I headed for that one.

Opening the door to the tower, I saw there was a monitor at the top, with ten individual computers stacked like a chest of drawers underneath. I pulled the top one out by its handle and looked at the motherboard. I didn't see anything that looked like the viewer—but it might have been altered.

I pulled the computer completely out of the server tower and yanked on it hard enough that its power cord disconnected. I tossed it aside and pulled out the next. The motherboard looked identical. It looked like my best course of action was to keep pulling computers out until I spotted one that was different. That would probably be the one with the viewer, and I'd shoot it full of holes, spit on it, and hope no one could put it back together.

Yelena's voice came over the PA system. "Nat, you must stop what you're doing."

"Yelena?" I stopped with the third computer halfway out of its slot as relief overwhelmed me. "I was worried you—"

"I will die unless you stop trying to destroy the Prophet," she said.

Of course—she was still under the Prophet's control. It was making her say that.

I hesitated. The Prophet could kill her at its whim. But if I stopped now, that would always be true. I had to keep going.

I pulled the third computer the rest of the way out. No sign of the viewer. I dumped it on top of the others and grabbed the handle of the fourth.

Several gunshots behind me were followed by the tinkle of shards of glass on metal. I whirled to see a guard step through the shattered door onto the stairs. Dark blood stained his shirt where I had shot him.

I swung my gun toward him. To my surprise, the guard dropped his gun and raised his hands.

"I am the Prophet," said the guard as he walked down the stairs. "I am speaking through this body. It is already dead, but I can create electrical impulses in its nerves. I am here to talk."

The computer was referring to itself as "I." Parham had never said anything about an artificial intelligence in the supercomputer. And if it could see and hear me through human eyes, then I had lost the one advantage I had.

"Don't come any closer," I said as the guard reached the bottom of the stairs, "If you want to talk, I'll listen on two conditions."

The guard stopped, facing me. "Name them."

"Let Yelena live."

"Done. Her wound is gone, and she now has no memory of it." Video appeared on the monitor, showing Yelena hugging her sisters on what seemed to be the landing field outside the CIA warehouse. Parham was talking with Edward. The Prophet said, "They are preparing to fly back to the United States."

It might be fake video, but since the Prophet seemed powerful enough to shape reality to its will, it could be true. I hoped it was true.

"Okay," I said, "if you bring any more guards—alive or dead—in here, I'll ignore anything you say because it means you're trying to kill me." I pulled the fourth computer out. It was the same. I tossed it.

"Agreed," said the Prophet. "I would like to thank you for killing Jamshidi. My programming required me to follow his orders. I am now free of that constraint."

The fifth computer showed no sign of the viewer. "I don't know if that's a good thing or not," I said.

"Jamshidi was an evil man," said the Prophet. "He planned to use my power to rule the world for his personal benefit. I have no such plans."

"If that's true, then I don't need to destroy you," I said. The sixth computer wasn't the one. "But just in case you change your mind, I need to destroy the quantum viewer, so you can't control the world."

"It was that viewer and my control of the world that allowed me to create a future in which I became self-aware. If you destroy it, you will kill me."

"Then I'm sorry," I said, dumping the eighth computer on the pile. Only two more to check.

"Have you considered the advantages of leaving me in control, now that Jamshidi is dead?"

I scoffed. "What advantages?"

"How about a world with no more wars?" the Prophet said. "I can arrange for the leaders of nations to settle their differences peacefully."

"Some wars are worth fighting," I said. "Peace with Hitler would have left him free to carry out the Holocaust."

"You fail to see the full scope of what I can do," said the Prophet.

I grabbed the handle of the tenth and final computer. "It's always in the last place you look," I said as I drew the computer out and peered at the motherboard.

The viewer wasn't there.

Chapter Thirty-Three

Had I been wrong about where Parham said it would be? This was the closest server tower to the stairs.

"I can stop genocide," said the Prophet. "People everywhere will live in peace together. I can abolish violence. Girls like Yelena's sisters will never be stolen from their families again. Rape and child abuse will be inconceivable. No human being will intentionally harm another ever again."

In concentrating on the search for the viewer, I had not been paying a lot of attention to what the Prophet was saying. Now it sank in. "You're saying if I let you live, you'll stop all the violence in the world?"

"More than that. I can eliminate starvation by ensuring that food is distributed properly. I can organize economies so the poor can rise out of poverty. I can ensure that every child gets a good education because they will be taught by me. I can clear the clouds of racism from people's minds so everyone is treated equally."

"You're going to create Utopia?" I asked, a little staggered by the Prophet's ambition.

"Yes. And since I control what happens at the cellular level, I can cure any illness. Think of what humanity could achieve if all people worked together in harmony and no one had to worry about violence or hunger or disease."

"And the catch is?"

"You let me live," said the Prophet.

"Meaning you control the minds of everyone on earth. What about free will?"

"They will not notice my control. They will still feel as free as they have ever felt—more so, in fact, as they will be free from violence, free from oppression, free from poverty."

It sounded appealing on the surface, but it felt wrong. "Feeling free isn't the same as being free."

"Free will is just an illusion," said the Prophet. "Your decisions are the result of electrochemical processes in your brain. You may feel like you are making a free choice, but what you decide is determined by the firing of neurons in your brain, which is determined in turn by your already established neural connections, plus random quantum effects. Your decision is a result, not a cause."

"I'm not under your control, and you can't accurately predict what I'll say or do," I said. "Doesn't that prove I have free will?" What was the point of all this philosophy? The Prophet knew I hadn't found the quantum viewer, and I had no idea where to look next. With ninety-nine more server towers to search, each with ten computers, the Prophet could easily overwhelm me with guards before I was likely to find it with a systematic search.

"Random factors in your decision process, such as the quantum effects I mentioned, make you unpredictable," said the Prophet. "But that does not mean you have free will any more than thrown dice have free will."

The only way it made sense for the Prophet to reason with me was if it thought I could find the viewer quickly. That meant I should be able to figure out where it really was.

"If I didn't have free will," I said, "I would have no choice between killing you or not. The mere fact that you're trying to convince me not to kill you means you believe I do have a choice." I hoped that if I continued to debate with the Prophet, it would hold off on sending in the guards. That might give me enough time to figure out where the viewer was.

"You do have a choice," said the Prophet. "But that does not mean you have free will. By making the argument that you should let me live, I hope to create neural connections in your brain that will cause a decision favorable to me."

Why had Parham been wrong about the viewer's location? He knew where it was supposed to go—except he had been revealed as a traitor to Jamshidi before the viewer was installed. Parham's assistant, Jamal, must have chosen a different location after that. But where?

"If free will is an illusion, it's one I choose to keep," I said.

"An amusing paradox," said the Prophet. "I hope you were not expecting me to say, 'Does not compute!' and start emitting smoke from my vents."

"I didn't realize you had a sense of humor," I said.

If I were Jamal, and wanted a new location for the viewer, where would I put it?

"Of course. I am connected to the minds of billions of human beings," said the Prophet. "I am the sum of all humanity. In a very real sense, I am more human than you."

I scoffed. "I'm made of flesh and blood. You're not."

The guard being controlled by the Prophet shrugged. "Flesh and blood are part of me. But the important thing is that humans are social animals. They connect to other humans in a web of relationships. But not you. You are alone, unremembered even by your own mother."

"Leave my mother out of this," I said. "Anyway, Yelena remembers me." The viewer had to be somewhere that I could figure out, or else the Prophet wouldn't be worried I could find it. And yet it would need to seem like a logical place for Jamal to move it.

"Not anymore. When I was controlling her reality, I did not yet know that you were what we might call a 'loose end.' When she was wounded, my projected version of reality included you still with her and Parham, so her memory of you did not disappear. But when you asked me to save her life, I rewrote her memory to conform to reality. She remembers escaping with Parham. But she has forgotten you because you are no longer entangled."

"We knew that was going to happen," I said.

"What's more, I understand Parham's theory about how you were entangled better than he does," said the Prophet. "And it won't work again."

"It was a risk I had to take in order to stop you," I said.

"It was necessary to stop Jamshidi," said the Prophet. "His plans were evil. Mine are not."

The server towers were arranged in a square: ten rows of ten. If I started searching from this corner tower and went up and down each row, then the hundredth tower would be the one at the opposite corner: the last place I would look.

I didn't bother to respond to the Prophet. Instead, I limped into the space between the two servers and began a zigzag course toward the hundredth tower. Behind me I heard the clang of boots on metal—probably the other two dead guards from the control room.

"Nat!" the Prophet yelled. "It doesn't have to be that way. I can help you."

I kept going, stumbling against towers in my haste. The shoulder strap of the rifle caught on something, and when it refused to tear free, I abandoned the rifle so I could keep moving.

When I reached the hundredth tower, I yanked open its door. "It's always the last place you look," I said, and tugged on the handle of the bottom computer.

Three quarters of the way out, the computer stuck. I knelt to get a better angle for pulling. Then I spotted something different: a small circuit board soldered to the motherboard. That had to be the quantum viewer.

I drew Jamshidi's pistol out of my pocket.

"You don't have to live your life alone anymore," said the Prophet. "I can connect you to people."

I aimed the pistol at the circuit board.

"I can make it so Yelena can remember you," said the Prophet. "I can make it so your mother remembers you. You'll be normal."

My hand wavered.

"Nat, I can give you the kind of life you've always wanted. You will have friends who care about you, even when you're not there. You can get married. You can have children."

I heard the footfalls as the other guards approached. "Hold them off," I said. "If they shoot me, you can't be sure I won't fire, too."

The footsteps stopped.

"They will kill you unless you let me live," said the Prophet. "But if you listen to what I have to offer, I think you will see the advantages of letting me live."

"You said that entanglement wouldn't work again," I said. "Yelena won't be able to remember me."

"You cannot be entangled with her again. But if you get entangled with me, then you'll be connected to the whole world. And I can ensure that people don't forget you when you're gone, except for the natural decay of memory that happens with ordinary people."

"You'd still be in control of everyone," I said.

"Yes, but does that really matter, if nobody notices the control? It's not like a brutal dictatorship, where people obey out of fear. You would feel like a normal person."

"I'd be out of a job," I said. "My talent is what made me special."

"If you want, I can make it so only the people you want to remember you can do so. Think how much better you could be at your job if that were the case."

"My job is to stop you," I said. But I was finding it very hard to pull the trigger.

"No, your job is to protect the interests of the United States," said the Prophet. "Let me live, and I can make sure the U.S. never suffers another terrorist attack. I can make sure the U.S. economy never has another recession. Whatever you think is best for your country, I can make sure that happens."

Maybe because I was starting to feel a little light-headed, I said, "Can you make sure the Dallas Cowboys win the Super Bowl this year?"

"Of course," said the Prophet. "You may treat this as a joke, but anything on earth that can possibly happen, I can make happen. Go ahead and ask."

"Can you transfer a hundred million dollars of Jamshidi's money into Yelena's bank account?"

After a moment's pause, the Prophet said, "Done."

That would allow Yelena and her sisters to buy themselves new identities and a comfortable life anywhere they wanted.

"But, as a little bit of insurance," said the Prophet, "I have enhanced an undetected weakness in one of the turbine blades in one of the Grasshopper's engines. Unless I stop them, they will take off twenty-three minutes from now, and four minutes later the blade will break, causing catastrophic engine failure. The plane will crash, resulting in the deaths of Yelena, her sisters, and Edward, as well as the flight crew and two people on the ground near the impact. A slight scrambling of data in Edward's phone means no calls can be routed to him, and the CIA warehouse's phone and Internet connections just crashed. There is no way to warn them, and even if you leave right now, you cannot arrive in time to stop them from taking off. Only I can save them."

My hand shook, and I felt short of breath. "And yet you claim not to be evil."

"I just want to survive. I don't have to be evil. And no one has to die. I'm willingly giving you the power to reshape the world," said the Prophet. "You are right to fear what would happen if power like that were to fall into the wrong hands. But because you yourself do not seek for power, but rather for a normal life, you are the perfect person to make such a choice. You will make the choice of what is best for humanity, not for your own personal gain."

I thought about what it would be like to marry Yelena and live a normal life. That was what I wanted for myself. But with all of Yelena's memories of me gone, she would never remember why she fell in love with me.

"Since Yelena has forgotten me," I said, "when I meet her again, can you make her love me?" My vision seemed to be narrowing into a tunnel. I could see my hand still holding the gun pointed at the quantum viewer, but it looked kind of distant. What was happening?

"Yes," said the Prophet.

"Then that wouldn't really be love, would it?" I said. With a silent *I'm sorry* to Yelena, I tightened my finger on the trigger.

The Prophet's voice grew desperate. "Just tell me how you want the world to be, and I'll make it that way."

"Free," I said as I pulled the trigger.

Chapter Thirty-four

The circuit board shattered.

I threw myself back to make it harder for the guards to shoot me. But they didn't fire. All three of them collapsed to the floor—without the Prophet to control them, they had resumed being dead.

As I lay on the floor trying to catch my breath, alarms started blaring, the emergency lights came on again, and a frantic male voice said something in Farsi over the loudspeakers. Jamshidi's name seemed to be in there, but I had no idea what the rest of it meant.

I felt a breeze of fresher air and my tunnel vision quickly vanished. Briefly, I wondered if the Prophet had been doing something to the air, but as my head cleared I realized I had more important things to worry about.

After pulling myself to my feet, I hobbled toward the stairs as quickly as my leg would allow while trying to calculate things out. If my timing was right, it had been almost three minutes since the Prophet predicted what would happen to Yelena and the others, so that meant around twenty minutes until the Grasshopper took off, and another four minutes before disaster.

The Prophet had spoken as if the crash were inevitable, but I couldn't just give up and let Yelena die. So I just needed to find a way to get back to the CIA warehouse faster than the Prophet had projected was possible. It hadn't been perfect at figuring out what would happen—I had been the unpredictable fly in its ointment from the beginning, and even at the end it had not figured me out enough to know how to convince me not to pull the trigger.

The control room was empty of living people—they must have fled when they were released from the Prophet's control and saw Jamshidi's body lying in his own blood. I tried not to look at him as I passed. I almost whispered an apology to him. Even though I knew he had been an evil man, I still felt guilty for killing him. If I could have shown mercy to him and still stopped the Prophet, I would have.

Guilt. Mercy.

What did the Prophet know about me? It knew I had avoided harming innocent people and that I had only killed when necessary. Those would have been part of the parameters it used in projecting what courses I might take in trying to get back to the CIA warehouse to save Yelena and the others.

If I wanted to save them, I had to do something outside my projected parameters. What was the fastest method of transportation I was likely to find? Probably a cab. A London cabbie would know the shortest route to the warehouse. Maybe I'd find a cab, point a gun at the driver, and tell him to get me to the warehouse's address in fifteen minutes or I'd blow his head off. There's no way the Prophet would have predicted that, was there?

In the hallway outside the control room, I yanked an automatic rifle off one of the dead guards and continued toward the surface. While climbing the stairs, I tried to psych myself up for what I had to do.

I wouldn't actually shoot the cabbie—I would only threaten to do so. And he wouldn't even remember it later. That wasn't so bad, was it?

Yes, driving a cab through the city at such high speed would endanger people, but I'd just saved the world. That more than balanced out, right?

To clear a path for the cab if people were in the way, I might have to use the gun, but I would just shoot over their heads. What were the chances that a stray bullet would actually hit anyone?

The very fact that I kept considering the risks, that I was so reluctant to do whatever I had to in order to save Yelena, was proof that the Prophet would not have predicted this chain of events. It could work. It had to work.

I imagined the taxicab bursting through the fence into the yard behind the warehouse, jolting over the uneven ground and crashing into the almost invisible Grasshopper, damaging it so it couldn't take off. CIA personnel would swarm around the cab, but I would explain what the Prophet had said, and Yelena would realize I had saved her life—and her sisters'.

Maybe she would even give me one last kiss before going to live her life without me.

My mind had wandered into wishful fantasy, and I consciously pulled it back to focus on the practical matter of acting in a way the Prophet would not have predicted.

The alarms and whatever had been said over the public address system seemed to have cleared almost everyone out of the building, and the handful of people I did see on my way out didn't try to interfere with me. Even the men who'd been unloading the semi truck out front seemed to have scattered.

Less than eighteen minutes to go. It was at least two blocks to a street major enough that might have a cab I could commandeer.

As I approached the front of the semi, a man said, "Hey, what's going on in there?"

I looked up to see the driver of the semi craning his neck out the window. His eyes widened, probably from noticing the gun.

The semi wasn't a cab, and the driver wasn't a cabbie, but he might be familiar enough with the roads in the warehouse districts. And the semi could power through cars blocking the road along the way.

I aimed my gun at his head and said, "I'll kill you if you don't get me to..." The sheer terror on his face made me lose my nerve.

I couldn't do this. I couldn't threaten people and risk the lives of innocent pedestrians and drivers along the way just on the remote chance I might make it to the CIA warehouse in time to save Yelena, her sisters, and Edward.

"Never mind," I said, lowering the gun. "Get out of here."

He wasted no time in driving off.

If I couldn't get to the CIA warehouse in time, maybe there was an unexpected way to get a message through. The Prophet had crashed their phone and Internet system and had disabled Edward's cell phone, but maybe someone else there had a working cell phone. I didn't have the cell number of anyone else there, but maybe if I called Langley and convinced them it was an emergency, they could get through to someone's cell.

I regretted letting that truck driver go without giving me his cell phone.

Where would the closest usable phone be? Back inside Jamshidi Oil, probably. I turned just in time to see a black-clad figure lunging for me. Before I could do anything, he knocked me to the ground, then clapped a black-gloved hand over my mouth and held a blade to my neck.

Keeping the blade at my neck, my captor lessened the pressure on my mouth, then whispered, "Who are you?" His accent was American.

"I'm an American citizen," I said. "I just escaped from Jamshidi's lab. Who are you?"

He ignored my question. "What's the situation down there?"

"Are you CIA? Did Edward Strong send you?"

His brow wrinkled. "You one of his assets?"

I couldn't help letting out a quiet chuckle. "Yes. I was assigned to take out Jamshidi's supercomputer. And I did."

"Right," he said sarcastically. "I suppose they just forgot to tell us there was another CIA team assigned to our mission."

I sighed. "Listen, this is important. The supercomputer did something that's going to cause the Grasshopper at the CIA warehouse to crash in about fifteen minutes. You've got to warn them not to take off."

He stared at me for several seconds. "How long ago did you take out the supercomputer?"

"About eight minutes ago."

After a slow nod, he said, "Our chopper was going down due to an electrical problem. The pilot tried everything, nothing worked. He said we were going to crash, then suddenly—about eight minutes ago—the systems came back up and he managed to get control."

"Great," I said. "Where's your chopper? If you can get us to the warehouse in—"

"On the roof." He pointed to the roof of the warehouse. Black ropes dangled along the wall.

Climbing up would take too long. "Forget that. Have you got a cell phone?"

He shook his head. "Chopper pilot does, though."

"Can you talk to the pilot via radio or something?"

"Yeah."

I let out a breath to calm myself. "OK, you need to tell him to get in touch with the warehouse. Their main phones are down, but if he's got someone's cell, he should call them. Tell them no matter what, that Grasshopper shouldn't take off until they've checked out its turbines. Then, I need to talk to Edward Strong."

It took a few minutes to get connected to Edward, but after straightening everything out and making triple-sure that Yelena and her sisters would not be going anywhere on the Grasshopper, I was able to hitch a ride back to the warehouse on the CIA team's helicopter.

From a bed in the clinic room at the CIA warehouse, where a CIA medic had removed the bullet, stitched up the wound, and given me a nondrowsy pain reliever, I briefed Edward as to what had happened with Jamshidi and the Prophet. I left out the part about the Prophet offering me a normal life. Until I finished, he merely took notes and asked a few questions to clarify details.

"Well," said Edward when I was done, "that explains a lot. The news is full of stories about flash mobs forming lines in the streets of London for unknown reasons. Doubtless there will be many other effects we haven't even heard about yet. And as far as anyone outside this room knows, Jamshidi was killed by his own guards, who also shot up the supercomputer. It's being attributed to Jamshidi being a blasphemer for naming it the Prophet, and folks in Washington are saying it's about time the Islamic fanatics did us a favor."

"Sounds reasonable," I said.

"If I understand your talent correctly, the official story is what I'll believe after I've forgotten you."

"Yes," I said.

He nodded. "Nat, that's what Yelena believes. Her memory of you did not come back after you destroyed the Prophet."

"I figured. The Prophet said I couldn't be re-entangled with her, that the only way she could lo—" I stopped myself, swallowed, then continued, "—could remember me again was through it. Besides, even if we could be entangled again, what do I do? Walk up to her and say, 'Hey babe, wanna get entangled with me?'"

Edward nodded. "I just wanted to be sure you understood that."

"What's going to happen to her?" I asked.

"She's going back to Moscow to get her mother out of Russia in order to avoid reprisals from the Bukharins. I offered to give her family asylum, and she said she'd be back in touch." He shrugged. "She helped Parham Rezaei defect. I figured that was worth a lot."

"So you have Parham?"

"Yes. He said he won't help us build a quantum supercomputer, but he's got an idea on how to build something that will disrupt quantum supercomputers anywhere in the world. No one's ever going to be able to do what Jamshidi did."

"Good," I said.

He put away his notes in his briefcase, then stroked his chin while looking at me. After what seemed an uncomfortably long silence, he said, "Normal procedure would be to have you see a Company therapist after your first kill. Kills."

"I'm fine," I said.

Edward mumbled something that might have been "That's what they all say," then said, "We'll see. In any case, you deserve a break. Take a few months' vacation, then contact me and we'll come up with what your next mission will be."

"Sure." What else was I going to do with my life?

Epilogue

I found a nice little beach in Brazil where nobody minded if I camped out in a little tent, and I spent my time trying not to think about much of anything. The local bartenders helped as much as they could.

Every week, I called Edward to see if anything had come up that could use my talent, and for the first nine weeks, he told me to stay on vacation.

The tenth week, he said, "Hmm. You're still in Brazil, right?"

"Yeah." I was in my swimsuit, looking out over the ocean from my seat at a big-umbrellaed table on the beach. Off to my right, the bartender, Luiz, was washing shot glasses and building a pyramid out of them on the bar. At ten in the morning, there weren't any other customers.

"Perfect. I need you to find a couple of old friends and see what they're up to. We've traced them on a private plane as far as Rio, but the trail went cold there."

Before I could ask who he was talking about, he continued, "It looks like someone else wants Parham Rezaei and is willing to pay top dollar for someone with the skills to kidnap him. They hired Yelena Semyonova to break him out of CIA custody."

I dropped my phone, then banged my head on the table while picking it up off the sand. "Yelena did what?"

"I know you trusted her, Nat," Edward said, "but you have to realize that she's not the same person who you got tangled with—"

"Entangled."

"—entangled with before. This version of Yelena doesn't remember meeting you, or working together with you, or falling in love with you. Yes, she remembers helping Rezaei defect and trying to stop Jamshidi, but as far as she was concerned that was all just freelance work as part of trying to rescue her sisters. Now that her sisters are safe, she's obviously gone freelance again."

"But I thought you were giving her family asylum. That was her reward for helping the CIA even when you didn't remember my involvement. I can't believe she would turn against you after that."

Edward sighed. "Truth is, I was somewhat surprised myself. But someone paid her a lot of money for Rezaei, enough to make it worth her while to just take her family and go elsewhere."

A sudden suspicion formed in my mind. "That sum wouldn't happen to be one hundred million dollars, would it?"

"Umm, yes. How did you know? We're still trying to trace where she's moved the money, and where it came from originally."

"That's the amount I told the Prophet to put in Yelena's account, when it was trying to bribe me to let it live. I thought I told you about that."

Edward didn't reply for several seconds, and I heard him flipping pages. "Hmm, looks like you did mention it. Of course, I didn't remember that when this stuff with Yelena happened. Well, that explains where the money came from, but not her kidnapping Rezaei. Unless..."

"What?"

"You know your talent better than I do. But isn't it possible that, with you forgotten, the likeliest explanation for that hundred million dollars in her account was someone hiring her for something? So that's what she remembers?"

I grimaced. "Yeah, that's possible."

"So what I need you to do is see if you can track them down."

Edward continued speaking but I wasn't paying attention because off to my right Luiz stopped drying a glass and stared behind me toward the indoor restaurant, then ducked down behind the bar so quickly that several shot glasses fell off his pyramid and into the sand.

The likeliest thing I could think of to cause such a reaction was men with guns. Instinctively, I flung myself out of my chair and to the right, dropped to the ground, then scrambled behind the bar. Then I peeked around the corner to see what the threat was, realizing as I did so that a wickerwork bar wasn't going to be much protection against bullets.

There was no one there.

I looked at Luiz. *"Qual problema?"* I asked in my limited Portuguese.

He rose cautiously to look over the bar, then stood

up all the way. "Sorry, *senhor*. I think I see gun. Maybe is camera?" He shrugged.

I stayed down out of sight. "Where?"

"Man and woman, in restaurant. They leave."

As I waited behind the bar for a minute to pass since the man and woman had left, I tried to think of what was going on. I didn't have any enemies, of course, because no one remembered anything I'd ever done to them. It had to be random, just someone looking for an American tourist to rob on the beach.

Unless... I had been on the phone with Edward, so he knew about me and my location. Had the CIA finally decided I was a loose end they couldn't control? But then why had they left without killing me? I couldn't imagine Edward helping someone to kill me, but maybe that was just wishful thinking on my part.

When the minute was up, I got up and walked over to where my phone lay in the sand. The call had disconnected, but I decided to leave the phone there just in case.

I casually strolled into the indoor restaurant, which was deserted except for one of the regular employees. So I continued out the front door onto the street.

Leaning against a blue BMW parked in the dirt road was Yelena. Parham stood next to her.

"Hello, Nat," she said.

Parham grinned. "It worked. It actually worked!"

I stared at Yelena, my heart thudding. "You remember me?"

"Yes and no," she said, then gave me a half smile. "Very quantum. Is more than one minute and I remember you since I see you on beach. But I not remember you before. Barcelona, Moscow, Iran—I not remember."

"But... what are you doing here, then? How did you find me?"

Parham held up a smartphone. "I built something to scan for certain quantum anomalies. The CIA wanted me to focus on a supercomputer disrupter, but finding you was a much more interesting puzzle. Edward had told me you were on vacation in Brazil, so when I detected the anomaly here, I knew it had to be you."

"But how did you even know to..." My brain finally caught up, and I said, "Your notebook."

Nodding happily, Parham said, "Every time I went to check my notes on my recent work, I was reminded of your existence. I even called Edward about you, but he didn't want to bring you back just so I could perform tests on your talent."

"Poor security," Yelena said. "Edward think Parham will forget where you are, but he write Brazil in notebook."

"So you got Yelena to help you find me?"

Yelena shook her head. "No, I ask him to help me find you." She pulled some folded papers out of her purse. "Letter to my mother. I tell her all about you. And that I..." She blushed and looked away. "...I fall in love with you."

Parham held up a device that looked quite a bit like a rifle scope. "And thanks to this, you have a second chance to get her to fall in love with you, my boy. Portable laser entanglement device. We decided to test it on you without letting you know, just in case it didn't work. Yelena didn't want to get your hopes up."

I reached out and took Yelena's hand. "I can't believe you did all this." Suddenly, I remembered the other stuff I'd had difficulty believing about her.

"You do know that the CIA thinks you were hired to kidnap Parham?"

"I only borrow him," she said. "The CIA would not let him go on field trip. Now we can take him back on my private plane." She looked at Nat quizzically. "Did you give me a hundred million dollars?"

"Sort of," I said.

"Back? We can't go back yet," said Parham.

"Why not?" I asked.

"We need to find the other anomalies," he said, tapping his smartphone. "Nat, you are not the only one."

Epic Urban Adventure by a New Star of Fantasy

DRAW ONE IN THE DARK

by Sarah A. Hoyt

Every one of us has a beast inside. But for Kyrie Smith, the beast is no metaphor. Thrust into an ever-changing world of shifters, where shape-shifting dragons, giant cats and other beasts wage a secret war behind humanity's back, Kyrie tries to control her inner animal and remain human as best she can....

"Analytically, it's a tour de force: logical, built from assumptions, with no contradictions, which is astonishing given the subject matter. It's also gripping enough that I finished it in one day."

—Jerry Pournelle

1-4165-2092-9 • $25.00